PRAISE FOR *T*

The End of Feeling is a story that will stay with you long after
you finish reading it. Charlie is a strong, independent
young woman, guarded as she protects those she loves.
Benjamin is tough, resilient, a fighter in every sense
of the word. *The End of Feeling* is haunting, heartbreaking,
in other words, another winner for Bennett!
—Sherry Gammon, author of *Unlovable*

The End of Feeling was a rollercoaster ride of emotion. From the
moment I picked it up, my heart was warmed, melted, broken,
and pieced back together again. Cindy C Bennett has crafted
a beautiful story of love, loss, and acceptance that will leave
you aching long after the last page.
—Jamie Canosa, author of *Falling to Pieces*

The End of Feeling is another beautiful story crafted by
Cindy C Bennett. She weaves a tale of hope and love about
a couple of teens who have every reason to believe in neither.
It's raw and real, but she leaves us believing
in the power of redemption.
—Juli Caldwell, author of *Psyched*

Too often in young adult romances, the comedy and teenage angst take center stage and get in the way of the real story, but Cindy C Bennett does an amazing job balancing everything out, drawing the reader into the heart of the story. The high school quarterback and the new girl in town scenario may seem stereotypical, but the reality both characters live makes their story captivatingly unique and emotionally powerful. Benjamin and Charlie's story demonstrates the beautiful truth that two people can learn to be true to themselves, no matter what— especially while falling in love.
—Heather Frost, author of The Seers trilogy

The End of Feeling is a remarkably heartfelt and touching story. I instantly fell in love with Charlie and, against my better judgment, fell in love with Benjamin as well. The struggles in their story bring to light the fact that beauty and truly miraculous things can be found in the everyday, and that the most important thing any one of us can possess is love. This story proves that we can find a cathartic space by coming to terms with the reality of our lives, when compared to the fantasy we wish we lived. It shows that the greatest gift we can give someone is acceptance and understanding. Cindy C Bennett writes a beautifully told tale that will not disappoint.
—Shannen Crane Camp, author of *Under Zenith*

OTHER BOOKS BY CINDY C BENNETT

Rapunzel Untangled
Geek Girl
Heart on a Chain
Immortal Mine
The Experiment (with Sherry Gammon and Jeffery Moore)
Whispers of Razari (with Jeffery Moore)

A Fantasy Christmas (with Sherry
Gammon and Stephanie Fowers)
It's a Love Thing (editor)
Screams in the Night: Tales of Terror (editor)

THE ENCHANTED FAIRYTALES SERIES

Beautiful Beast
Red and the Wolf
Snow White
The Unmasking of Cinderella
The White Swan

SHORT STORIES

"Halfling"
"In the Beginning"
"Watched"
"Reluctance"

THE END OF FEELING

Cindy C Bennett

SKYSCAPE

SKYSCAPE

Published by Skyscape, New York

www.apub.com

Amazon, the Amazon logo, and Skyscape are trademarks of Amazon.com, Inc., or its affiliates.

ISBN-13: 9781477821015
ISBN-10: 1477821015

Cover design by theBookDesigners

Library of Congress Control Number: 2014915353

Printed in the United States of America

*To my daughter, Lexcie, who lives with the struggles of diabetes
day in and day out and does it with bravery and an aplomb that I admire.*

You are my hero.

PROLOGUE
BENJAMIN

I don't feel anything anymore.

If I were going to feel something, it would be for my sister, Mia. She's gone now, has been for the last eight years, since I was ten . . . and I somehow doubt she's coming back.

I loved her when she was here. I tried to protect her.

I failed.

When he finally hurt her so badly that she nearly died, torn up inside and out, *she* came and took her. *She* left me here, left me with him, completely at his mercy. As far as I know, she didn't even come back to see if I was okay, if I needed help, if I needed to go, too.

I don't hate her for that. I don't even envy her that she got out so much earlier even than Mia. To do either of those things requires feeling, and I don't feel. Anything. So I live with him still, numb and beyond caring.

How else could I be?

ONE
BENJAMIN

Daniel and I relax at a table in the center of the common area. School begins in less than fifteen minutes, so many of the other students have already begun to gather their stuff and move toward their first-period class. Those who remain behind, unhurried and unworried, are the seniors. It's the sophomores and juniors who worry about being late.

Daniel sits on the bench, his back facing the table, elbows propped on the edge and his legs sprawled in front of him. I'm lying flat out on top of the table, arms propped behind my head, as we discuss the upcoming football game. Some of our other buddies are sitting around with us as well, but they're almost unimportant. Daniel and I rule the school and they know it. The others serve the purpose of having a crowd to rule.

"Whoa," Daniel says, sitting up straight. I turn my head in his direction. "Hot new girl at ten o'clock."

I turn my gaze to the ten o'clock position and see nothing and no one unusual. I sit up and see that Daniel is staring straight ahead, and I roll my eyes. I should have known. Clearly Daniel has no idea how to read an analog clock. Every time he gives a position in relation to a clock, he's nowhere near correct. I follow his eyes and see exactly who he's looking at.

Alexis, Phoebe, and Cozi are emerging from the main office, and at their center is a stranger. Granted, with a school as large as ours, it's not possible to know everyone, but she's one I would have noticed. She's about the same height as Phoebe, which puts her around five and a half feet. She has straight, blonde hair. Nothing extraordinary in either of those features, but she's definitely on the gorgeous side of life, I can see that even from here. She laughs at something one of the other girls says, and Daniel turns to look at me, grinning. Her laugh carries across to us, throaty and joyful, one of the greatest laughs I've ever heard.

"We should go say hi," I say.

"That's what I was thinking," Daniel replies, scooping up his backpack from the floor as he rises. When we near the group, Alexis sees our approach. Her gaze finds mine and I see a flash of anger mixed with hurt. Her eyes flick to the new girl and then back to me as understanding dawns. She knows I'm not coming to see her, but to meet her new friend.

"Hey, guys," Daniel says.

They all respond, except the new girl. I've got my gaze locked on her and she's looking back.

"Hi, Benjamin," Phoebe says.

"Hey, Phoebe," I say, my gaze flicking to her quickly, dismissively, before returning to the new girl. She's even better looking up close. Her eyes are a hazel green, wide and almond shaped, surrounded by thick, dark lashes. I wonder if they're fake. Plenty of girls have fake lashes. "Who's your new friend?"

"Oh, um, this is Charlie. Charlie, this is Benjamin and Daniel."

I hold a hand out and she looks at it. She hesitates just a nanosecond before placing her hand in mine. She grasps my hand tightly, gives it a single, firm shake, then pulls her hand back before I have a chance to give her my usual soft squeeze and gentle brush of the thumb across the back of her hand. It always works to throw girls a little off, when they're not sure if they've had their hand shaken or caressed.

Alexis bites the inside of her cheek, and I can see she's trying not to laugh over Charlie's handshake. Alexis is one of my most recent heartbreaks—her heart, not mine. To be fair, I only went on two dates with her. That's my absolute maximum. Any more than that and the girl might think I'm interested in some kind of relationship. Sometimes they fall too hard for me. If I'm being honest, *most* times they fall too hard for me. Not my fault. Alexis smiles at Charlie's apparent rejection of the vibes I'm trying to project.

Charlie turns and juts her hand toward Daniel, giving him the same brusque handshake, but smiling at him as she does. Alexis laughs outright this time. I ignore her, awed by Charlie's smile. It reveals deep dimples in both cheeks, with smaller ones at each corner of her mouth. Her smile is even better than her eyes and her laugh.

"Charlie?" I say. "That's an unusual name."

"Short for Charlotte," she says, gazing directly at me. I try using my most intense, come-hither look. She remains unmoved.

"Down, Benjamin, she's new here," Cozi says, linking her arm through Charlie's and leading her away. Daniel and I watch her go. Daniel is grinning, but I watch intently. It's not usual for a girl to be immune to me, particularly when I'm pouring on the charm.

Well, I decide, nothing like a good challenge to begin the football season.

TWO
CHARLIE

I'm home," I call, stepping through the front door. I drop my backpack by the door, then remember my aunt's obsession with order and pick it up again. I can hear the TV in the family room at the back of the house. I look around the strange entryway, allowing myself one moment of longing for my grandma and her home, where we lived until her death a month ago.

I walk into the family room and see my mom, sitting on the couch watching *Barney*. I dig my nails into my palms. Man, I hate that stupid, annoying, dense purple dinosaur. "Hi, Mom," I say.

Mom jumps at the sound of my voice. She'd been too intent on *Barney* to hear my earlier greeting. She turns my way, a wide smile splitting her face. I smile back. Her eyes crinkle with joy as she jumps up from the couch, stray, wiry gray hairs escaping her messy ponytail. I grit my teeth at my aunt's lack of care of her.

"Charlie!" my mom yells brightly, running to me and throwing her arms around my neck, kissing my cheek noisily. I hug her tightly, cringing at the slightly sour smell.

"Mom, did you take a bath today?"

"Mimi says I don't have to bath today."

"Mom, we talked about this, remember? You need to bathe every day."

She shakes her head, mouth drooping. She refuses to shower, has ever since the *incident*. So we compromise with a bath, followed by a lotion rubdown. If she could manage to go a night without wetting her adult diaper, she could skip a bath. In all the time I can remember, she's been able to skip only a handful.

"Should we go take a bath now?" I ask.

"*Barney's* on," she whines.

"Yes, and if you take a bath, you can play with your Barney toy. Doesn't that sound like fun?"

As fast as her mouth drooped, it now is replaced by a big smile. She claps happily and skips to the bathroom. I follow and run the water while she undresses, singing the annoying theme from the TV show. When she's in the tub, I pull the rubber band from her hair and dump water over her head. She blows bubbles as I do so. I get her washed as she happily plays with the big purple dinosaur, and then I have to convince her to get out of the tub. Convincing her to get out is as difficult as getting her in.

Once she's dried and dressed, she sits back in front of the TV to watch cartoons, *Barney* long since forgotten, while I start dinner. I'm angry that my aunt is still not home. I wonder how long my mom sat here alone, unsupervised, until I arrived.

She comes in when I'm just about done with the spaghetti, acting like nothing is wrong.

"Hi, Charlotte," Naomi says. I bristle at the name. It's not that I dislike the name; my grandma chose it for me because it was her own mother's name. It's because my aunt refuses to call me Charlie like everyone else does simply because it's the nickname my mom gave me.

"Where were you?" I ask.

She stops in the act of setting her purse down to stare at me. "That's none of your business."

"It is when you leave my mom home alone," I retort. "She can't be left on her own."

"I was gone maybe ten minutes before you got home from school. What can happen in ten minutes?"

A lot, I think. I refrain from telling her, though, knowing our living here is precarious and based on staying in her good graces.

"I have a life, Charlotte. Allowing you two to move in didn't include the requirement that I give up all my freedom."

"I understand that," I say, biting my tongue to keep from telling her how selfish she is. "I'm coming home directly after school. I haven't signed up for any extracurricular activities or anything. I'll even get up early to bathe her if that's too much to ask of you. All I *do* ask is that you watch her while I'm gone."

Naomi sighs. "We need to talk."

"It's time to eat," I say. I have a feeling I know what she's going to say. I move past her to call my mom when she places a hand on my arm.

"Not all homes are bad places," she begins, and fury consumes me.

"I will *not* place my mother in a *home*," I spit.

"You shouldn't have to give up normal teen things to take care—"

"I don't care!" I'm shaking with anger. "I don't care about any of that. I'll drop out of school if I have to. I'm *not* putting her in a home!"

Naomi sighs again, and I'm tempted to punch her. What does she know of taking care of my mom? She abandoned ship as soon as she graduated from high school to get away from the embarrassment of having my mom for a sister. Plus, she *knows* what happened when my grandma did buckle under pressure—from Naomi, no less—and put her in a home. How could she possibly subject her to that again?

"I know it's not ideal—"

I spin away from her, refusing to listen to another word. I walk into the living room where my mom sits, curled up on the couch, a blanket pulled up to her ear in one hand, sucking on the thumb of her other. My shoulders sink in dismay as I walk over to her. Her eyes are glued to the TV, but I know she's not watching it.

"Mom," I say softly, sitting down and placing a hand on her arm. Her wide, innocent eyes turn to me.

"Does Mimi hate you?" she whispers, voice trembling. Mimi is her nickname for Naomi.

"No, Mom, she doesn't. Were we talking too loud?"

She shakes her head. "You were yelling." Gotta love Mom's honesty.

"I'm sorry, Mom. We were just having a disagreement. I love Mimi, and she loves me." Blatant lie. "Everything's fine now. I'm sorry we scared you. You want to come have some spaghetti now?"

She nods and takes my proffered hand, rising from the couch. When we enter the kitchen, Naomi is outside, pacing, smoking a cigarette. I bite the inside of my cheek. I *hate* that she smokes, but at least she no longer smokes in the house with my mom and me. I suppose I can give her a few points for that.

I sit my mom at the table and fix a plate for her before taking the time to check my blood sugar. I prick my finger at the counter with my back turned because it tends to freak my mom out. She thinks I'm hurting myself. A few minutes later, Naomi comes in. My mom brightens.

"Hi, Mimi," she says happily.

"Hi, Cora." Naomi gives her a tight smile, then fixes herself a plate. "I'm going to eat in my room," she says. At the doorway she pauses, and without looking back says, "Thanks for dinner."

If my mom weren't sitting here, I'd probably scream. Instead, I smile and play a word game with her while we eat.

THREE
BENJAMIN

Dinner is a lonely affair as usual. I don't care. I prefer it that way. The microwave beeps, my burritos nuked. I open the fridge door and pull out the crusty bottle of salsa and container of sour cream. Green fuzz coats the top layer of the sour cream. I consider scraping it off and eating what's beneath, but then decide I can't afford food poisoning right now. Not with the game in two days.

I dump what little salsa is left across the burritos and toss the empty bottle into the trash, where it crashes loudly against the other bottles that fill the can—empty beer bottles. Guess I'd better take that out.

My cell buzzes as I sit down and take my first bite. Lava-hot beans and cheese burn my tongue and the roof of my mouth. "Argh," is the sound that comes out of my mouth as I open wide, trying to blow around the bite of burrito, as if that will somehow relieve the burning. I quickly swallow the hot bite and follow it with a large swig of water, hoping it will prevent the burning from continuing down my esophagus.

My phone buzzes again and I pull it out of my pocket. As I suspected, it's a text from Daniel.

Dude, meet me at Mega-Cinema at 9.

I text back: *On a school night? What would your mother say, Danny boy?*

C'mon, man, what if hot new girl shows?

That stops me from texting my auto refusal. What if hot new girl *does* show? She intrigues me. I've spent a lot of years honing the charm, as well as the biceps and abs, which means it's a rare girl who can resist me. And yet, Charlie . . . uh, Charlie . . . what did she say her last name is? Anyway, Charlie seems to have no problem resisting. I sense a challenge.

I glance toward the trash can, remembering the sound of the bottles within. I know *exactly* what that means. My life is nothing if not predictable, and I know the bottles in the can mean I'm not going anywhere tonight.

Sorry, bro, gotta get a report done or my butt's in a sling, I text. *Give her a kiss for me. Wait, strike that. Talk me up to her.*

My phone is silent for a few minutes. I know he's debating trying to convince me to come, but I also know he's well aware it won't work. Finally it buzzes.

Your loss, man. If she's there I'll be talking ME up.

I laugh, knowing that's not true. Daniel and I have a very clear understanding about girls—I get first pick, and he gets either the leftovers or my picks once I'm finished with them. I glance at my phone and realize I don't have much time left.

I quickly finish the now tolerable-temperature burritos, then rinse my plate in the sink and put it in the dishwasher. After hiding all of the big knives in the freezer, I gather the bag full of bottles and take it to the large can outside. Back inside I look around to see what items make the worst weapons and place them in the backs of various cabinets. I can't move too many items where it's obvious, or it'll set him off. Avoiding setting him off is priority one.

Then I settle in to wait.

It doesn't take long. I hear his car and I grab a notebook and sit at the kitchen table, pretending to do homework. I can't have any real homework out on the off chance he decides to target that. He's done it before. He'll do it again. He stumbles through the front door and I clench my jaw. Why has he never gotten a DUI? The man drives drunk more than he does sober, and yet he's never been pulled over. Makes me wonder if the cops are simply waiting for him to kill someone before they do. It wouldn't kill *him*—I'm not that lucky.

He barrels his way into the kitchen, and in spite of myself, I cringe. Shame fills me that I do, but in my defense, I've spent a lot of years on the receiving end of his fists. My dad is a big man, roughly the size of a grizzly, or so it seems. I'm pretty tall at six-four, but he towers over me. As much as I work out to build my muscles, I can't hold a candle to his brawn or his meaty fists that are already clenched before he even sees me.

"Damn loser," he says in greeting. No worries for him winning Father of the Year. I don't respond. I don't even bother looking up, but I watch his feet furtively. I need to be prepared when he nears, which he does rather quickly for an enormous, drunk man.

His fist lands on the side of my head, but the blow isn't so bad. Because I'm prepared, I duck as he swings, causing his blow to glance off the side of my head. I stand, moving back from him as he swings again, this time catching my shoulder. I grimace in pain, in the back of my mind thinking about the possibility that a bruise might affect my playing in the game.

"Stop, Dad," I say, the words coming in spite of my trying to keep them back.

"Stop what, loser?" he slurs, swinging again, connecting with the center of my back as I turn away. "Fight back, coward."

I don't want to. And yet, without a doubt I know what will happen if I don't obey the command. He's told me before in no uncertain terms. He even began a convincing demonstration on more than one occasion until I caved. I've also learned, though, not to fight back until he requests it.

I turn his way. Because he's drunk, I at least have a small chance to, if not win, at least escape mostly unscathed. And so I fight back, no emotion coming into play as I do. I don't feel any more or less for hitting him or receiving his blows than I do when I stand in the boxing ring. Finally, he swings at my head and misses, the force knocking him to the floor. He's passed out cold as soon as he lands. I wipe the blood that drips from my lip with the back of my fist as I stare down at him. I want to hate him, I genuinely do. But that requires feeling I don't have. I feel nothing for him.

Shamed at the life I live, the life not a single soul outside of my father knows about, I drop a blanket over his prone form and then drag myself to the shower. The hot water will loosen my tight muscles, and hopefully I won't show too many signs tomorrow. Since I've made a rep for myself for hitting up the local boxing club quite frequently, no one questions the random bruises or cuts I might show up with.

Before stepping into the shower I stare at myself in the mirror. I touch my lip gingerly, turning my head to the side to examine the red mark where he managed to get a blow in. I press against the mark. Not too sore, so likely no bruise or black eye, or at least not too bad.

I avoid looking myself directly in the eye. I can't do it. Haven't been able to for years. My life is sick, twisted, at the mercy of insanity and absence of reason. I pick up the bar of soap and drag it back and forth across the mirror until I'm obliterated.

FOUR
CHARLIE

First period is a killer. I'm dead tired. I was up late, worrying about whether Naomi was going to kick us out, and what my mom and I will do if she does. I woke up extra early to get my mom bathed, trying to stave off anything that might make us seem like a bigger pain to Naomi. Being tired can throw off my blood-sugar levels, so I'll have to watch it today, pay attention to my body.

Naomi is pretty well-off because of a wealthy husband who died and made her the beneficiary of a large life insurance policy. She doesn't work. I'm not sure what she does all day since we've only been here a few days. Either she stays home with my mom or she goes somewhere and refuses to say where she's been. Like it's some big secret or something.

Staying awake while the teacher drones on about absolute convergence while writing a series of numbers on the board is nearly impossible. I lean on one hand, trying to decide if I can sneak in a little nap without it being obvious. A sharp pain in my side wakes me up. I glance around to see Cozi smiling while she wiggles the pencil she poked me with between two fingers. She mock-yawns behind one manicured hand.

Cozi is definitely unlike anyone I've ever met. She's absolutely gorgeous with her ebony skin, golden-brown eyes, and long, black hair—created by a weave she has redone once a month. She dresses in clothes fashionably mismatched, with a wide, studded belt and high-top sneakers that are clearly not cheap. And yet she's one of the kindest people I've met. She's not conceited in even the vaguest sense of the term. She genuinely loves everyone. As I watch, she turns her attention back to the Bible on her desk. School is a bore to someone as smart as Cozi. She prefers to study and mark her religious text. Cozi is the furthest thing from what I imagined a Jehovah's Witness to be.

As I move my gaze from her to turn back to the front, my eyes are caught by Benjamin, who stares intently at me from two rows over. My mouth drops as I see the fat lip and bruise around his eye. A lazy smile crosses his face and I snap my jaw closed, eyes locked quickly back on the board that the teacher continues to scribble on. I can feel his gaze boring into me, but I refuse to look at him again.

I have to admit that Benjamin is an extremely good-looking guy. Dark hair cut short, curly on top, with green eyes. His smooth skin is olive, giving him an exotic appearance as if his heritage is something different from that of most of the white people who live in the area. His wide, slightly crooked smile shows deep grooves around the corners of his mouth and full lips. He has a strong jaw and a straight nose. He's tall, and because of his athleticism, his body is hard with muscle. He'd be hard for any girl to ignore—and he seems to know it.

When the bell rings I stand and turn to Cozi.

"Rough night?" she asks.

"Something like that," I say. I don't mean to, but my gaze flicks to Benjamin.

"He's trouble," Cozi says, following my look. "I saw him staring at you."

"It's because I'm new," I say.

"That's true," she confirms as she gathers her books. "But I'm giving you fair warning. You're hot, so he's going to pursue you hard. Then, when you've gone out with him once or twice, he'll drop you without a backward glance. He does it to everyone."

We move toward the door. "Did he do it to you?" I ask.

"Of course not. He's not of my faith, so I wouldn't date him." She grins. "Plus, I'm way too smart to fall for his shtick."

I laugh at her just as the object of our conversation catches up to us in the hall.

"Hey, Cozi. Hey, new girl," he says.

Cozi points at his face. "What does the other guy look like?"

A look flashes through his eyes, gone too quickly for me to determine what it means. "Worse than me, as always," he says with a smile, his face returning to lazy charm, eyes blank.

"You should quit going to that place," she says with a head shake. "Violence is not attractive."

"Aw, c'mon, Coze," he says, slinging an arm across her shoulders. "You know you love the bad-guy look."

Cozi shrugs out of his hold. "You could definitely learn a little humility, Benjamin Nefer."

"Nefer?" I ask, repeating the unusual name.

"Ahhh, she speaks," he drawls.

"Turn off the charm, Benny, I've already warned her about you," Cozi says, hooking an arm through mine and dragging me away.

‿

Lunch finds me sitting with Cozi and Alexis. Phoebe doesn't share this lunch period. Soon we're joined by a few other girls and some guys—including Benjamin and Daniel. It seems pretty obvious that these guys usually eat together since no one remarks on their appearing. It kind of surprises me since Cozi doesn't seem fond of Benjamin at all, and yet she accepts his presence easily.

Everyone mills about the table, seeming more interested in socializing than actually eating. But I'm starving. I didn't get a chance to eat this morning since I was trying to get my mom ready, only having time to chug some juice to keep my sugar levels up. I also didn't have a chance to make a lunch, but my blood-sugar level is now a little low, so I'm eating a salad of wilting lettuce and questionable strips of meat and cheese that I have to eat for the protein, with a stale roll I have to eat for the carbs, and drinking a warm soda for a quick sugar boost.

Suddenly Benjamin is next to me. He slides his long legs beneath the table, sitting a little too close for comfort. He props an elbow on the table and leans his head against his fist, turned my way.

"How can you eat that crap?" he asks.

"Because I'm hungry," I say simply. I glance at the empty table in front of him. "Where's your lunch?"

"I don't eat lunch," he says. He sits up and pats his tight abdomen. "Gotta watch the figure, right?" He leans closer. "Unless you want to watch it for me," he murmurs.

I narrow my eyes at him. Is this guy for real? "Does this approach really work on girls?" I hear myself asking. I'd been thinking the words but hadn't meant to speak them.

He looks a little taken aback but quickly recovers, a grin spreading across his face. "Is it working now?"

I roll my eyes and turn my attention away from him.

"You're a hard one to crack, aren't you?" he mumbles. I glance at him. "Well, I appreciate a good challenge."

I smile at him, my shoulders dropping a bit. Thinking he's making headway, he smiles back. I almost flinch, though, when I realize that the smile doesn't come anywhere near his eyes. They're almost . . . dead. I lean toward him.

"Don't hurt yourself, big guy," I say, popping the last bite of roll into my mouth. I stand up, dragging my tray with me as his smile fades. "I'm not falling for it." I wink at him as I turn away, not looking back when I hear Cozi and Alexis laughing at my shutdown.

FIVE
CHARLIE

When I get home from school, my overwhelming desire is to take a nap. But my new resolve to make sure my aunt doesn't place my mom back into a home keeps me from giving in to my desire. Plus, it'll be another late night with homework. I'd really, *really* like a nap.

"Hi, Mom," I say, stepping into the family room, where she watches *Mary Poppins*. I smile at her rapt attention on the TV.

She grins delightedly at me, pausing the movie before coming from the couch to hug me enthusiastically. "I missed you," she says.

"I've only been gone a few hours, Mom." She continues to hold me before abruptly releasing me and skipping happily back to the couch, her words forgotten. I sigh. "Where's Mimi?"

My mom points toward the hallway. I follow where she indicates and find my aunt in her bedroom, working on her computer.

"Hi," I say, stopping in the doorway. "I'm home now."

"Hi, Charlotte." Her tone is relaxed, which immediately puts me on edge. As I turn to leave the room her voice stops me. "Can I talk to you for a minute?"

I clench my fists. I really don't want to talk to her, but since I'm trying to play nice, I paste a smile on my face. "Sure."

I walk into the room, sit on the small bench at her vanity close to her desk, and wait.

"I know you're opposed to putting your mom into a home because of what hap—"

I abruptly stand, not wanting to listen.

"I have custody of her," she says as I swing away, striding from the room. Her words stop me just outside the door. I turn back, not bothering to hide the anger on my face. She holds her hands up in surrender.

"Look, Charlotte, legally I can have her placed if I want, but it's not what I want to do." She pauses as I suck in deep breaths, trying to control the emotion threatening to overwhelm me. I hate that she's right—she can do what she wants and I can't do anything to stop her. Even once I turn eighteen I'll have to go to court to get custody.

"I'm not going to have her put into a home, Charlotte. I'm well aware of what happened to her . . . before." She looks down, refusing to meet my gaze. I'm guessing she's not sure of just exactly how much I know. "I just want to talk to you about some options."

I fold my arms. "What options?"

"There are some places where she can go during the day. Be with others . . . like her."

"No." My word is short. Final.

"Charlotte, she—"

"Charlie," I say, though I know it's a wasted effort.

She takes a deep breath and blows it out. "Cora just sits here all day, watching TV. Is that really the kind of life you want for her? Just sitting and waiting for you to get home?"

I admit her words make me pause for just a second. Then I remember what happened to her eighteen years ago when she *was* in a home, and the reason for my existence. I'd never subject her to even the slightest chance of that kind of violence again.

"She likes watching TV," I say.

"She'd have friends there," Naomi argues.

I lean against the doorjamb. "I don't know if you think you're helping her, or if you're just trying to get rid of her, but do you honestly think being there only during the day will protect her? Are you selfish enough to put her at risk again just so you don't have to deal with her?"

Naomi pales. Her voice is strained. "It's not that at all, Charlotte."

"Whatever," I say, straightening. "I'll fight you on this. I won't let you do it to her." Fear worms into my gut that this will be the thing that makes her kick us out. Without waiting for a response, I turn to go join my mom in whatever she wants to do that will make her happy.

SIX
BENJAMIN

Sweat drenches my shirt and beads on my forehead as I bear-crawl across the field. My usually intense and singular concentration is broken today. The reason for that flashes through my mind yet again.

The new girl. Charlie. She's unlike any girl I've met before. I've never had a problem getting a girl to like me. One smile and a few well-placed looks or words, and I can have anyone I want. Not her. Why?

That question is what breaks my concentration. It bothers me more than it should. It's not like I really like her or anything. That isn't even possible, for her or anyone. But the fact that she's immune to me . . . that *really* irritates me. Beyond reason. If there's one thing in my life I'm sure of, one place I have power, it's this.

Suddenly it occurs to me: *She's not into guys.* I stumble at the realization. Abruptly everyone turns to look at me. I don't stumble. Ever.

"Everything okay, Nefer?"

"I'm good, Coach," I say, waving a hand dismissively. He looks at me oddly but gestures for everyone to return to their exercises.

I'm able to relax and focus better now that I have a pretty good idea of how she's able to stay so cold. That has to be it. There can be no other explanation.

❦

I see Charlie at her locker and hurry over, wanting to test my theory. She's standing with her back to the hallway, hunched just a bit.

"Hey, new girl," I say.

She jumps, looking over her shoulder guiltily. She quickly shoves something into her locker before slamming it closed. Only then does she fully face me.

"Hey, Benjamin," she says. Her voice is oddly tight, and she watches me closely as if waiting for a reaction of some kind.

"Everything okay?"

"Fine," she says, straightening and moving down the hall toward the lunchroom. I hurry to catch up with her. She sticks her middle finger into her mouth briefly, and the thought comes that maybe she's on some kind of drug or something. That would explain her guilty look and sucking on her finger, but it doesn't explain her resistance to me. Or maybe it could, I guess. I still believe my first thought is the correct one.

"So . . ." I begin, wondering how to ask. Should I be blatant about it, or should I fish for the answer?

"So, what?" she asks when I don't finish my thought.

"I was wondering . . . where you moved here from."

"Idaho," she answers, surprising me.

"Idaho, huh? Potatoes and all that?"

"Yes, there are potatoes in Idaho," she says, looking at me as if I'm slow.

"I mean, did you . . . grow potatoes?" I grimace at the awkward conversation. This isn't how I intended it to go at all.

She stops walking and turns to face me. I'm struck again by her natural beauty. She's not like one of the typical popular girls, covered in makeup, every hair in place. Instead the look on her face is open, fresh, her incredible hazel eyes fringed in long lashes. Right now those eyes are flashing at me.

"Do you really care, Benjamin? Why are you doing this? I told you I'm not interested."

I nod. "Yeah, I figured that out."

Surprise crosses her face. "You did?"

"Well, yeah, I mean, it wasn't that hard. I get it, okay? I get that you're, you know . . ."

"I'm what?" she asks suspiciously, her face darkening.

I suddenly realize that she might not be ready to let everyone know. So I shrug. "Immune to my charms," I say teasingly.

The smallest of smiles tilts the corners of her mouth. "And you're okay with that?"

"Of course," I say. "I mean, jeez, it's not the fifties or something. I'm totally fine with it."

Confusion flits across her face, pulling her brows together.

"So why are you still talking to me then?" she finally asks.

"I thought we could be friends," I say. Then I shrug. "I mean, there aren't a lot of girls I'm friends with. I've dated most of them, and now—"

"They hate you?" she supplies with a grin.

"Something like that," I say. "But since there's no chance of you wanting to date me, it might be nice to have a girlfriend . . ." At her lifted brow, I revise. "*Friend* that's a *girl* without any pressure."

"Huh," she says, leaning back, crossing her arms, a small smile playing across her lips.

"What?"

"Either this is some new game you've devised to try to get me to change my mind, or you're being sincere. I don't know you well enough to decipher the difference."

A thought flits through my mind. *Change* her? Huh. I shake my head.

"The second one . . . I think."

She laughs at my joke, and I laugh with her. She really does have a great laugh.

"All right, friend," she says. "Let's go eat lunch. I'm starving."

SEVEN
CHARLIE

After I have my mom tucked into bed, I sit in my room working on homework. It's late and my eyes burn with the need for sleep, but I've got to get this math done before tomorrow. I *hate* math. Seriously, when am I ever going to use this in my life? But I do it for my mom, so that I can go to college, get a degree, and support us.

I think about my strange day with Benjamin. I thought he'd caught me checking my blood sugar, especially when he started to say he'd figured it out. Then he said something about the fifties, or at least I think that's what he said. I didn't question him too much because I didn't want to give away my secret.

I know that sooner or later they'll all know. I can't hide it forever, and it's not really that big of a deal. I just kind of hate it, when they know. When they stop looking at me as just another girl and start to look at me with a tinge of pity, and I stop being Charlie and become *the girl with diabetes*.

I rub my eyes and try to focus on my laptop screen, where the impossible problems wait to be solved.

૦૭

Of course it would be Benjamin who's nearby when my pump goes off, alerting me to the fact that I need to refill the cartridge with insulin. It couldn't have been Cozi, Alexis, or Phoebe, who I could count on to keep quiet about it.

Since Benjamin's strange speech about figuring out that I wasn't going to fall for him, he's actually been pretty cool. He doesn't send me long, lingering looks or give me that crooked grin. And even under pain of torture I'll never admit I miss having that smile sent my way. He just hangs out near me, not even taking an especially close interest in me.

Today, though, he's walking by as my alarm goes off, and I glance up to see who's heard, making eye contact with him. He stops.

"Hey, new girl," he says, coming close.

I grit my teeth in frustration. I knew I was close to being out of insulin, but I didn't have time to fill my pump this morning after taking care of my mom, and then I sort of forgot about it until my alarm just went off. I seriously consider ignoring it, but my sugar is a little high and I'm hungry, so I plan to eat lunch. Plus I have a test in geography this afternoon, and if I let myself run high, I'm going to get a bad grade.

"Hey," I say, turning away, hoping he'll move on. Instead, he comes over, leaning against the locker next to mine.

"That your phone?" Benjamin asks, eyeing the pump in my hand.

I nearly roll my eyes. Seriously, can't he see the tubing coming from it? What does he think, that I carry a corded cell phone?

"No," I say, not offering any more info.

"Oh." He doesn't press, though the curious look doesn't leave his face. He also doesn't look like he's about to leave, so I sigh and pull out my supply bag.

"It's an insulin pump," I say, pulling out a new cartridge and a bottle of insulin.

"Insulin?" he asks with even more curiosity reflecting in his face. "As in, what people who are diabetic take?"

"Yup," I say as I tip the bottle up and insert the syringe inside.

"Are you . . . Do you have diabetes?"

He says it as most people do, full of questions but hoping I'll volunteer the information so he doesn't have to ask.

"Uh-huh," I answer, pulling the plunger back and watching as the liquid swirls into the cartridge.

"Huh." He seems stumped. I don't say anything, and avoid looking at him. I'm not looking forward to turning his way and seeing him staring at me like I'm fragile. Finally, he says, "So, you have to give yourself shots and stuff?"

"No," I say, tapping the air bubbles in the syringe to the top and pushing them out with the plunger. "I just use the pump. It gives the insulin to me."

"How?"

I finally look at him, and instead of giving me the usual "she'll break if I'm not careful" expression, he just looks kind of curious. Not even intensely curious, more almost as if he's required to ask these questions he doesn't really care about. Odd.

I lift the pump, pull out the old cartridge, and insert the new. "This. It's like a little machine, gives me insulin whenever I need it."

"How does it know when you need it?"

"It gives me small doses all day. When I need extra, I tell it," I say, pushing the buttons required to load the insulin, unclipping the tubing from the site in my belly without even looking. I finish the loading process, then lift the bottom of my shirt to reattach the tubing. Benjamin straightens beside me, his body going stiff. I glance at him and see he's staring at my belly where I've lifted my shirt. I quickly drop it, cheeks flushing. It was completely unconscious on my part. I've been doing this for so long I sometimes forget others aren't used to it. I know he saw both the inset and the little round scars that dot my belly. "Sorry," I mutter.

He clears his throat and when I glance at him again, I swear his cheeks are a little pink beneath his olive skin. His reaction isn't one of disgust as I'd suspected, or even the pity that I'd feared. It's something I haven't seen on him before, something the suave Benjamin manages to always avoid.

He's nervous, as if he's never seen a girl's belly before. *Right.* Like Benjamin probably hasn't seen *hundreds* of girls' bellies.

I shut my locker and turn his way. "Should we go?" I say, waving a hand toward the lunchroom.

He nods and we begin walking.

"Hey, Benjamin?" I wait until he looks at me. "Not that it's a secret or anything, but I'd just prefer people found out later rather than sooner about me. About my diabetes."

He looks at me oddly, but nods his consent. "Sure. Not a problem. It's not my place to share it."

I smile at him. "Thanks."

He smiles back, but it's a thin smile. As usual it doesn't come close to reflecting in his eyes.

EIGHT
BENJAMIN

Stars explode behind my eyes. I stagger a little and shake my head.

"You okay, man?"

I look at my sparring partner, a new guy who only recently began coming to the gym. He's shorter than me, but probably outweighs me by a good fifty pounds of muscle. I hoped he'd give me a good pounding. So far, he hasn't disappointed.

"I'm good," I answer, straightening my headgear and biting down on the mouthpiece. I lift my gloved hands and move into place. He backs off a bit, giving me some room.

I swing, catching his padded jaw in an uppercut. His head snaps to the side a little and he quickly returns a check hook against the side of my head with one hand and a kidney punch with the other. I grunt and he drops his hands again.

"Need a break?" he asks.

No, I want to say, *I prefer you beat me senseless*. But since I'm bent over trying to catch my breath it's a little hard to say anything. I lift a glove at him that can be interpreted as anything he wants, and he pats me on the back.

"Good session, man," he says.

I nod and he steps out of the ring. I stand and take some deep breaths. Glancing at the clock I see that it's almost ten. Time to get home. A quick shower and I'm out the door, walking over to my car. It's an old Honda, but it's reliable and cheap, and gets good gas mileage.

I throw my gear into the trunk before sliding into the driver's seat. I stick the key in the ignition, but don't turn it. The beating didn't help. I can still picture it. Charlie, lifting her shirt just a little, exposing a small portion of her stomach, the white circle with a hard plastic center and thin tubing leading from it.

Placing my hands on the top of my steering wheel, I lean down until my forehead rests on my hands. "What is wrong with me?" I mutter into the silence. I can't figure it out. I've seen plenty of girls' abdomens. The cheerleaders are always showing theirs during games. Girls wear short shirts to school sometimes. At the swimming pool they're exposed on almost every girl. Magazine covers, TV shows, movies . . . there's no lack of skin to be viewed.

And yet, something about Charlie so innocently lifting her shirt, seeing a completely vulnerable place on her body that I suspect she keeps hidden from the world, it . . . did *something* to me. Something I can't name. And that scares the crap out of me.

∽

"Coming to the game tomorrow night?" I aim the question nonchalantly at Charlie as we sit at lunch, acting as if I don't care what her answer is. And I don't, not really. Maybe a little. I'd like her to come and see me in the one thing I do that is completely mine, the one thing I shine brilliantly at.

She glances up at me. "No, I can't."

"Why not?" Alexis asks. "C'mon, we have a blast at the games. Gives us some reason for putting up with all the crap around here all week."

Charlie smiles, and I swear I can see regret in her eyes. "I wish I could, but I have to, um, babysit tonight."

"You still babysit?" Phoebe asks. Phoebe, small and petite with her auburn hair and dark eyes, has never known what it means to have to earn money. Her parents give her everything she wants, and most things she *doesn't* want.

"Wait," Alexis says. "Little brothers and sisters?"

"No," Charlie answers, almost hesitantly. "Someone . . . else."

"Hope it's good money," Phoebe says. Apparently bored with any conversation regarding work, she asks me, "Gonna win this one, Benjamin?"

"Don't we always?" I grin. But I'm watching Charlie from the corner of my eye. Something's off with her.

"You try, anyway," Cozi says flippantly. The girls all laugh, except Charlie, who just keeps eating.

"I wish you could come," Alexis says. She glances at me and away again quickly. I know she's still smarting from my rejection of her. Maybe I'll have to sic one of the other players on her to give her someone else to focus on. Alexis is very pretty, no doubt. Straight, dark hair, big, green eyes, taller than most girls, which is nice for a tall guy like me, and a great body. If there ever were a candidate for a girlfriend, she'd be one of the top runners. But since it's not possible for me to have a girlfriend, it's a moot point.

"Me, too," Charlie says. "Maybe some other time."

"We have another game next Friday," I say, not sure why I'm speaking up.

She glances at me. "We'll see."

Well, thanks a lot, Captain Vague, I think cynically.

After lunch is the one and only class Charlie and I have in common. I didn't walk with her the first few days she was here, but now that we've become "friends," it seems silly to walk separately. And since we walk together, it also seems strange to separate once we enter the room, so now I find myself sitting next to or behind her most days.

PSYCHOLOGY is written in large, decorative letters on the chalkboard, has been since day one. Makes me want to ask the teacher, Mr. Snow, what he's trying to compensate for. I lean over and share my thoughts with Charlie.

She glances at me and lets a small giggle escape, her eyes shining with laughter. And I'm gut punched. Her open humor takes me by surprise. She's not trying to get me to notice her, or get me to ask her out, or get me to fall in love with her. Just simple enjoyment of my bad joke.

Mr. Snow walks up to the head of the class, and Charlie turns to the front, a small smile still playing about her mouth.

"Well, people, as you know, psychology is as much about observation as studying those thick textbooks they make us give you at the beginning of the year. To that end, you'll need to partner up with someone in this class for some observation exercises." He pulls out a clipboard and holds it up. "I'll send this around. If you have someone in mind, put your names together on a single line. If you don't have a preference, just list your name and I'll assign you a partner." He places it on the front corner desk, then turns back to the board to begin writing.

I happen to be sitting in the first row. When the clipboard is passed to me, I write my name down. Then I glance to the side, toward Charlie. She looks up at the same time and our eyes meet. I tap my pen against the board, my eyebrows lifted in question. Her eyes flicker to the list, then back up to me. She smiles and gives a small nod, and I write her name next to mine.

Benjamin Nefer & Charlie

I stare at the paper, realizing I don't remember her last name. I tip the board toward her and point at the blank spot. She takes it, writes her last name, and passes it back.

Benjamin Nefer & Charlie **Austin**

Her handwriting next to mine is clear and neat, her pen pressed harder than mine—strange for a girl. Usually girls' writing is lighter, not heavier.

Our names, side by side on the paper. For some reason it brings back the memory of her lifting the bottom of her shirt, and a flush heats my cheeks. Almost angrily I toss it on the desk behind me. *Get a grip.* Even if I want her—which I don't—she's got zero interest in me.

Man, I need to find me a new girl to date.

NINE
CHARLIE

I sit next to my mom on the couch and allow my eyes to slide shut, just for a minute, while she's distracted by *The Little Mermaid*. I really should be working on my homework, but I'm just too tired to care right now. Suddenly I'm being shaken awake.

"Charlie, I'm hungry," my mom whines. I glance at the window, surprised to see that it's dark outside.

"Oh, Mom, I'm so sorry," I say. "I didn't mean to fall asleep."

I jump up and hurry into the kitchen, and stop short. Naomi is there.

"Sorry." I repeat what I just said to my mom. "I didn't mean to fall asleep. I'll get dinner started."

"I already ordered a pizza," she says. As if her words conjure the delivery guy, the doorbell rings. Naomi hands me a twenty. Clearly she wants me to play butler and get the door. I take it from her and try not to be irritated, since she's at least paying for it. I swing the front door open, and freeze.

"One large pepperoni and a side of garlic bread," Benjamin says, not looking at me, but rather at the pizza bag he's wrestling the boxes from. "That'll be . . . Hey!" He sees me now.

"Hi," I say as I pull the door behind me. I can't quite close it all the way without stepping onto the porch, which I can't do with him standing there.

He glances up at the house. "So, this is where you live?"

I nod. "Yeah."

He nods. "Nice place."

"It's not ours," I say. "We live with my aunt." I'm not sure why I'm telling him this, since it can't possibly matter to him.

"Huh," he says. He points behind him and down the road to the west. "I live down that way about a mile and a half."

"Almost neighbors," I tease.

"Almost," he agrees, grinning. "Of course, any of the houses in my neighborhood would fit inside the garage of this house." He looks away as if embarrassed to have told me that.

"So would the house I moved here from," I say.

His eyes come back to me at that. We stand there, awkwardly silent for a few seconds. Then he lifts the pizza boxes a little. "Well, I guess here's your dinner."

"Oh, yeah, thanks," I say, taking the boxes and handing him the money. "Is that enough?" I ask. "You didn't say how much it was."

"It's too much, actually," he says. "I owe you some change."

I hold up a hand. "Keep it. My aunt's paying. She can afford the tip."

"Thanks," he says, shoving the money into his front pocket. He shuffles a little. "Well, guess I better get the rest of these pizzas delivered." He waves a hand toward an old red Honda sitting in the driveway with a temporary lighted sign on top advertising Tony's Pizzeria.

"Your car?" I ask, not sure why I'm dragging this out. I should just let him go.

"Yup." He looks at it. "It's old, but it's reliable."

I nod. "I don't have a car, so I wouldn't complain about *any* car, no matter how old."

He looks back at me. "How do you get to school?"

"Walk or ride the bus, depending on the weather."

"Oh." He doesn't seem to know how to answer as he takes a step back off the porch. "Well, see ya."

"Bye," I say, pushing back against the door, ready to go inside.

Suddenly he turns back. "I could give you a ride," he says.

"What?"

"To school. I pass right by here on my way. I could pick you up so you won't have to walk or ride the bus."

"Oh, um, I don't—" My words are cut off as I hear my mom calling me from inside. "Gotta go," I say quickly, withdrawing into the house. "Bye." I hurriedly close the door, knowing it's a little rude, but preferring that to him hearing my mom.

I stand with my back pressed against the door, balancing the hot box on one arm. I hear his car start as he pulls out of the driveway and I breathe a sigh of relief. Then I straighten and move to feed my mom.

❦

"You can't keep this up."

I sit upright at Naomi's words. It's nearly two a.m. and I'm trying to finish my homework. She's standing in my doorway.

"I didn't hear you knock," I accuse.

"Your door was open," she says.

I look at my door in surprise, as if it somehow opened itself. Didn't I close it?

"You have to be up for school in a few hours. You have your health to think of," she says.

My jaw clenches as she says the words. Like she knows anything about my health. "Yeah, well, I have to get this done."

"Charlotte, this is ridiculous. Neither one of us can take care of Cora properly—"

"I take care of her just fine," I say loudly, offended.

Naomi sighs. "I'm not saying you're not *capable* of taking care of her. You are. So am I. But we both have other obligations—"

"Yeah, I'd hate for taking care of Mom to cut into your luncheons." I know I'm acting like a sullen child, but I can't seem to help myself. "Why don't you go . . . smoke a cancer stick or something?"

She stands silently for a minute, not looking at me. Finally she gives one single nod and pulls my door closed. I stare at the backside of my door, weariness pulling at me, and a little guilt. That was pretty rude of me. Not for the first time I realize how much my grandma did for my mom and me. She took care of almost everything, which gave me time to be a semi-normal teenager. I didn't know at the time how much of the burden she carried. It's clear now.

I wonder how long I *can* keep this up. *Forever*, I answer myself. I'll never abandon my mom, no matter the cost. I feel a surge of anger at my aunt for her refusal to help other than staying home during the day with my mom. I take care of her before school and from the time I get home until she goes to bed. I do her laundry and keep the house clean as much as possible so my aunt can't say we aren't pulling our weight. My mom's paltry disability checks go completely to my aunt. I don't spend anything on myself.

I look down at my history book. The pages are blurry, so I close it. I'll have to try to work on it during some of my other classes tomorrow. I grab my monitor, check my blood sugar, grunting when I see it's only 81. I'm forced to get up, go to the kitchen, and grab a juice. If I'm not over 100 when I go to bed, it's almost guaranteed I'll wake up low.

I chug the apple juice and then go to bed without waiting to check my levels again. I'll take my chances.

TEN
BENJAMIN

I drive slowly down Charlie's street, not sure if I should pull in to see if she wants a ride. She didn't say she did, and we didn't clarify a time. The way she pulled back into her house when her name was called made me pause and wonder. Was her situation like mine? It sounded like whoever called her might have been drunk.

As I near her house and try to make up my mind whether to stop or not, I see her up ahead, hurrying down the sidewalk toward the corner where the bus stop is. I speed up to catch her before she gets there. Turns out not to be necessary since we both see the big yellow bus come by, slow, then speed up when the driver doesn't spy any students waiting. Charlie's shoulders slump.

I roll down the passenger-side window. "New girl! Need a ride?" I call. She startles, then relaxes when she spies me. She walks over to the car and leans down. I notice her jacket slung over her arm, and an apple clenched in her hand.

"Following me, Nefer?" she says with a grin.

"Maybe," I shrug, waggling my eyebrows. "Would it help my chances with you if I were?"

She laughs as she stands, opens the door, and climbs in. She gives me a wry look. "Thought we were past that."

I shrug as she pulls her seatbelt on. "Can't blame a guy for trying."

She shakes her head as she takes a bite of her apple. "You know, Nefer, if you treated *all* girls like this, you might actually have a few who still like you."

"But then none of them would date me," I argue, ignoring the warmth her words cause.

"See, that's where you're wrong," she says, waving her bitten apple for emphasis. "Girls like *nice* guys, not guys who think they need to constantly ooze charm. There's nothing real in that."

There's not supposed to be, I think. What I say is, "Well, it's *really* gotten me plenty of girls, so I think I'll stick with what I know."

She laughs and takes another bite. "You're a hopeless cause."

She has no idea.

"Thanks for the ride," she says as we near school. "I probably would've been late otherwise. Glad you happened by just then."

"No problem," I say. "You know, I could just happen by every morning."

She looks at me for long seconds as if trying to decide. I can feel her gaze, even though I keep mine on the road. Finally she holds out a hand. "Give me your phone."

I glance at her, brows lifted. "For what?"

"I'm going to put my number in so you can text me before you leave your house, then I can wait on the curb for you. Sheesh, paranoid much?"

I hand my phone over. "I'm not sure if you noticed or not, but I do have two feet. I can walk up to the door to get you."

She's silent long enough I glance over. She's typing her name and number in my phone but her face is scrunched, as if she's uncomfortable or upset. Finally, without looking my way, she says, "No way, Nefer. That's too date-like. I'll meet you outside." She's going for nonchalant, but I can hear the real stress beneath. I think about how she'd stood outside her closed door and how quickly she went back in when called. I wonder again how similar our home lives are.

"Well, we wouldn't want that," I say easily. "I'll text then. It takes only a couple minutes to get to your house. Is that enough warning?"

She hands my phone back to me. "Maybe give me ten minutes before you're ready to leave?"

"Can do," I say as we pull into the school parking lot. Charlie climbs out and waits for me at the front of the car. I kinda thought she might hurry inside to avoid being seen with me, but she just waits, then walks next to me.

Once inside the school, she gives me a wave. "Thanks again for the ride," she says before jogging over to catch up with Alexis and Phoebe. I watch her go until Daniel jumps on me from behind.

"Dude!" I stagger beneath the unexpected weight.

"What's up?" he asks, mock punching my shoulder. He glances to where I'd been watching Charlie. "Making headway with the new girl?"

"No, she's—" I stop, realizing I'd almost unthinkingly outed her. I relax my shoulders and grin with a shrug. "Maybe. Gave her a ride to school."

Confusion crosses Daniel's face. "Really?" I know where his confusion comes from. I don't give girls rides to school. That crosses too close into relationship territory.

"She's different," I say. When interest crosses his face, I correct him. "Not different in that I want her for a girlfriend. That isn't going to happen. I just mean that Cozi and Alexis got to her first, planted some bad seeds. Now it's a matter of pride to prove them wrong."

"But after you prove them wrong, you're going to prove them right."

His words stop me. He's right. What's my ultimate objective here? Charlie is either not into guys, dealing with crap at home, or both. Plus she has her diabetes. So my plan is what? To get her to like me—even if it goes against her instincts—so she'll go out with me, and then dump her, breaking her heart?

Seems cold, even for me.

❦

We win the game by four touchdowns. My teammates lift me on their shoulders, pretty normal since I'm the QB and made the passes. Of course, there's another guy who managed to catch them all and run them in, but I'm the one on their shoulders. I find it odd, in a detached sort of way, but allow it, grinning and fist-bumping whoever I can reach.

My eyes travel to the stands. Cozi, Phoebe, and Alexis all stand together, cheering. Charlie's not with them. I know she said she couldn't come, but I'd hoped she'd show anyway. I continue to scan the crowd, knowing *he* won't be here. He's never come, not once. I'm not sure what I'd do if he did. Walk into the crowd and have a good, rousing fistfight with him?

They finally let me down and we move into the gym to shower. Afterward, we all head to Tony's Pizzeria to celebrate. The last place I want to be on my day off is the same place I work, but I get a discount, so it's usually where we end up.

The place is already packed with students from school who cheer as we walk in. We lift our hands in victory as expected. Not for the first time I realize the futility of our lives. Strut around school like we're kings, helped by the attitudes of most of the other students, play a game that we receive accolades for, then work making and delivering pizzas. This might be the highlight of many of our lives. Suddenly I don't feel like being a part of it.

"Daniel, I gotta go, man."

He turns to me, a frown on his face. "Go? Go where?"

I quickly form a lie. "The old man called. I need to pick him up."

Daniel nods. He's aware of my dad's tendency to overdrink, though he's kept it quiet. He's not aware of the other side of my life, and has never been to my house to meet my dad. Still, it's not the first time I've had to go pick him up.

He places a sympathetic hand on my shoulder. "Try to come back, okay?"

"I'll try," I say, knowing I won't.

Behind the wheel of my car, I find myself driving down Charlie's street. It's not on my way home. I pull over across the street and cut the engine. Pulling my cell phone out, I scroll through the numbers to find hers. I grin when I see what name she's given herself: Charlie the Great and Powerful. I push send, looking toward her house before remembering she's not even home.

"Hello?" Her voice is hesitant.

"Hey, new girl, this is your stalker."

I can hear the smile in her voice. "Nefer, leave it to you to stalk me by phone as well as in person."

"I do what I can," I say. Then, "How's the babysitting going?"

"What?" She sounds confused.

"You're babysitting, right?"

"Oh, yeah, right. Babysitting."

"Are the kiddies in bed yet or do you need to get back to them?"

"No, they're in bed," she says.

"Where are you? I'll come over."

"No." Her response is quick. "Um, I don't think that's a good idea."

"Strict parents?" I ask. A sudden light coming on in the upper level of her house catches my attention. A figure moves in the background, and I suddenly see Charlie. She sits in the window where the light came on. She's *not* babysitting. She's home.

"Not so much that," she teases. I watch as she pulls one foot up and folds it beneath her, then tucks a long strand of hair behind her ear. "It's more the serial-killer thing."

I watch her. Why is she lying about babysitting when she's clearly home? Wait, did she just call me a serial killer?

"Serial killer?"

She laughs. I hear the sound through my phone as I watch her body shake with the motion in her window. "Yeah. Isn't that how it always happens in scary movies? The babysitter gets the kids in bed, her boyfriend comes over, and then they're both killed while they're making out or . . . more."

I swear I can hear her blush through the phone. "Are you calling me your boyfriend, new girl?"

She straightens in the window, her free hand going to her cheek. "Ugh, no!" Then a nervous laugh. "Sorry, I didn't mean that to sound like it did, like you're repulsive or something."

"I'm wounded," I tease. "Unless of course you're saying you find me the opposite of repulsive, which would be attractive."

Her body relaxes and she pulls her second foot up, sitting sideways in the windowsill with her knees propped up. She plays idly with the hem of her pants.

"C'mon, Nefer, you don't need anyone telling you you're attractive. You've completely convinced yourself of that. I don't think anyone can change your mind about that now."

"Besides, I'm not boyfriend material," I say lightly, though I'm intensely curious to see what she has to say to that.

She glances out her window before answering, and I shrink down in my seat, as if that can stop her from seeing the car.

"Not for me, Nefer."

"Okay, then, tell me what your type is? What is boyfriend material for new girl Charlie?"

Charlie leans forward, resting her forehead on her knees. Her back expands and relaxes as if she's taken a deep breath.

"No one is boyfriend material for me," she says.

Her words confirm at least part of my theory.

"Well then, that only disputes your serial-killer theory, new girl. I'm not your boyfriend, not even boyfriend *material*, so no making out or . . . *more*, as you say. I'll just be good company."

"Nice try, Nefer," she says, lifting her head. "I've gotta go. I've got tons of homework to catch up on."

"Fine, killjoy," I tease.

"See you Monday," she says.

Monday. Seems like forever away.

ELEVEN
CHARLIE

I slide into Benjamin's car, hoping my mom isn't holding her face at the window and waving as she sometimes does. I'd put the dreaded *Barney* on, hoping that would hold her attention enough, then hurried to the sidewalk, moving to the opposite side of the garage to hopefully hide me from view. I glance over at him, and see the huge bruise on his cheek.

"Whoa," I say, holding a hand up and lightly touching the edge of the bruise. "What happened to you?"

He doesn't meet my eye. "Boxing."

I shake my head. "You seriously like that? Getting hit?"

He twists one corner of his mouth up wryly. "I'm not always the one getting hit."

"Still," I say. "It just seems so . . . violent."

"It's a great stress reliever, and it's even better exercise. You wanna be in peak physical condition before you step into the ring with someone bigger than you so you can be faster."

"So I'm guessing you weren't fast enough to avoid this guy?" I point to his cheek.

A funny look crosses his face. "No," he finally says. "I'm not usually fast enough to avoid *this* guy."

"You fight him often?" I ask, trying to figure out his mood.

"Too often," he says, a heavy tone in his voice. We pull up to a red light and suddenly he looks at me. "You should come down sometime, to the gym, I mean."

"And watch you get hit? No thanks."

"There're plenty of girls who get in the ring."

"Get hit myself? That's an even bigger no thanks," I say, watching him. He holds my gaze, something there I can't read. A car honks behind us and he quickly turns forward, seeing the light's changed.

When we arrive at the school, I wait for Benjamin so we can walk in together. He glances at me. "You look tired," he says.

"Flattery will get you nowhere," I return.

"Come down to the ring. You'll sleep better."

My eyes go to the bruise on his cheek. "I'll take the exhaustion," I say as I hear Cozi call my name. "See you later."

"You rode to school with Benjamin?" Cozi asks as soon as I come up to her.

"Yeah. He delivered pizza to us last week, discovered my house is on his way, so he picks me up. Saves me from riding the bus."

Cozi takes my arm urgently. "Charlie, I truly want you to be careful. He's . . . well, let's just say he got his reputation for a reason."

"I know, Cozi. Don't worry, I'm well aware of what he can be like. I've heard it from plenty of people. But he seems like he's accepted I don't want to date him and he just wants to be friends."

"Or he could be just trying to get you to relax enough for him to make his move. He'll shred your heart."

Impulsively I hug Cozi. "Have I thanked you for taking me under your wing?" I say. "You, Alexis, and Phoebe saved me from that whole awkward-new-kid thing."

"Just lucky for us you turned out to be such a nice person," Cozi says. She's probably the only person who could say that and sound sincere instead of cheesy. "That being said, be careful. You haven't sat with someone he's broken while she cries heartbreaking sobs all over your shoulder."

I admit it's a powerful image Cozi paints, and seems so out of character for the Benjamin I know. Or that I think I know. I guess I really don't.

⁓

By Friday I'm walking around in a haze. I've had to stay up extra late for too many nights, catching up on homework since I started school a few weeks late. I have to wait until I have my mom in bed first because if I try to work while she's up, she keeps interrupting and it gets too frustrating. Then I only sleep a few hours before I have to be up to get her ready for the day. Naomi said she'd do it, of course, but I'm not about to let her hold it over our heads and threaten a home for my mom again.

It doesn't help that lack of sleep is messing with my sugar levels. I'm having a hard time keeping them in check, running either too low or high at odd times of the day. All of that makes me even more tired. Sitting in psychology in front of Benjamin, I decide the better decision would have been to sit behind him. He's tall enough I could sleep at my desk and Mr. Snow wouldn't see.

Snow drones on about some assignment. I don't care. I'll find out later what it is from Benjamin. I lean on my hand and let my eyes drift. Benjamin pokes me in the back and I jerk awake. I notice others in the class are visiting while Mr. Snow sits at his desk. I turn toward Benjamin.

"Were you just *sleeping* in *class*, new girl?" He manages to sound scandalized, and I roll my eyes at him. He just laughs. "Late night?"

"Late week," I say.

"So when do you want to do it?"

I shake my head at him. "You never give up, do you?"

He looks genuinely confused, then he smiles. "Oh, right, you were sleeping. We're supposed to decide when we want to do our observation."

"Observation of what?"

"Wow, you really weren't paying attention, were you?" At my blank look, he continues. "We have to pick five different things or places to observe people, do one per week for the next five weeks, and write a page on each one."

"A *page*?"

"Yeah, apparently Mr. Snow doesn't think we have any other classes or life outside of psychology."

"We do it during class time?"

"Nooo," he draws the word out as if explaining to a child. "We go somewhere on our own time to do it."

My heart picks up tempo in panic. When am I supposed to do homework outside of class where I have to partner with someone?

"I can't go tonight, obviously."

Still worried about when I'm supposed to fit this in, I distractedly ask, "Why?"

"The game."

"Oh, right."

He looks a little upset that I didn't remember it.

"Are you coming?" he asks.

"I can't," I say, frantically searching my brain for a plausible excuse. But I can't think of anything, completely distracted by the other issue.

Benjamin surprises me by saying, "Okay. So for the assignment, how about tomorrow?"

I just stare at him, surprised at his easy capitulation of my refusal. "Um, I don't know. It might be hard to get away."

He nods as if expecting my answer. "Well, we'll just play it by ear. Any ideas what we can do?"

"Did he give us ideas?"

"Yeah, a bunch."

"Okay, well, since I wasn't paying attention, what sounded good to you?"

"Go to a restaurant and observe a specific table, go to a movie and observe people's reactions, sit on a street corner and observe aggressive driving, go—"

"That one," I say. "Observing drivers." It sounds the best to me because it's the only choice he's given so far that doesn't cost anything.

"Passionate about aggressive driving, huh?"

"No, it just . . . sounds like fun."

He looks at me oddly. "You have a strange sense of fun, new girl."

"Can I text you tomorrow and let you know?"

"Sure," he says. "I work at five, but I'm available before then."

I think about asking Naomi to watch my mom on what she considers her day off and shudder at the thought. I could of course take my mom with me, but then I'd have to explain to Benjamin, and I can't do that. Someone who lives a life as blessed as Benjamin can never understand what my life is like, and why I feel such love and loyalty to my mom.

TWELVE
BENJAMIN

I check my phone for the fiftieth time. It's not that big of a deal, really, if we get the assignment done today. It just has to be done in the next week. Then I think of her at home, and why she might not be calling. I imagine someone, her father or uncle, laying heavy hands on her in anger, hitting her the way my father hits me. I try to picture her fighting back like I do, but can't see it.

At twelve thirty I get a text: *I can go now if you can. I only have an hour.*

I can leave right now and be there in 2 min, I text back.

Thanks. Meet you at curb?

See you in 2.

If my dad were home I'd probably have a hard time leaving right away, but since he didn't come home last night, I hurry out the door before he does. When I get to Charlie's, she's waiting on the curb with her backpack slung over her shoulder. She climbs in the car.

"Sorry for the last-second notice," she begins, looking down to buckle her seatbelt.

"No worries. I wasn't doing anything, just watching some TV."

"Okay, good. I wasn't sure if I could get away or not until just then."

She's looking out the window, not at me. I consider asking her if she needs help, if things are that bad. That would be the height of idiocy. What can I possibly offer? I can't get myself out of my own situation, how can I possibly help her? Besides, she might mistake that as caring rather than as just a fellow human offering help.

"So what exactly are we supposed to do?" she asks.

"Find a busy corner, and sit and make observations."

She laughs, still looking out the window. "As if we're qualified to observe behavior and determine what it means."

"Future Psychologists of America."

"That's not a real thing." She pauses, then, "Is it?"

I laugh. "Not that I know of. Maybe we should start a club."

"I don't think I'd be a good candidate for a psychologist."

"Why not?" I ask, genuinely curious about her answer.

"If I could figure out why people do the things they do, and influence them otherwise, my life would be a lot different than it is now."

I glance at her. She still hasn't looked my way.

"This intersection looks good," I say, pulling into the parking lot of an ice-cream parlor.

"Okay," she says, finally looking my way. I catch sight of her face for the first time.

"Have you been crying?" The words are out before I can stop them.

She shakes her head.

"Yes, you have. Did someone . . . hurt you?" I stop short of asking the real question: Did someone *hit* you?

"No, it's no biggie, Benjamin."

"It is if it made you cry."

She smiles thinly at me. "Just an argument with my aunt. I swear, it's not a big deal."

I stare at her, trying to determine if she's telling the truth. It's been so long since I cared if anyone was telling me the truth it's hard for me to decide. She smiles wider.

"C'mon, Nefer, it's not a big deal, okay? And the clock's ticking. I've gotta be back in an hour. Let's go." She turns and opens her door, climbing out.

I pop the trunk and pull out two chairs, which I set on the sidewalk near the street. She plops in one and pulls her notebook and pen from her backpack. I sit next to her.

"Okay, now what?" she asks.

I point to the street. "Observe."

Almost immediately we see a car run a red light.

"Someone's in a hurry," I say.

She writes it down in her notebook as she says, "He's late for a work meeting. If he doesn't get there in time, he's fired and his family will be forced from their house."

"Oh, yeah?" I ask. She grins at me. "Just one problem with your theory."

"Only one?"

"It's Saturday. Who has a work meeting on a Saturday?"

"That guy," she says, pointing her pen in the direction the car went.

We spend half an hour observing cars making completely bonehead moves, both of us surprised we haven't seen a single wreck yet.

"You wanna go in and get some ice cream?" I ask, pointing to the parlor. "I think we have more than enough material for a page."

She glances at the ice-cream parlor, but shakes her head distractedly. "I should probably go." She shivers.

"Are you cold?" I ask.

She just looks at me, not answering. Her eyes are blank.

"Charlie?"

"I don't feel good," she says, moving to get up.

"I'll take you home." I stand and turn to grab one of the chairs when she makes a strange noise. I look back and see her falling. "Charlie!" I call, stepping forward in panic. My arms shoot out to catch her, but she's going too fast. Before she hits the ground I manage to get my hand partially under her head, my hand crushed between her skull and the cement.

Her back is arched, hands clenched tightly next to her shoulders. That's bad enough, but her face terrifies me. She's whiter than the sidewalk beneath her, her teeth are clenched around ghostly lips that look parched as if she hasn't had water in days, and spittle forms around her mouth, running down her cheek. Strangled moans issue from her throat.

"Help!" I yell, panic choking my words. I look up wildly. "Help!" Suddenly a woman crouches next to me.

"What's wrong?" she asks.

"I don't know!" My words sound crazed, but they reflect how I'm feeling.

"She's having a seizure," the woman says. "Does she have a seizure disorder? Epilepsy?"

I can only shake my head, but she doesn't wait for my non-answer, simply pulls up Charlie's hand that is banded with the silver bracelet she always wears.

"Diabetic," the woman says. "Do you have Glucagon?"

"What?" Her words sound as clear as Japanese.

"Does she have a purse or something?"

I point to her backpack, my other hand still beneath her head. The woman searches through it and it occurs to me to tell her to stop, but I'm beyond words now.

"No Glucagon," the woman says, turning back. She turns to a man who is standing close by and watching. "Call 911," she says.

"Tell them we have a diabetic seizure." She sees Charlie's pump clipped to her front pocket and pulls it up, pushing some buttons on it.

"Is she dying?" I ask fearfully.

"No, of course not," she says soothingly, placing a hand on my arm. "I'm a nurse. I've seen this before. She's having a seizure from low blood glucose, so we need to get some glucose in her quickly. Since she doesn't have any Glucagon, we'll have to wait for the para-medics."

I return my gaze to Charlie's face, contorted in pain, strangled moans coming from her lips. She still arches, teeth clenched tightly. I swear she's even paler than before. "Tell them to hurry," I com-mand. This woman claims Charlie's not dying, but she sure looks like she is.

The woman continues to talk calmly to me, asking me ques-tions, but I can't tell her anything. I don't know *anything* about Charlie, including her home phone number. Someone else takes Charlie's cell phone from the woman and begins scrolling through the numbers.

"I don't see anyone named mom or dad," the man says.

"Do you know her parents' names?" she asks me.

As with every other question, I can only shake my head. "I only know her from school."

Forever later, the sound of the sirens reaches us, and then there are three men pushing me out of the way. The woman speaks to them, and they attempt to stick a needle in her arm attached to a long tube and a bag of fluid. Apparently it doesn't work because they have to stick her again. I really want to punch them for the pain they're clearly causing her if her face is any indication. Finally they place her on the stretcher. The woman comes over to me.

"They'll have to take her to the hospital since she doesn't have a parent here. Can you go with her?"

I nod, my eyes following Charlie as they wheel her to the waiting ambulance. She shoves Charlie's backpack into my hand.

"I think everything is in here except the chairs. They'll keep them in the ice-cream place until you can come get them, okay?"

I stare at her, trying to process her words.

She rubs my arm. "She'll be fine, I promise. Just go with her. I'll bet she'll be awake before you get to the hospital."

I nod, unable even to open my mouth to thank her, and follow the paramedics to the ambulance, climbing up inside with Charlie, who's still so pale she blends in with the sheets. At least she's not arching anymore. The paramedic sitting next to her doesn't seem all that concerned, writing on his clipboard.

"What's her name?" he asks.

"Charlie Austin."

"Is Charlie short for something else?"

I tear my eyes from her face to look at him. "I don't know," I mutter, shamed that I don't, my eyes returning to Charlie's. I think I should know, maybe I've been told, but I can't remember.

"How about an address?"

I search my mind, trying to remember her address from my pizza delivery.

"I know she lives on Fifth West," I offer. "Between 200 and 400 North, but I'm not sure of her exact address."

He nods. "We'll probably be able to find her in the system since she does have diabetes."

Suddenly, Charlie's eyes open. She looks wildly around, until finally her eyes find me. "She's awake," I say.

The paramedic leans forward. "Welcome back," he says. Her eyes flick to his face. "Do you know this guy?" he asks her, pointing at me.

Her gaze comes back to mine. She nods.

"Do you know his name?" the paramedic asks.

She stares at me, then squints her eyes closed, tears coming as she shakes her head.

"It's okay," I say, automatically grabbing her hand. She clings to my hand as if it's a lifeline. She's still crying, but her eyes open again and fix on me.

"Charlie, do you know your mom's phone number? Or your dad's?" he asks.

Without taking her eyes from me, she shakes her head again, tears falling harder.

"Don't worry," the paramedic says. "We'll find them."

Suddenly her address pops into my mind. I give it to the paramedic, who calls it in. He turns to me. "Someone will go by her house and see if they can find one of her parents."

Relief flows through me. She'll be fine. Everything will be fine.

THIRTEEN
BENJAMIN

Charlie's aunt finds me in the waiting room. I'd gone back with Charlie when we first arrived because she refused to let go of my hand. But as time went on and she became more aware of her surroundings, she relinquished her death grip on me. When they started examining her, I told her I'd wait outside.

"Benjamin?" a woman asks, stopping near me.

I stand. "Yes."

She holds a hand out. "I'm Naomi Austin. Charlotte's aunt."

Charlotte. I suddenly remember her telling me that the first day I met her.

"Hi," I say.

"I wanted to thank you for everything you did for her today."

I sink back down onto my seat. "I didn't do anything. I stood there like a statue while someone else took care of her."

"I was told you caught her so she didn't hit her head on the ground."

"I wasn't fast enough. I think she still hit a little."

"Yes. She does have a bump on the back of her head, but it's small. It could have been worse." I nod, and she asks, "They said you came in the ambulance with her. Can I give you a ride somewhere?"

I glance at the double doors that Charlie lies behind. "Is she staying?"

"Only overnight. Usually she'd be able to go right home, but since she hit her head, they just want to be extra cautious. She'll be able to go home in the morning."

I nod again, wondering if this is my new form of communication.

"Do you want to go tell her good-bye?" she asks.

I really don't. This is all feeling too personal. Instead, I nod again and stand to enter through the doors.

Charlie lies on the hospital bed. They've taken the IV out and she's sleeping. I consider just leaving, but then her eyes open.

"Hey," she says softly.

"Hey," I say back, stepping farther into the room. "How're you feeling?"

"Stupid," she says. "And really tired."

"Why stupid? It's not your fault."

She looks at me with a grimace. "It kind of is." She blows out a breath. "I didn't eat lunch because of the argument with my aunt. I really thought I'd be fine while we did our assignment. I can usually feel when I'm getting low, but today I didn't. I felt fine, last I remember."

"Still, it's not your fault."

"It's embarrassing, knowing all those people were watching. Knowing you . . ." Her eyes drop to her hands. "I'm really sorry, Benjamin."

"You must be, since you called me by my first name," I tease.

She smiles. "Don't get used to it."

"I won't," I say, holding my hands up.

"Is this . . ." She trails off, playing with the blanket's edge. "Is this something that will stay between us? I mean, you don't have this burning need to run home and call everyone you know on your cell phone, right?"

"I've kept my mouth shut so far," I say. Then I add, "Might not be a bad idea to let people know, though. Maybe if I'd known what signs to look for . . ."

She sighs deeply. "I know. You're right, I know. I'm just not looking forward to becoming *that* girl."

"What girl?"

"The girl with the disease that makes her fragile. The girl who's treated differently because she has this thing."

"I think you've proven you're not that fragile, Charlie."

"Thanks . . . I think," she says with a smile.

"Well, your aunt said she'd give me a ride back to my car. Are you going to be okay?"

She waves a hand to ward off my words. "This is nothing. I'll be fine. I wish they'd just let me go home, but they're worried about my head. So I'll stay here and try to sleep until they realize I'm just fine."

"Okay, I guess I'll go then. Call if . . . call if you need anything."

"Thanks, Nefer. I appreciate it."

I smile at her, then leave, checking the time on my cell phone. If I don't hurry, I'm going to be late to work.

FOURTEEN
CHARLIE

You look better today," Benjamin says as I slide into his car.

"You mean, better than lying on a sidewalk?" I ask with a smile.

"Not quite so tired," he says.

"Two days of sleep will do that for you."

"I wasn't sure if you'd come to school today or not. How are you feeling?"

"Tired mostly, and really sore, like I ran a marathon or lifted weights for a few hours, or something. I'm fine." Not wanting to keep dragging it out, I say, "I forgot to ask, did you win the game on Friday?"

"We did," he says. I glance at him, noticing the lack of pride in his voice.

"Good." When he says nothing else, I say, "So, Nefer, is your life taking you to the NBA?"

He looks askance at me. "Why in the world would it take me to the NBA?" Then he laughs. "You mean the NFL?"

I shrug. "Is that the football one?"

"Uh, yeah. The other is basketball."

"You could play basketball," I say. "You're tall."

"Not tall enough for the NBA. I'd be a shrimp next to those guys."

"Okay, the NFL then. Think you'll keep playing?"

"No." I look at him at his abrupt answer and wait. "I hope some college scouts will come around, but even if they do, that'll probably be the end of it. *If* I get a scholarship to play in college, I might play there, but I'm not holding my breath on that."

"If college scouts come, that's good, right?"

"It's my only chance for getting out of here," he says. "I won't be able to afford college otherwise."

"Well, I hope you get a scholarship, then."

"What about you?" he asks, glancing at me. "What are you doing after high school?"

"Working, I guess. I can't afford college, either, and since I can't play football . . ."

"What about scholarships?"

"Those require going to school fulltime, and that's not possible."

"Why not?"

"Because I'll have to work."

"You don't work now?"

I look out the window. How do I explain that I can't work right now because I have to take care of my mom, and that every day I worry about how I'm going to work and take care of her after I graduate?

"They're hiring at my work," he says. "It's not glamorous, but sometimes the tips make it worthwhile."

"I don't have a car," I say.

"Oh, yeah. I guess that doesn't help, then. You could still work there, just not doing delivery."

I shrug noncommittally. As much as I don't want to bring up the seizure again, there's something that's been bothering me.

"Um, can I ask you something?" He nods. "About Saturday . . . I mean, *after* . . . Did I *say* anything or do anything that's, well, weird?"

He glances at me. "You mean besides having a seizure and scaring the crap out of me?"

"I'm really sorry," I say.

"I told you, and I mean it, that it's not a big deal. I'm just glad you're okay. But what do you mean, did you say or do anything weird?"

"It's just . . . when I have a seizure, I'm not really me for a while, you know? So I might say or do something that's odd, something I don't mean."

"Well, you did tell me that you thought I was the best-looking guy you've ever met and that you believe you're falling in love with me."

My mouth gapes open. "I said *that*?"

He glances at me, trying to look hurt though I can see through the lie. I grin and punch his arm.

"Ouch," he teases. "Are you telling me you didn't mean it? That wounds me, new girl, it really does."

"You're such a jerk, Nefer," I mutter, still smiling.

After a minute, he says, "No, you didn't say anything weird, but I'll take advantage of the situation in the future to get you to tell me your deep, dark secrets."

"I don't think it works that way," I say wryly, though honestly I'm not sure whether it does or not.

"Do you have seizures often?" he asks.

"Nope. In fact, this is only the second one I've had. But that's two too many."

"Kinda scary, huh?" he asks.

I don't answer. I don't want to tell him how hard I work to avoid having seizures, that even on days when I've had enough of dealing with my diabetes and just want to take a day off, I can't because the risk of seizure is always present. And they *hurt*.

When we arrive at school, Cozi and Alexis are waiting near my locker. I figure they're here to lecture me more about Benjamin. Whatever they say, it's nothing I haven't thought of. But then I remember that he's the one who got me the help I needed on Saturday, who rode in the ambulance with me and stayed until my aunt came.

"Hey, guys," I say. Before they can begin, I decide to tell them. "Listen, there's something I wanted to tell you, something I should have told you the first day I came." I pull my sleeve up and expose my pump site.

"What's that?" Cozi asks.

"I know," Alexis says. "My cousin has diabetes and he has a pump. Is that what that is?"

I nod.

"You have diabetes?" Cozi asks.

"I do. I've had it since I was nine."

"Why didn't you tell us?" Alexis asks.

"I don't know," I say. "When I was diagnosed, everyone knew. Because I kind of grew up in the same area with the same people, I guess everyone just always knew. I was afraid that once I told you guys you'd treat me different, kinda like I'm breakable or something. I just liked being normal for a while. And then I didn't know how to bring it up."

"My cousin has had it since he was a little kid. He plays basketball and swims on his college team. I *know* you're not breakable."

"I don't know enough about it to think you're breakable, either," Cozi says. "What does that thing do?" She points to the site and tubing.

I give her the shortened version of what my diabetes is and how I take care of it. Phoebe joins us in the middle and Alexis catches her up. It takes all of about ten minutes before we've moved on to other subjects.

I realize how silly it was to try to keep it secret. There was no reason for it; they didn't react any differently than anyone before, with curiosity. By lunch it seems almost everyone knows. I get some curious looks, but most people don't seem to care as much as I'd worried.

In psychology, Benjamin sits behind me. He leans forward before class begins.

"So, you took my advice, new girl?"

"Your advice?" I ask, turning to look at him.

"To tell everyone."

"You told me to do that?"

"On Saturday, at the hospital."

"Huh," I say. I don't recall the conversation, but maybe subconsciously it stuck. "Good advice, Nefer."

He laughs softly as Mr. Snow begins his lecture.

❧

When I get home my mom, Naomi, and a girl I don't know are sitting in the family room playing Chutes and Ladders. It's the first time I've seen Naomi interacting with my mom on any kind of personal level. The girl is young, probably my age or maybe just a little older. She has long, straight, brown hair and one of those faces that sort of screams *nice person*. Her mouth stretches into a wide smile as I have the thought, solidifying the image.

"Look, Mimi, you get to climb!" My mom's voice is happy for her sister.

"Lucky me," Naomi says, only instead of the sarcasm I'd expect to hear with those words, she sounds genuine.

Finally my mom spots me standing in the doorway, watching.

"Charlie!" she calls. "Come play with us."

I step into the room. "That's okay, I'll just watch. You've already started playing." I walk over and sit on the couch next to my mom, who immediately throws her arms around me in a hug. "Who's your new friend?" I ask, eyeing the strange girl.

"That's Ma'am."

"Ma'am?" I ask.

"My name is Mariam," the girl says, "but Cora likes to call me Ma'am."

"She is one for nicknames, isn't she?" Naomi says. "This is Charlotte, Mariam."

Mariam holds a hand toward me and I take it. "Charlie," I correct.

"Mariam is the daughter of one of my friends," Naomi says. "She's a CNA. She came over Saturday to stay with Cora while I came to the hospital, and Sunday when I picked you up."

I flush. I hadn't even thought to wonder where my mom was while Naomi was with me, and since the whole weekend was a bit of a blur . . .

"Thank you," I say.

"She's my friend," my mom interjects.

"I was glad to do it," Mariam says. "I like Cora."

She seems like a nice enough girl, so I relax. Until my aunt speaks again.

"Mariam works at Dayspring. It's both a daycare and live-in for people who can't take care of themselves without supervision."

I shoot her a dark look. I'm angry she's bringing this up now, in front of both a stranger and my mom. "That's nice," I bite out.

"It really is," Mariam says, completely missing my tone. "I love it there. We have tons of activities for the residents, and field trips, movie nights, dances, things like that."

"That sounds fun!" my mom enthuses.

"Can I talk to you for a minute?" I ask Naomi. "Privately?"

She stands and I follow her into the kitchen.

"What is this?" I ask, fury in my low voice.

"Just listen to her, Charlotte. That's all I ask. If you want, we can go down and visit."

"I told you I'm not—"

"This isn't a home," Naomi interrupts. "It's just a daycare, a place for Cora to go and have some fun with others like her. Do you really think it's fair to just keep her locked up here all day with nothing to do but watch TV?"

"She doesn't have to be 'locked' up," I say, making air quotes to emphasize my sarcasm. "Grandma used to take her places all the time."

"I'm not Grandma," Naomi says. "I have a life, Charlotte."

"I'm sorry we're disrupting your life, but it's only temporary, I promise. If there were any other way, believe me, we'd be gone."

Naomi grits her teeth. "I'm not unhappy having you here. I'm not," she says urgently at my rolled eyes. "And I'll do whatever is needed to take care of both of you. But I think you're being extremely selfish."

My jaw drops. "Selfish? Are you kidding me?"

"I'm dead serious. She's *bored*, Charlotte. She needs to have a life, too. Look how excited she is just to have Mariam here playing a game with her."

Her words stop me. I haven't ever really thought about my mom having a life. I mean, outside of me. Is she bored? Does she need something else?

"Besides, you can't keep going on like this. You're going to have a meltdown. You already had a seizure."

"My seizure had nothing to do with her."

"Didn't it? You're getting hardly any sleep, you're stressed about things you have no control over, and you're not taking care of yourself."

"This isn't about me."

"No, it's about her. Let her find some small measure of happiness, even if for only a few hours each day."

Abruptly, the fight drains out of me. I'm so tired of fighting.

"Fine, I'll go look at it. But that's all I'm promising."

"That's all I'm asking," she says.

"Mimi! It's your turn," my mom calls from the other room. We both turn toward the sound, and with a final look, Naomi leaves to finish their game. I stay in the kitchen for a few minutes, overwhelmed. The thought of exposing my mom to possible danger terrifies me. The only thing that scares me more is the idea that she's not happy because of me.

FIFTEEN
CHARLIE

I stand in the corner, watching my mom play duck-duck-goose with a group consisting of four residents of Dayspring and three employees, one of whom is Mariam. Naomi is still talking with the director of the facility.

I don't want to admit Naomi was even anywhere in the neighborhood of right, but I can't deny my mom's been in the thralls of pure joy since we arrived. She played in the common room while we took a tour, then we all ate dinner with the residents—a surprisingly good dinner. Now I watch her play until Naomi is ready to leave. The light and laughter in her face is like a physical blow to me. Maybe I really have been selfish by hiding her from the world, from people who *want* to play the same things she wants to play.

"Are you ready to go?" Naomi asks.

I nod and walk over to let my mom know.

"Mom, it's time to go."

"Can't I stay? I want to play," she whines.

"Maybe we can come back some other time, okay?"

She's pouting, but Mariam stands. "I'll walk you to the door, Cora. Would you like that?" She holds out a hand, which my mom reluctantly takes. She stands.

At the door, my mom hugs her. "I'll come back tomorrow, okay?"

"It probably won't—" I begin.

"Tell Ma'am good-bye, Cora," Naomi interrupts me. She shoots me a look. I clamp my jaw.

༄

After my mom is tucked in bed, which took longer than usual since she was so excited, I think about how happy she was, playing games. The director showed us the exercise room, which I admit my mom needs. She doesn't really exercise, which can't be good for her. She showed us some photos from previous field trips. I think about letting Naomi have her way, and putting my mom in Dayspring during the day. It feels wrong—and right—all at the same time.

Naomi knocks on my bedroom door, and comes in when I tell her to.

"What did you think of Dayspring?" she asks, sitting on the corner of my bed.

"She was happy there," I admit.

"I know you question her safety, Charlotte. But I want you to know I don't take this decision lightly. I've known about Dayspring for quite some time, and I've looked into it extensively." She hands me a sheaf of papers she's holding. "This is their track record for safety. There isn't a single case or complaint of a resident being attacked by a staff member, or any kind of abuse. There are lots of testimonials from family members."

I take the papers and leaf through them. Then I look up at Naomi to ask the question that's been bothering me since we visited. "How much does it cost? You've seen my mom's checks. They aren't exactly very much. I can get a job, though, to make up the difference . . . maybe. It seemed like it might be expensive."

Naomi smiles. "It doesn't matter, Charlotte. I can afford it."

"I know you can," I say. "But I don't want there to be an obligation."

"She's my sister," Naomi says, tucking a strand of blonde hair behind her ear. "How can there be any obligation?" Before I can respond, she says, "I want to do this for her, Charlotte. And I can easily afford it."

I look down at the papers she handed me. "I need some time to think about it," I say.

Naomi stands. "Read those papers, and if you have any more questions, the director's card is in there. She said to call anytime."

After she leaves my room, I read each of the papers she gave me. In the back of my mind I know I should be doing homework, but this is more important. I read pages of reports and testimonials, as well as their program plan for the next few months. Finally, I set them aside and lie on my bed.

My decision is made. I won't fight Naomi on this—for now. I'll give it a chance and see how it goes, as long as my mom isn't hurt. As I roll over to go to sleep, I feel lighter, as if a burden has been lifted.

SIXTEEN
BENJAMIN

Y ou look . . . different," I tell Charlie as she gets in the car.

"Different bad or different good?"

I waggle my eyebrows at her, talking in a nasally voice, holding an imaginary cigar. "Always good, darlin'. Always good."

Her forehead scrunches. "Who is that supposed to be?"

"Hello? Groucho Marx?"

"If you say so," she says with a laugh. "What movie is that from?"

"It's not from . . . never mind. Hey, we need to get together to work on that paper for psychology. When do you want to do that?"

"Oh, um, well, I'm not sure . . ."

"I can do it tonight," I tell her, "or tomorrow or Friday. But Saturday I work."

"No game Friday?" she asks.

"Nope. We have a bye this week. Maybe I can come to your house later."

"Oh. Not tonight," she says, catching my attention with her tight voice. "I could come to your house, maybe."

"No. Not my house."

She looks at me, waiting for an explanation. She's not going to get one. Finally, she says, "You could come to my house after school tomorrow. I'll double check with my aunt to make sure it's okay, but that works for me."

"Sounds like a plan," I say, extremely curious to get an inside peek at Charlie's life.

∽

Charlie is definitely nervous as we enter her house. Belatedly, it occurs to me that I should probably offer just to go to the library with her. But after spending a good portion of the night lying awake, wondering about her home life, it never crossed my mind.

When we walk into the kitchen, a woman stands from where she was sitting at the table. I would have pegged her for Charlie's mom if I didn't recognize her from the hospital. Other than having darker hair, she looks similar to Charlie, with the same dimples when she smiles, and the same big, hazel-green eyes.

"Oh, um, Benjamin, this is my Aunt Naomi." She swings a hand my way. "This is Benjamin."

Naomi steps forward and shakes my hand, smiling at me. "We've met." At Charlie's look, her aunt says, "At the hospital. Nice to see you again, Benjamin. Charlotte told me you'd be coming over today to work on a report?"

"Yes, ma'am," I say, smiling widely and giving her the smallest of winks. "Thanks for having me." I'm in my element here, charming a female, something I'm unable to do with Charlie.

She gives a little bashful tucking of her chin, meaning I've managed to charm her. "Well, you're welcome anytime, Benjamin." She tilts her head. "You look familiar. I mean other than the hospital. Do I know your parents?"

My jaw ticks just once before I relax and smile. "I've delivered a few pizzas here," I say. "Though last time it was Charlie who answered the door. It was some time before that since I've been here."

"That must be it," she muses, continuing to look at me as if trying to figure me out. "You'd think I would have remembered you."

"Naomi, *please*," Charlie says, sounding very much like a petulant teen, something I haven't heard in her before.

"Well," Naomi says. "I'm going to meet with a friend for some shopping and dinner. I'll be home around eight, Charlotte." She looks at Charlie meaningfully, a look I can't interpret.

After she leaves, Charlie turns to me. "You want something to eat? Or drink?"

"I'd take a soda," I say.

Charlie hands me one, and grabs a water bottle for herself. She snags a bag of chips and leads the way into the family room, dropping her backpack onto the couch.

"Before we start," I say, "I'd love to see your room."

"I'm sure you would," she says, her words rolling in sarcasm.

I hold my hands up. "Give me a little credit, Charlie . . . or should I say *Charlotte*?"

She narrows her eyes at me. "If you call me that ever again, I'll . . . cut your tongue out."

"Not quick with the threats, are you? I mean, you had to think about that one for a minute." She glares at me and I laugh. "Okay, okay, *Charlie*, can I please have a tour of this amazing house that's bigger than anything I can even dream of?"

She thinks it over for a minute, watching me. Finally she nods and leads the way. The house really *is* amazing. Just the furniture in any one room is probably worth more than my entire house and its contents.

"And this is my room," she says as we enter the last bedroom—at least, the last one she's shown me. We passed a few closed doors that she didn't open. She looks around and shoves her hands into her back pockets.

I walk in and look around. It's a nice room, not as large as some of the others we've seen. The bed is big, probably a queen, and she has her own desk. In my room, my bed serves as a desk when needed. In one corner she has an iPod dock and a TV, surrounded by CDs and movies. I walk over to see what kinds of things she listens to and watches.

Unable to believe my eyes, I pick up a specific CD and turn her way, holding it up.

"Seriously? Def Leppard?"

She walks over and pulls the CD from my hand. "Mock all you want. I happen to like them, and most classic rock."

I turn back to the rack. "You have all their CDs."

"Yeah, I do. Most of them were my . . . wait a minute, how do you know I have them all?"

Without looking at her, I begin tapping the edge of the rack with my fingers and singing the first lines of "Rocket."

She laughs. "You're a fan, too!"

"I'm a bit familiar with the Sheffield boys—Joe, Phil, Vivian, and both Ricks."

"A little more than familiar, if you can name them all."

"Got a player out there?" I ask, pointing toward the family room. "We can listen while we work." She nods and I add, "I can honestly say I've never met anyone my age who actually owns a single Def Leppard CD, let alone all of them. They might be familiar with the music, but they don't *know* the music."

"Bet I know more lyrics than you," she says, cocking an eyebrow.

"Bet you don't," I say. "In fact, I'd wager on it."

"Oh yeah?" she asks, a small smile playing across her lips.

"I'll bet you that I know more lyrics than you on the *Hysteria* album. If I do, then you have to treat me to a movie sometime."

She studies me. I can practically see the wheels turning behind her eyes as she tries to figure out my motives. I lift a single brow in challenge and that seems to decide her. "Too easy," she says. She steps past me and grabs another CD, lifting it. "*High 'n' Dry.*"

I laugh. "Aha, a true aficionado."

"And what do I get when I win?"

"*When* you win? Don't you mean *if*? Moot point, isn't going to happen."

"*When* I win," she says, emphasizing the *when* strongly, "you take me to your house to see *your* room."

My abdomen tightens at her words. She has no idea what she's asking. I force a smile. "That's it? That's nothing. Don't you want dinner, or a dozen roses or something?"

"Nope. Just a tour of your house."

My instinct is to tell her no, to walk out of here right now. *No one* ever comes to my house, not even Daniel. I can't remember the last time I had a friend over—if ever. It's just something that's always been an unwritten, unspoken rule with my friends, from even before *she* left. No one has ever called me on it before. No one has dared.

"You're on," I hear myself say. Then I decide it doesn't matter, there's no way she can win. I know every song inside out.

"Let's go," she says, leaving the room.

I follow slowly, glancing around once more. My eyes fall on the window seat, where I watched her talking to me from below, unaware of my presence, unaware of having been caught in her lie.

SEVENTEEN
CHARLIE

When I get into Benjamin's car on Friday morning eating a muffin, Def Leppard is blasting from the speakers. Not just any Def Leppard song, but "No No No," the song he beat me on. It's the last track on the album, and I got messed up on the second verse.

To be fair, it was a bit disconcerting to be sitting in my family room with Benjamin Nefer, singing along to Def Leppard, getting zero homework done. I was having too much fun to take the contest as seriously as I should have. Plus, I was intent on getting a tour of his house. Apparently it's a big mystery, no one has ever been inside, and few even know where he lives exactly. Alexis had been happy to share that info with me. Now I'm going to have to figure out how to come up with the money to take him to the movie.

Which sounds way too much like a date.

"Very funny," I say loudly over his high-volume singing. He laughs and turns the sound down.

"Sorry, just had to rub it in a bit," he says.

"We didn't get anything done on the paper," I say.

"Well, we might have if someone hadn't thrown me out before her aunt came home. Were you worried I was going to seduce her, or what?"

"Har-har," I say, not looking at him but infusing my tone with as much sarcasm as possible. I can't possibly tell him my mom was coming home with my aunt, and that's why he had to be gone before she arrived. "You are far too full of yourself, Nefer."

We're stopped at a light and I glance over. He's examining his face in the rearview mirror. "Hard not to be when you look like this," he says.

"Excuse me while I get out and throw up," I say. He just grins at me. It's disarming, that grin. I really don't think I've ever seen anyone as good-looking as Benjamin. Too bad he knows it. "What are you, anyway?"

"Um, human, I believe," he says. "Unless you're saying I'm god-like, which is of course not only possible, but probable." When I choke theatrically, he relents. "What do you mean?"

"I mean, what's your heritage? Mine is Scandinavian and Nor-wegian, but you're . . . exotic looking."

"And by exotic you mean extremely handsome, right?" I make gagging sounds and he laughs. "Fine, sorry. Half-Egyptian, half-Caucasian."

I stare at his smooth, olive skin. "You have skin most girls would kill for."

He winces. "You're saying I look like a girl?"

"Please, you know you don't look like a girl. You just have great skin is all."

"You were partly right," he says.

"What do you mean?"

"Most girls would kill to *touch* my skin."

I toss my wadded-up paper towel at him, which bounces harm-lessly off his shoulder.

"You're beyond help," I mutter.

"That's the nicest thing you've said to me yet." When I only roll my eyes, he says, "We really need to get that paper done. Are you available tonight?"

"What, no hot date?" I ask while my mind frantically scrambles for an excuse to say no.

"Only if you say yes," he says, waggling his eyebrows.

"I'm not dating you, Nefer."

"So I've heard," he says mildly as we pull into the parking lot.

"I can't tonight, anyway," I say. "How about tomorrow?"

"So you're saying you've got a hot date?" His tone is teasing, but I can hear the genuine desire to know.

"Yup," I say. "Me and my mom." I bite the inside of my cheek. I hadn't meant to say that.

"Ah, girl's night," he says.

"What do you know about girl's night?"

"Absolutely nothing. And I'd like to keep it that way." I laugh while climbing out of the car. "So, should I pick you up again tomorrow?"

"Um, I'll let you know, okay? I'm not sure when I can go. What time do you have to be to work?"

"Five."

"All right, I'll know by later tonight."

He places a hand across his heart. "I'll be waiting with bated breath for your call."

"Yeah, I'm sure you will," I say, rolling my eyes again as I hurry inside to find Alexis, Cozi, and Phoebe.

❦

We're sitting at dinner when I finally have the courage to ask my aunt about staying with my mom tomorrow so I can meet with Benjamin.

"Are you doing anything tomorrow?" I ask her.

"Yes, I have my monthly garden party."

"Oh. When's that?"

"It begins at eleven thirty."

"In the morning?"

She stops in the motion of lifting her wine glass to her mouth and stares at me. "Well, it wouldn't be at eleven thirty at night, would it?" I realize the stupidity of my question and shake my head. "What's going on, Charlotte?"

"Nothing, I just . . . I wanted to get some homework done with . . . a friend," I finish lamely, cheeks flushing. "It's no biggie, we can do it another day."

She looks confused. "Do you need my help with it or something? Or a ride?"

"No, I was hoping you could, you know," I say, cutting my eyes toward my mom, who's happily playing with her Jell-O squares.

Naomi's face clears. "Obviously you've forgotten what tomorrow is," she says. I scrunch my forehead, trying to remember what tomorrow is. Not anyone's birthday, unless it's Naomi's. I can't say I know when hers is.

"Tomorrow is Cora's field trip," Naomi says.

"I get to go to the park," my mom adds. Apparently she isn't as oblivious to our conversation as I thought.

"I know you do," I say, suddenly remembering. "Are you excited?"

She claps her hands and bounces in her seat. "And we're gonna see the ducks, and eat on a blanket, and Josie said she wants to sit by me on the bus."

Her enthusiasm is contagious and I smile with her. Surprisingly, so does Naomi.

"I guess I forgot," I say to Naomi. "What time does she go?"

"I'll drop her off on my way to the party. Then she's there until ten tomorrow night."

"We're gonna watch movies on blankets in our jammies," my mom says. "And eat *pizza*."

The word *pizza* reminds me of Benjamin. Guess I can meet him now, without worrying about my mom. Not that I won't worry about her. I always do when she's away from me. So far, Dayspring seems like a really cool place, and definitely somewhere she loves to go. But I'm withholding judgment, and probably always will based on what happened to her eighteen years ago.

"Which pajamas are you going to wear?" I ask. That opens the floodgates of discussion as to which pajamas she should wear, and what she should wear to the park.

Later, after she's in bed, I sit in my window seat and text Benjamin. This is one of my favorite places to be in the house because I can see above the single-story house across the street to the mountains in the distance. When the moon hits them, like it does now, they seem to glow, almost surreal in their blue color.

My phone rings, startling me. It's Benjamin. I smile.

"Are you still stalking me?" I ask without preamble.

"Kind of," he says. "You don't understand how important this paper is to me."

I laugh. "Whatever. I'd think you have enough going on socially that you hardly need to be calling your study partner on a Friday night." A car pulls up across the street, its lights shutting off. I don't even give it a glance, parked under the tree as it is. Lack of streetlights make it too dark to see much of anything, and I haven't met any of the neighbors, so it's not like I'm going to wave or anything.

"Well, I thought I was going to meet up with this hot girl, but then she told me she had a date already." My stomach tightens at his words. So he *did* have a date. "You know who with?"

I try to imagine who might be better looking than Benjamin who might get a girl to go out with him instead. I can't think of a soul. There are others who are *nicer*, definitely, according to the rumors I've heard about Benjamin. That could conceivably be a very long list.

"Daniel?" I guess.

"Nope. And you don't give Daniel enough credit. He's smarter than that." My forehead scrunches again. What does that mean? Before I can ask, he says, "Her date was . . . her *mom*."

The air whooshes out of me and my smile returns. I pull my feet up, resting my chin on my knees. "Don't you ever stop, Benjamin?"

"Where would the fun be in that?" Before I can give him the flippant response I have, he says, "So, what time can you go tomorrow? I only have until four thirty, so as early as possible."

"I can't go before about eleven thirty," I say, feeling that's a safe time to be certain my mom is gone. Since my aunt's garden party—whatever *that* is—begins at that time, they'll for sure be gone.

"I'll pick you up at eleven thirty then. Don't eat before I get you—I mean, unless you need to. So you won't, you know, have another . . . um . . . anyway, if you can wait, I'll take you to this cool place I know that makes these amazing grilled-cheese sandwiches."

"Grilled cheese? Big, bad, football player like you eats grilled cheese?"

"More often than you know," he mutters, something strange in his voice. "I promise, they're the best grilled cheese you'll ever taste."

"Hmm, well, I guess I'll just have to trust you on that."

"See you tomorrow, new girl."

"Bye, Nefer."

I hang up and fold my arms around my knees. I know I shouldn't be looking forward to seeing him tomorrow, I *know* that. Logically. Still, butterflies flutter inside my belly at the thought. I turn away from the window when the car across the street starts its engine. I glance back for only a moment, mostly uninterested. Guess it was just someone picking someone up or dropping them off.

EIGHTEEN
BENJAMIN

Charlie hangs up as I watch, then hugs her knees. She was more correct than she thought when she asked if I was her stalker. I'd already been driving to her place, hoping she'd be in her room when I called her. I almost hoped she'd catch me and come outside to talk.

I start my car when she turns away from the window and drive home. I'm troubled by this strange . . . *obsession* I have with her. It has to be an obsession, because what else could it be? No doubt I'm attracted to her. Who wouldn't be? She's beautiful. And she's surprisingly fun to talk to. But I don't *like* her. I don't like anyone. I don't hate anyone, either. I don't feel anything for anyone, not Daniel, not any of my other friends, not my father, and most certainly not Charlie.

I pull into the gravel drive next to our mobile home, my stomach dropping when I see my dad's car already there. I was hoping he'd still be gone until long after I was asleep. Not that that'd keep him from wanting to fight, but sometimes it discourages him enough to leave me alone.

I consider sitting in my car in the driveway until I'm sure he's out, but he peels back the sheet that covers the window and sees me. With a grunt I open my door and climb out. I walk in through the back door and he blindsides me with a blow to the head. I let him pound on me until he yells, "Fight back!" then do my best to defend myself. Since he's not completely drunk, it's a while until he tires of hitting me and simply walks away, without so much as a word or backward glance, to go to bed.

I walk into the bathroom, exhausted, and examine my face in the mirror. A goose egg on my forehead near my hairline and a split in the middle of my bottom lip seem to be the worst of the damage. It's hard to imagine that my life is my reality. It feels, sometimes, like a bad movie. I've created this public image for myself that makes my life seem the opposite of what it really is.

I stare at my reflected image. I look similar to my father in my skin and hair coloring. Even my smile is the same as his—when he manages to smile.

But my eyes. They're *her*. Green, wide, with long, thick lashes. I've seen pictures to reinforce my weak memory of her. My dad's eyes are dark and small. There's no doubt where this particular feature comes from, and I'm reminded of her each time I see them in the mirror.

I turn away from me and go to bed, wishing I could escape into sleep. That doesn't seem to be possible. The violence riddling my dreams keeps me from ever getting any real rest.

๛

When I pick up Charlie, she's waiting for me at the curb as usual. I'm pretty sure at this point that her home life is nothing like mine, the way I'd suspected. There is something weird with her and her aunt, and I haven't met her mom. She never speaks of a dad or uncle, though I don't know for sure if anyone else lives here.

"Did you come hungry?" I ask her.

"Of course." She holds up her backpack. "But I also brought a pb&j in case you lied."

"I hate to tell you this, but you're going to waste a perfectly good sandwich."

She smiles and I turn away. For some reason her smiles give me a strange feeling in the pit of my gut, something I can't name and don't want to examine too closely.

An hour later, Charlie tosses her napkin on the table and leans back in her chair. "You win," she says. "That was an amazing grilled cheese."

I shrug and hold out my hand.

"What?" she asks.

"Give me the pb&j so I can toss it in the trash."

She grins at me. "I was just kidding you, Nefer. I didn't bring a sandwich. I fully trusted you and your culinary sense."

"My culinary sense?" I ask, laughing.

We decide to go to the library to work on the paper since it's quiet there, and we can access the Internet if we need further information. Charlie is surprisingly easy to work with. She has great ideas but isn't so stubborn that she refuses to listen to my opinion. The paper actually gets finished pretty quickly. Too quickly.

"So," she says as she places her items back into her backpack. "They still hiring at your work?"

"I think so. Why, you interested?"

"Maybe," she says. "But I can only work a few hours a week and on certain days. Do you think that's weird for me to apply for a job then tell them I'm limited on when I can work?"

"Ninety percent of the employees there are in high school. They're not only used to working around weird schedules, they're really good about it. I can put in a good word for you."

"A good word from Benjamin Nefer? That can either be a really good thing, or the thing that keeps me from getting the job."

I roll my eyes at her, but say, "The manager is a woman."

"Did you date her?"

"Of course not! She's, like, old. She's married with kids. Maybe even grandkids. But she loves me." At her look, I say, "Not in that way."

"Thanks, Nefer. I appreciate it, but don't say anything just yet. I need to talk to my aunt first."

"Your aunt?" I say. "Not your mom?" Maybe I was wrong. Maybe there is something weird going on at her house.

Charlie doesn't look at me as she says, "My mom's okay with whatever I want to do."

"Must be nice," I say.

She shrugs. "We should get going so you can get to work."

"Can't wait to get rid of me, huh, new girl?"

She studies me for a minute in mock seriousness. "Nah, you're pretty tolerable."

I choke out a laugh. "Wow, the compliments you pour on me . . . a guy could get a big head."

I stand and follow her from the library. "You already have a big head, Nefer. You don't need me to help in that department."

"See what I'm talking about?" I say. "It's just compliment, compliment, compliment."

❦

I roll out a new chunk of pizza dough, preparing to put it on a pan. I'm not particularly happy right now. I was supposed to be on delivery tonight, but someone else called in sick, which means they need someone with half a brain to stay in the store to keep things running. I don't make any tip money standing in the store, putting pies together.

"Hey, Benjamin, guess who's here?"

I barely turn at the sound of Casey's voice. She's sixteen, and as immature as a twelve-year-old. Gossip rules her life. Working here where most high school kids hang out at some point or another during the weekend puts her in her own personal heaven. I grunt a noncommittal response.

"A-lex-is," she sing-songs.

"Cool," I say, gritting my teeth. Daniel and I were talking about Alexis and my breaking things off with her a few months ago, and Casey overheard. Now she feels it necessary to point out every time she comes in, to try to get me to confide in her. She makes it all seem much more dramatic than it really is. It's nothing—less than nothing, in fact.

"She's with those other two she usually hangs out with," she continues her running commentary. I'm about to tell her to get back to work when she says, "And some new girl that I've never seen before."

I whip around and follow her line of vision. Sure enough, Alexis, Cozi, and Phoebe are sitting in a booth. So is Charlie. I feel a smile creeping across my face and quickly push it away.

"Well, go take their order," I tell Casey. "Unless you already know what they want."

"I know what Alexis wants," she sing-songs again as she turns to walk to their table. I watch her for a minute—or not really her, but Charlie. Charlie's laughing with the other three as they give Casey their order.

I suddenly have an idea. I finish the pizza I was working on, then pull another chunk of dough and shape seven breadsticks in the shape of the letters spelling "new girl." I glaze them with garlic butter and put them through the oven. It takes ten minutes while I work on other orders and try to keep my eyes from their table. Finally they finish and I arrange them on a plate. I hand them to Casey, who informs me they didn't order breadsticks.

"I know," I say, exasperated. "These are from me."

"Should I tell them that?" she asks, grinning slyly at me.

"No," I say. "They'll know who they're from."

Casey glances down at the breadsticks, then grins at me. "Welcoming the new girl, huh? Did you get the idea from me calling her that?"

My eyes move from their table to Casey. I open my mouth to tell her no, but remember how well she keeps information to herself. "Yup. Good idea, Casey."

I send her one of my winning smiles, and she blushes as she picks up the plate, carrying it to their table. She seems to be explaining to them that the breadsticks are free when they try to reject her. Then Charlie looks down at the plate, turning her head to see the message better. Suddenly she smiles, her eyes lifting, searching me out. I smile when she mouths, "thank you." I'm aware the others have finally realized where they came from as their gazes turn my way.

I'm stunned by the anger in Cozi's eyes. She seriously looks like she'd be just as happy to come back into the kitchen and take a knife to me. Phoebe looks disgusted, but Alexis's expression causes the smile to drop from my face. Hurt fills her expression, reaching me across the expanse of the room, through the noise of the jukebox, talking, and laughter, beneath the heat of the lamps that keep the pizzas hot. My eyes flick to Charlie to see if she can see it also, but she's simply smiling at me. She picks up a piece—looks like the R from here—lifts it in mock salute, and takes a bite. I manage to smile back thinly before giving one last glance at Alexis, who's now turned away.

A weird sensation fills my chest, similar to the feeling I have when we lose a football game. I rub my fist across my chest, trying to banish it before I get back to work.

☙

It's almost an hour later before I have a chance to take a break. Good thing, though, since it takes me that long to come up with a good reason to visit their table. When I do think of it, though, it seems so obvious.

"Hey, everyone," I say, addressing the whole table. By now, the four girls have been joined by several other people until there's about ten of them squished into the booth. Charlie is squeezed between one of my teammates named Mario and a hot cheerleader named Tonya. I'm not sure which one I should be jealous of.

Several of the guys fist-bump me, Daniel saying, "Workin' hard for the money, man, or hardly working?"

"What money?" I ask as everyone laughs.

"Thanks for the breadsticks," Charlie says, giving me the excuse I need to turn my attention to her.

"Not a problem," I say, giving her one of my charming grins, the kind that usually melts girls' hearts—well, most girls. "Hey, glad you came in, new girl. Now I can give you this." I hand her an application. She takes it, looks at it, then ducks her head when she realizes what it is, as if ashamed. What's up with that?

"You're going to apply here?" Cozi asks.

Charlie shrugs. "I was thinking about it. I need a part-time job."

"The downside to that is that you have to work with this loser," Daniel says, giving her an exaggerated wink.

"Better than hanging out at the table with you losers," I joke back, though his words hit a little close to home. If she's here, working, where I'd see her more often, then that means even more confusion for me. As if the thought brings her to mind, my eyes slide over to Alexis. She's pointedly ignoring me, though I can sense her discomfort. Not sure why this bothers me, but I rub a fist across my chest again, trying to push the strangeness there away.

A loud crash from the kitchen area catches my attention. I sigh and look back at the group. At Charlie, actually, if you want to get technical.

"Might want to reconsider applying," I tell her with a wink. "Guess I better go make sure no one was maimed or wounded."

I wave at the group and head back into the kitchen, not surprised at all when I find the cause of the noise to be Casey.

NINETEEN
CHARLIE

I wake late on Sunday, jerking out of bed at the bright sunlight streaming through my window. I barely take the time to stop in the bathroom before rushing to my mom's room.

Empty.

Then I hear laughter coming from somewhere else in the house. I walk slowly down the stairs, feeling like I've been dropped into the Twilight Zone. My mom and Naomi sit on a large blanket in the family room, eating waffles—and laughing. Naomi glances up and sees me.

"Well, look who decided to join the land of the living," she says. I can't detect any malice or sarcasm in the words.

My mom turns around and sees me, a wide grin splitting her face. She waves happily, but doesn't get up to greet me.

"Would you like to join our picnic?" Naomi asks.

"Our *waffle* picnic," my mom corrects.

"You're having a picnic—I mean, a *waffle* picnic—in the middle of the living-room floor?"

"It's fun," my mom calls.

"Cora had so much fun at her movie picnic last night, we thought it'd be fun to have a breakfast picnic," Naomi explains, as if this isn't *way* outside her norm.

"Uh-huh," I say, continuing the rest of the way down the stairs. Mom had been really tired and fallen immediately asleep last night when Naomi brought her home, so she hadn't told us about it. That meant Naomi had been up with her even longer than I'd thought.

"Come sit," my mom says, patting the floor next to her. It looks rather sticky with syrup, but I sit anyway, leaning to give her a hug.

"Tell me about your movie picnic, Mom."

"We sat on the floor," she says happily, practically glowing.

"I figured that," I say. "What else?"

"And we watched *Brave*, and ate popcorn. And we ate pizza, with *pineapple* on it." She says this with a joyful roll of her eyes, fists clenched at her chest, as if it's the best thing she's ever had. It suddenly occurs to me I've never thought to ask her what she wanted on a pizza. Something so simple to bring her this much pleasure. I just always assumed that what my grandma ordered was what she liked, so I simply followed suit.

"Did you sit by Josie on the bus?" I ask, slightly choked up over my selfish discovery.

"Yup, and she's my bestest friend," she assures me.

"You really like it at Dayspring, don't you?"

"I love it," she says. "I love it more than chocolate-chip cookies."

"That's quite a bit, isn't it?"

She nods vigorously, having stuffed her mouth full of waffles.

"Well, I guess I'll go get some waffles, too," I say, standing.

"I'll come with you," Naomi says, following me into the kitchen. When we're out of earshot, I ask, "So, what's this all about?"

"The picnic?" Naomi asks. When I raise my eyebrows, she shrugs. "She talked nonstop about it while I was making breakfast, so I figured it would be fun for her."

"But *why*? That's really not . . . normal for you to do."

"Believe it or not, Charlotte, I do love my sister."

"But you—" I cut myself off. I don't want to get into this with her right now. So instead I say, "Thank you, that was a really nice thing to do."

I grab a plate and place a couple of waffles on it, covering them with peanut butter and a small amount of syrup.

"I was wondering," I begin hesitantly. "Do you think . . . is it okay if I get a part-time job as long as it doesn't interfere with times when Mom's home?"

"You don't need to work, Charlotte. I have the means to take care of you. Anything you need, or want, just ask."

I bite the inside of my cheek. Like I'd ask her to give me money to take Benjamin to the movie. "Um, thanks, but I'd rather have a job where I can earn a little money and get some experience."

She studies me silently for a few moments before nodding. "I think that's a great idea. In fact, I was going to tell you I have an extra car that you can use whenever you need it. It just sits in the garage, so someone might as well be driving it. It's not good for cars to sit unused for long periods of time, right?" I have no idea if it's good or bad. "And now that you'll have a job, you can use it to get yourself there and back."

My first instinct is to flat-out refuse. There must be some angle, something she wants from me. Then I think about the freedom a car would afford me. Not always dependent on someone else for a ride. And to be honest, I hadn't really considered how I'd get to and from Tony's Pizzeria. Plus, the best bonus of all, I could take my mom to Dayspring on the weekends and pick her up on the weekdays.

"Okay, yeah, that'll be very helpful. Thanks."

"Not a problem," she says. She begins to walk from the kitchen, pausing in the doorway. "Why don't you bring your waffles and picnic with us?"

∽

As much as I hate to admit it, Benjamin's word was my in at Tony's Pizzeria. I applied one day, was called in for an interview and hired the next. My first scheduled shift is tonight, and I'm nervous. I've never worked anywhere before. I've never had a need to—my first priority has always been taking care of my mom.

The "uniform" is simply a white shirt and dark blue or black pants. Luckily I happen to have what I need. It's been amazing having the car to drive as well. My grandma could never afford to have a car for me in the year and a half that I had my license before she died. Which didn't seem like that big of a deal. But the thought of asking my aunt for a ride whenever I needed one filled me with dread. So to be able to not only have a job to begin to save money for my mom and me, but also a means of transportation, however temporary, to drive us around, is more than I hoped for.

Mom is at Dayspring tonight until nine. My shift ends at eight thirty, which means I can pick her up. She doesn't know I'll be coming. She's used to being picked up by "Mimi." I can't wait to see her face.

When I pull into Tony's, I'm relieved to see Benjamin's car in the parking lot. At least there will be a familiar face here tonight. I only hope he doesn't decide to tease me like he usually does. I really need some calm.

Debbie, the manager who interviewed me, greets me with a nametag and an apron. "We're going to start you easy tonight," she says. "You'll be working with Benjamin, who I believe you know, on putting toppings on the pizza crusts after he rolls them out."

I can't decide if I should be glad I'm working directly with Benjamin, or if I'm nervous about looking like an idiot in front of him.

"Hey, new girl," he says as Debbie leads me into the back. "Looks like you're *new* new girl now."

I smile nervously at his lame joke, not even able to form a sarcastic reply.

"Well, good luck," Debbie says. "Take care of her, Benjamin."

"You got it, Deb," he says, charming her with a smile. I swear the woman actually blushes as she leaves.

"Come on," Benjamin says, actually sounding like he might take it easy on me. "Let me show you the basics."

An hour later I'm finally figuring out how to put the toppings on the pizza. It's far more technical than I ever suspected. There are certain amounts of each topping to be placed on a "pie," as Benjamin calls them, no more and no less, evenly spaced. Then they have to be placed in a specific order for optimal taste. I can make one pizza to Benjamin's every three but he assures me that it's normal for a newbie to be slow.

Benjamin treats me professionally and yet friendly all night, without teasing me or trying to flirt with me. I'd never admit, under pain of torture, that I kind of miss his usual corny banter. This responsible, in-charge Benjamin seems more unapproachable than the usual Benjamin.

As the clock nears eight thirty, I find myself checking it frequently. I definitely don't want to be late on my first night picking my mom up. I'm not sure what the usual protocol is for leaving when one's shift is over. Do I just punch out and leave, or do I have to wait for someone to tell me to go?

"Got a hot date tonight?" Benjamin asks, teasing me for the first time as I glance at the clock once again.

I feel my cheeks heat at getting caught looking. "No, I just need to pick my mom up at nine." Now, why in the world did I just tell Benjamin *that*?

"Using her car, huh?" he assumes. "No worries, we'll get you out in time."

As if conjured by his words, Debbie appears. I really like her. She's older than even my mom, probably early to mid-fifties, but she has this cool auburn-and-blonde-streaked hair, cut short and spiked up in the back. She's friendly and fun, and apparently quite the cook. I've overheard her talking about her recipes for a variety of foods with some of the other workers.

"How's it going?" Her question is directed at me.

"Good. I've learned a lot, I think," I say.

"Of course she has," Benjamin says cockily. "She's learning from the best."

"Your humility is ever amazing," Debbie says, smiling at him. "So since you're such a good teacher, take her in the back and—" When Benjamin waggles his eyebrows rather exaggeratedly, Debbie shakes a finger at him. "Control yourself, Benjamin. Take her back and show her where to check the schedule, how to request time off, and how to punch out."

"Sure thing," he says. He tosses a last handful of cheese on a pizza he was making and places it in the oven. "Come with me, new girl." He leads the way and I follow.

He shows me the required things, once again professional. It's a strange contradiction from his usual relaxed, flirty self. He shows me how to punch out—pretty much the same as punching in. Before I leave, he says, "We need to get together again for our next experiment. Any ideas for that? Or a time when we can meet?"

I shrug. "I guess we could sit in an eating establishment and watch how people interact," I say. "Maybe even just do it here."

"Not here," he immediately responds. "We'd never get any work done since I know everyone and would spend all my time having others talk to me."

It's an arrogant statement, and if I didn't know the utter truth of his words I might roll my eyes. "Where, then?"

"How about Firenzi's?"

Firenzi's is an upscale restaurant in town. "Uh, yeah, I don't think I can afford that on my current wages," I say.

"I know the owner," he says. "I'll see if I can get her to comp us some meals in the name of homework."

I look at him skeptically. I guess if anyone could talk a restaurateur into free meals, it'd probably be Benjamin. "Well, you see what you can do. If not, we might have to shoot for something more like Barney's Burgers."

TWENTY
CHARLIE

I head to Dayspring to pick my mom up. It's the first time I've picked her up, but I know the place well enough to know where to find her. I walk into the rumpus room, which at this time of night has only a few people in it.

She spots me and her face lights up as she runs over to hug me. "Charlie!" she cries happily. I wonder if every kid in the world is met with the same joy each time their parent sees them, and I realize I'm one of a very lucky few. Another woman, younger, with long, dark hair comes timidly up. She has Down syndrome.

"Josie, see? My Charlie," she says to the woman, who smiles shyly at me. So this is the infamous Josie.

I squeeze her hand and smile at her. "Hi, Josie. My m—Cora tells me you're her friend."

"She's my bestest friend," my mom says.

Josie nods enthusiastically.

"Do you live here, Josie?" I ask.

She nods as my mom says, "She has her own room. Can I sleep over with her?"

Her question throws me. "Um, well, you have your own room at home."

"I don't want my own room. I want to stay with Josie."

This is completely unexpected. "Not tonight," I say gently. "You have to come home with me. You'll be back tomorrow."

"No!" Her adamant refusal stuns me.

"What?"

"I want to stay with Josie and my friends here. Why can't I have my own room here?"

"Because we live with Mimi, remember?"

"I don't want to live with Mimi. I want to live here."

I stare, gape jawed. She's throwing a tantrum like a little kid.

"You can't live here. You live at Mimi's . . . with me."

I admit it. It hurts a little that she'd rather stay with Josie than come home with me, her daughter.

"You stay, too."

"I can't. I can't live here. I have to live with Mimi."

"Okay, bye," she says happily, turning away, taking Josie's arm as they walk back toward the activity area.

"Wait, Mom . . . Cora," I call. She doesn't turn back and I have to jog to catch her, grabbing her arm. "It's time to go home now. Come on."

She turns on me, stomping a foot. "I'm staying!"

Frustration, hurt, and anger well up in me. "We're going," I demand, feeling very much like the mother here.

"No!"

Mariam, the aide who'd come to our house before, comes over. "Hi," she says to me. I blink rapidly against the tears, clenching my jaw. "Sorry, Cora gets more and more like this each time she's picked up. I guess Naomi didn't warn you?"

I shake my head, not trusting myself to speak.

"Sometimes it takes a while to get her to go. Let me try?" she asks. I give a terse nod and she turns toward my mom. "Cora,

Charlie came to bring you home with her. You want to go with Charlie, don't you?"

"No, I want to stay here," she says.

"Did you have fun today?"

The change in subject stops my mom's tantrum. It even takes me by surprise.

"Yup. I played with Josie all day."

"Do you want to play with Josie some more?" Both my mom and Josie nod vigorously at her question. "Well, if you want that to happen, then you have to let Josie go to bed now so she can get plenty of rest to play again tomorrow. And you need to sleep, too, so you can play again. Do you want to play again in the morning?"

"Yup, I want to play with Josie and Edie and Darlene and Marie."

"And they all want to play with you," she continued, her voice soothing. "But first everyone has to sleep. So you go with Charlie and sleep in your bed, while they sleep in their beds, and you'll be back bright and early tomorrow. Isn't that right, Charlie?"

It takes me a second to realize I need to answer. I clear my throat. "Yes, that's right. Bright and early." I can hear the choked sound of my voice, but Mariam doesn't comment on it.

"See?" she asks my mom. "Now give Josie a hug so she can go to bed, and we'll see you tomorrow."

She's not happy about it, but she does as asked, then sullenly follows me out to the car. I don't know what to say. I've always been the center of my mom's world, never rejected in favor of anyone else. I bite my cheek, trying to force the tears back as I help her into the car and make sure she's buckled. It isn't until after we're home and she's tucked into bed that I lock my bedroom door and allow the hurt to spill.

"Why didn't you tell me?" My first words to Naomi as she enters the kitchen in the morning. My mom is eating her bowl of oatmeal at the table while I wash the pan in the sink.

She doesn't pretend to not know what I'm talking about. "Because you wouldn't have believed me. You would have thought I was exaggerating because you think I have some underhanded motive to try to get her out of my house."

Just because she's right doesn't make me any less angry with her. "A little warning would have been nice. I had no idea how to handle her. Mariam had to do it for me."

"She usually does," Naomi says mildly. "Her or one of the other aides."

"It was . . . embarrassing."

"You mean hurtful." I clench my jaw and don't answer. "Charlotte, there's nothing personal in it. She just really loves it there, and in her mind it isn't fair she has to leave when everyone else stays. She doesn't understand that simply sleeping there isn't going to make that much of a difference."

"And you know all this after spending no more than a few weeks with her?" I know I sound petulant, and look it, too, with my arms crossed tightly. I don't care.

She ignores my jab and says, "If you think that was bad, pick her up on a Friday when she won't be back until Monday."

I want to refuse to ever pick her up again, refuse to put myself in the path of her utter rejection. But I also know that to do so would be to admit that Naomi is right. Instead, I say, "I'll pick her up tonight."

"You don't work again?" she asks.

"Not tonight. They're good about scheduling me when I *can* work."

"You can work whenever you want," she says. "Just let me know so if I need to pick Cora up, I—"

"No worries," I say, using Benjamin's phrase. "I can take care of it. It's one of the purposes of me using the car, right?"

"No," she says. "The purpose of allowing you to use the car is for whatever you need it for. Not just for running Cora around."

"I'm done," my mom announces, pushing her bowl away from her.

I clean her up, get us both ready for the day, and pack her into the car. We drive to Dayspring.

"See, Mom?" I say when we arrive. "I brought you back like I promised last night."

She gives me a hug and a slobbery kiss on the cheek. "'Kay, bye," she says, opening her door and scrambling out. I quickly follow.

"Wait, Mom, I need to . . ." I'm talking to empty air. I walk inside and see the same smiling woman at the front desk. "Hi, Nancy."

"Hi, Charlie. Guess she was excited to get here, huh?"

"Guess so," I say, signing the entrance sheet. "See you tonight."

I climb back into the car and take a few deep breaths. A war brews in my chest. On the one side, I'm happy my mom has a place that gives her so much joy. She has friends here, activities to give her something to do all day rather than just veg in front of the TV, something to look forward to. On the other side, my selfish heart wants her to be that excited to just be with me. I know it's beyond egocentric for me to want that. I don't begrudge her having her own thing, but I'm her *daughter*. I just kinda wish she knew that.

TWENTY-ONE
BENJAMIN

Nefer!" I turn toward Coach's booming yell. He strides up to me, grabbing my face mask. "Get your head in the game, kid. Where are you today?"

"Sorry, Coach. Short night. Lots of homework."

He examines my face through the guard, seeing the many cuts and bruises there, more than usual. "Been hitting the boxing gym again?"

"Always," I say with a cocky smile.

His mouth thins disapprovingly. He's fine with brutality on the football field, expects it in fact. But step into a ring and suddenly it's mindless violence.

"Well, Nefer, maybe next time you have a lot of homework you can skip the gym."

"I'm good, Coach. Call the next play and watch."

He stares at me for long seconds, but finally releases me. I can't tell him that I had a particularly fierce fight with my dad last night. He wasn't drunk enough to go down easy, but was drunk enough to refuse to give up. I should have just gone down myself, but something in me refused. Because he'd gotten so many good swipes in I was forced to drag myself to the gym in case anyone asked if I'd been there. After several rounds and poundings by guys who I knew were particularly ferocious, and weren't sticklers for rules, I'd gone home and *then* done my homework. I wasn't lying when I said it was a short night. I'd maybe gotten two hours.

I step my game up extra hard so he doesn't question me again, then gratefully hit the showers. I hate these early-morning practices. As I leave the gym, which is a separate building from the main part of the school, I see Charlie pull in. I debate ignoring her and just going inside. Instead, forgetting about my face and exhaustion, I jog over in time to open her car door for her.

"Hey, new-new girl," I say. Then I notice the look on her face. She's upset about something. She looks on the verge of tears. I should have followed my first instinct to go into the school when I saw her. I lean down. "Is everything okay?" I ask, forcing gentleness into my tone.

She turns stricken eyes to me, then her expression changes. Her eyes skim my face and a look of horror crosses her face, eradicating whatever upset her. She stands up and one hand lifts, her fingers lightly caressing the huge lacerated goose egg on my right temple, held closed by two butterfly bandages. I flinch and suck in a painful breath through my teeth. Her hand immediately drops.

"Sorry," she breathes. "What happened to you? Are you okay?"

"Just an extra-hard round at the gym," I answer lightly.

"Benjamin, that's horrible. Why would you subject yourself to that?"

"It's fun?" I ask with a wide, goofy grin.

She shakes her head. "You are one warped person, Nefer." Her hand comes up again and she nearly brushes her thumb across my split lip, stopping just shy of contact. I find myself holding my breath, wondering if she will—hoping she will. "Maybe we should find you a better hobby," she murmurs. Her eyes lift to mine, seeing how close we're really standing. It would only take a minute movement for me to lean in and kiss her. Her pupils dilate and she steps back, fumbling her backpack strap onto her shoulder.

"So, Nefer, what interests you that doesn't involve violence?"

I remain silent until she glances at me then I slide my eyes down her body. She sighs and elbows me in the ribs. It's a light touch. I'd have barely felt it, except that I suspect I might have a few bruised ribs, compliments of my dad's boots. I grit my teeth, holding the hiss in.

"Fine," I say laughingly. "Since you refuse me *that*, I suppose I'll have to think of something else. Just how unviolent does it have to be?"

"Seriously?" she asks. "What do you do for fun besides football and boxing?"

"Girls."

"Well, I'm not going to help you with that. Why would I subject some poor girl to Benjamin Nefer? What else?"

Her words bring to mind Alexis's eyes that night at Tony's as she looked at me, pain reflected as clearly as my own cuts and bruises. I push the image away. "What else is there?"

She laughs. "Bowling?" At my grimace, she says, "All right, not bowling. Skating? Rock climbing? Dancing?"

"Please tell me you didn't just suggest I take up dancing."

"Hey, don't knock it until you've tried it," she says.

"Do you dance?" I ask.

"Well, no . . . but that doesn't mean you shouldn't."

"What do you do for fun, new girl?"

She looks at the ground, a little spot of color in her cheeks. Okay, now I'm *very* curious about what she's thinking. I wait.

"I, you know, go to movies and . . . stuff."

"I like movies," I say. "In fact, I believe someone owes me a movie."

"I haven't forgotten," she says. "I just need to earn some money first."

"I know the manager at the theater," I say. "I could—"

"Oh, no," she interrupts. "I lost, so I'll pay. I'm not using one of your favors."

"We could have another contest, double or nothing," I suggest.

"Yeah?" she asks. "What kind of contest?"

"What other bands do you listen to?"

"Taylor Swift."

"Yeah, no, that's not gonna happen. Seriously, Taylor Swift?"

"She's good."

"All that chick sings about are her previous boyfriends. Who would be dumb enough to date her?"

She looks at me, eyebrows lifted. "I know someone who could give her a run for her money in writing about previous heartbreaks."

"I've never had my heart broken," I say proudly.

"Really?"

My mom's image flashes through my mind for a brief moment. Doesn't count. "Nope," I say.

"Wow, that's kinda . . . sad."

"How is that sad?" I ask.

"Because heartbreak helps to shape you. Helps you know how you want to be treated, and how to treat those you're with. Maybe that's your problem, Nefer, you need a really good heartbreak so you know how to treat the girls you date."

"I don't *have* a problem getting girls to date me," I say. It's true, I don't. Because I don't care if they date me or not. I don't care if they like me or not. I only date so that I appear normal, and to prove that I can. Otherwise I'd just as soon hang out with my buddies. "Other than you," I qualify. "Can't seem to get you to date me." When she doesn't answer, I ask, "Have you had your heart broken?"

"Of course."

"When? Who?"

"Freddy Tappmore. First boyfriend I had, when I was in fourth grade."

Boyfriend? Maybe I'm wrong about her—or maybe she just didn't know in fourth grade that she didn't really like guys. "*Fourth* grade?"

"Don't mock me," she says. "I remember it clearly. He told me he liked me, held my hand and everything. Then one day he told me he liked Sheila Chester better. So he started holding her hand instead. It was devastating."

I laugh at her and she mock-glares at me. "That's it?" I ask.

"No, but I'm not telling you any more when all you do is laugh at me."

The warning bell rings and I startle. I didn't realize so much time had passed.

"Well, see you at lunch," she says, jogging down the hall toward her class. I watch her go, wondering if I've ever lost track of time, *ever*, while talking to anyone.

ᑲ

"You should ask Alexis out."

Daniel pauses only momentarily in pulling his sock on as we sit in the dressing room.

"Oh yeah? Why?"

I glance at him. There's something funny in his voice. "Because she's beautiful, for one. And she's funny. I think you two would get along."

Daniel grunts and I peer at him closer.

"You've already thought about asking her out?" His eyes cut toward me and away again quickly. What . . . "Wait, did you already ask her out?"

He pauses again, then bends to grab his cleats. "Yup. She said no."

"She said *no*?" It's not that I think Alexis is easy, or anything. But Daniel is a pretty decent-looking guy and he doesn't have any harder time getting dates than I do. "Do you want me to talk to her?"

"No!" His answer is quick, firm.

I stare at him before it occurs to me. "Is it because of me? Is that why she said no?"

"Not because she's still in love with you or anything," he mutters.

"But because I hurt her," I say. It isn't a question. He nods. "Sorry, man."

"Well," he says, pulling his shoelace taut and grabbing his gear. "It is what it is, right?" Without waiting for an answer he heads to the field, leaving me sitting alone on the bench.

TWENTY-TWO
CHARLIE

I stare at Benjamin. "You're kidding, right?"

"I'm dead serious."

"Like a double date?"

"No, not a date. A homework assignment." He shrugs. "Alexis and Daniel might not be in our class, but they have to do the same thing we do."

"You're telling me you can get the owner of Firenzi's to comp you four meals?"

"Well, we'll have to tip the server, of course."

"What exactly do you have to do to get *four* meals at . . . never mind, I don't want to know." I shake my head. It sounds *way* too much like a date to invite Alexis and Daniel to Firenzi's with us. Not that it feels any less date-like for it to just be the two of us.

"You might have to talk Alexis into it," he says, voice hesitant.

I narrow my eyes at him. "Why?"

"She's not exactly a fan of me."

I laugh. "I don't know any girls who are a fan of you, Benjamin. Good thing you're graduating this year so you can move on to unsuspecting college girls."

He winces, the move practiced and not at all genuine. "Ouch. Leave it to you to tell it how it is."

I shrug. "Hey, it's your thing, Nefer. Now, had I come along years ago I might have been able to save you from yourself, but I fear it's too late to help you."

"You think I'm beyond help?" He tries for a joking tone, but as I look at him, I realize there's a seriousness beneath his grin. Does Benjamin *want* to be different? That stops my cocky reply.

"Well," I sigh, "I'll see what I can do. When do you want to go?"

"It'll have to be a weeknight. They're too busy on the weekends for me to wrangle free meals then. How about next Wednesday around six thirty?"

"What if we're scheduled to work?"

"Well, I just happen to know the manager of Tony's . . ."

I laugh. "Okay, fine, I'll talk to Alexis and see what she says."

❦

"Go to Firenzi's . . . with Benjamin and Daniel?" Alexis sounds dubious at best.

"Benjamin can get us free meals, and it'll be a great place for observation."

"Daniel's not my study partner for this assignment."

"Oh. Right." I should have thought of that myself. "I guess I just assumed you were and that's why he suggested it."

"You know why he told you to ask me, right?"

I honestly don't. Then I remember him asking if I thought he was beyond help. "Maybe he wants to make nice with you, Alexis, after what he did."

She shakes her head. "You're pretty blind where Benjamin is concerned. We've all noticed it, and we're worried about you."

"I'm not . . . I mean, we're just friends. I've made it very clear to him I won't date him." A vision of him standing outside my car door, inches from my mouth, looking very much as if he were going to kiss me, flashes through my mind.

Alexis laughs, though it's more scoffing derision than humor. "You're new, Charlie. You haven't been around long enough to see what he's capable of. He's trying really hard with you *because* you're refusing to date him. Benjamin doesn't have it in him to be a friend."

I bristle. "I'm not as naive as you think," I say. "I've known guys like him. I really don't think he's *trying* anything."

"Really?" she asks. "Think about it: he volunteered to be your partner for the assignment when he has plenty of guy friends in that class, he got you hired on at Tony's, and he's always hanging out with you at lunch and in the halls. That's not normal behavior for most guys, but definitely not for Benjamin Nefer."

"You're being really judgmental," I say.

"I have the right to be. Do you know what he did to me?"

I actually don't. I only know they dated and he hurt her. I shake my head.

"He did kinda the same thing he's doing with you, always wherever I was at, talking to me, smiling at me, making me feel like I was the center of his universe. I told him I wasn't interested because I know exactly what he's like. Didn't matter in the end. He wore me down. He can be extremely charming. By the time I agreed to go out with him, I was half in love with him.

"Two dates, that's his rule," she says bitterly. "I thought I was the exception, right? He'd pursued me pretty hard." She swallows loudly and leans against the side of the building. The pain reflected in her eyes is practically tangible. "So at school the Monday morning after our second date, I went to find him just as I had every day between our dates. He looked at me like I was trash beneath his feet. You know what he said to me?"

I shake my head, not sure I want to hear this.

"He said, 'You've had your two, now leave me alone.' Right in front of all his friends. They all laughed."

My heart cringes. "Oh, Alexis, I'm so sorry."

She straightens, blinking her tears away. "Doesn't matter anymore. You want to know the worst part? I used to really like Daniel. We got along really well, but he'd never ask me out. It's like some unwritten rule between Benjamin and all his followers. He gets first pick, then they can have what's left, or have whoever he's done with. I didn't want to date Benjamin, I wanted to date Daniel, but then I fell for Benjamin's crap. Now that he's done with me, guess who asked me out?"

My stomach roils. I feel sick. "Daniel?"

"Yup. I told him no."

"And now Benjamin's trying to get me to set you up with him." I feel like I'm going to throw up.

"Everyone gets used by Benjamin eventually."

I hug Alexis. "I'm so sorry. Really I am. Please believe me I wouldn't have even asked if I'd had any idea."

She hugs me back. "You didn't know. But you do now." She looks me in the eye. "Be careful, Charlie. He's good at what he does."

I nod. She's right, he is good. Because as much as I thought I've been emotionally aloof when it comes to Benjamin, I now realize that he's been working his subtle magic on me. I know this because the thought of not being friends with him anymore makes my heart hurt.

⁓

After school I text Benjamin and tell him Alexis can't go, so it'll just be the two of us. I don't feel like I can face him right now, so I take the coward's way and run to my car, getting in and driving away before he can find me.

At home, I lie on my bed listening to T-Swift singing about her heartbreaks. I don't want to listen to Def Leppard right now—too much Benjamin in that music. It really ticks me off, to be honest. What if he's ruined them for me forever?

I glance over at the photo of me, my grandma, and my mom. It was a year ago, before we knew about the cancer that would steal my grandma from us. She'd raised me. She was truly my mom. I wish she were here right now so I could talk to her, ask her what I should do. Should I stop being Benjamin's friend because he might be trying to do to me what he did to Alexis? Or should I just keep being his friend and stay strong in not dating him?

My eyes flick to my mom's smiling face in the photo. I imagine sitting down with her, spilling all of my problems, having her give me sage advice and stroking my hair while I cry out my confusion. Angrily, I punch my pillow at the fates that gave me a child for a mother and a grandma whose cancer put her in the ground, and let the tears flow.

TWENTY-THREE
BENJAMIN

Charlie insists on meeting at Firenzi's.

"It's not a date," she'd said when I pushed the issue of picking her up.

Something is wrong, and I can't figure it out. Since she now has a car, I don't pick her up for school anymore, and she avoids me at lunch and in the hallways. I miss our talks. She's been treating me a little cold—not quite cold enough to be considered rude. More like a polite freeze.

She's waiting on the bench in front of Firenzi's when I pull up. Her hair sits in soft waves on her shoulders rather than straight as she usually has it. She's wearing peach-colored jeans tucked into brown, knee-high boots, and a yellow T-shirt covered with a white knitted sweater of some kind, allowing the yellow to peek through.

I give a low whistle. "You look pretty amazing, new girl."

She stands and gives me an empty smile. "Thanks."

She turns and pulls the door open, entering the restaurant without waiting to see if I follow.

"Benjamin, *amore mio*," the manager, Elise, says with her Italian accent as she spies me. She glides over, placing her hands on my shoulders and kissing the air near each of my ears.

"Elise, *mia bella*," I say, smiling at her.

"One of these days you will pay for a meal, *si?*" She places her hands on my cheeks.

"When I'm rich and famous, I'll bring all of my rich and famous friends here and make your restaurant the toast of the free world."

She pats one of my cheeks. "Such crap, *mi amore*, but such beautiful crap it is."

I laugh and she turns toward Charlie.

"This is my friend, Charlie."

Elise glances at me with a wink. "Ah, she is very beautiful, is she not?"

"That she is," I say, only for Charlie to narrow her eyes at me. Not playfully like she usually does, but with true anger. "Uh," I say, feeling at a loss. "Um, she's . . . she's my lab partner at school. For this assignment."

"Mm-hmm," Elise says suggestively. Oddly, I'm embarrassed by her response. She turns back to Charlie. "Welcome, *mia bella*." She hooks an arm through Charlie's. As she leads her to a table, I hear her say, "Watch out for this charmer." She nods her head in my direction.

"Not to worry," Charlie says seriously. "There isn't *any*thing between us other than homework."

"We will see, we will see," Elise says as she hands Charlie into a booth. A server hurries over and hands a menu to Charlie, and then to me once I sit. "You order what you want, *mio bell'uomo*," Elise says. "Sadly, unlike Charlie, I am not immune to the charms of young Benjamin. And so, I pay for his meals." She winks at Charlie then leaves the table.

Charlie studies the menu, holding it up like a shield. I don't need to look. I already know what to order since I've eaten here many times, so I leave my menu on the table and watch Charlie as she scans hers.

"What?" she demands, peering at me over the top of the menu. "Why are you staring at me?"

"Did I do something?" I ask. "You seem really angry at me."

She slaps the menu down on the table. "Maybe it's not about you, Benjamin. Did that ever occur to you? Not everything in this world is about you." She jerks the menu back up in front of her face.

I sit in uncomfortable silence for long minutes, trying to remember if I *did* do anything to make her angry. When I can't think of anything, I begin to think her words are true, that it's not me but something else. While I'm relieved it isn't me, I wonder what else is bothering her. I've never seen her like this before.

"Do you want to talk about it?" I ask.

She shakes her head tightly. I can tell she's not even reading the menu, just pretending to.

"It might help," I say. "I mean, I don't know that I'll have any good advice for you, but I can listen. Maybe it'll help to get it off your chest."

She slams the menu down again. "Don't talk about my chest," she says vehemently.

My jaw drops. "I wasn't . . . I didn't mean . . . c'mon, Charlie. You know I didn't mean anything by that. I just want to help. Isn't that what friends are for?"

The server walks up to the table to take our drink orders. Charlie smiles at the server when ordering, and I'm jealous that the server is the recipient of her smile while I only get her temper. When she walks away, Charlie glares at me.

"You dare to call yourself my friend? You have no idea what friendship is."

This is genuinely unchartered territory for me. I've had plenty of girls mad at me in the past, but I've always known *exactly* why they were. It was deserved. But here's Charlie, claiming she's not mad at me, but then in the next breath telling me I'm not her friend.

"Okay, so clearly it *is* me you're mad at."

"Yes, it's you. How could you be such a jerk? You completely had me fooled."

Now I'm really scrambling, trying to figure out what in the world I did to tick her off so much.

"Well, I guess I had me fooled, too. I thought we were . . . *are* friends."

She lets out a disgusted sigh, then pastes a smile on her face when the server brings our drinks and asks for our order. Charlie asks what she suggests, then orders that as I study her. The server turns to me.

"Uh, yeah, I'll have that also," I say, though I'm completely unaware of what I just ordered. When she walks away, I lean toward Charlie. "As much fun as I'm having playing the 'Guess Why Charlie's Mad' game, it'd be much easier if you'd just tell me."

"Yeah, it would, wouldn't it? And we should all make Benjamin's easy life as easy as possible."

I nearly laugh. She has no idea how *un*easy my life really is. She'd cringe if she had an inkling of what I go home to each night, if she knew how hard I have to work to make sure I get top-notch grades, and that I'm the best on the team. All of that while working my butt off to make sure I have the money I need to pay for my clothes, car, gas, and food. Sleep is a luxury I get very little of. And this princess in her big house, driving a nice, expensive car, wearing clothes that someone else bought her, able to be picky about the shifts she works each week rather than picking up every possible extra shift, dares to judge me.

"Fine," I say. "Don't tell me. No worries." I pull a notebook and pen from my backpack and look around the restaurant. "Let's just work."

She pulls her own notebook and pen from her bag and opens the notebook to a blank page.

"So, what's our objective here?" I ask. "How people interact with one another, or how they treat the servers, or what kinds of food—"

"You used me," she blurts.

"What?"

"You knew Daniel already asked Alexis out, that she said no, and you used me to try to set them up anyway."

I set my pen down. "I didn't use you, or at least, I didn't mean to, not in the way you're implying."

"Then what was that?"

Alexis's hurt eyes flash into my mind again. "I just . . . I feel like they'd be good together, and I thought this was a good way to . . . it's, you know, a romantic place—not that I'm trying to be romantic with you . . ." I trail off. I feel completely like a floundering fish here.

"Why do you care if they're together?" she asks. Her tone has gone from angry to curious.

I shrug. Then I decide honesty—at least some small amount of honesty—is the only thing that'll work with Charlie. I watch my hands playing with the fork, bouncing it up and down lightly on the table.

"I don't know if Alexis has told you that we . . . dated . . . a couple of times." I glance up and she nods, mouth tight. I realize Alexis probably told her *every*thing, and shame runs through me. "Anyway, because of me, she won't go out with Daniel, but he really likes her. I thought maybe dating him would make her not so . . ." Alexis's eyes come to me again and I blink the image away. "He's . . . he's a really good guy, you know? He's not . . . like me," I finish lamely.

When she's silent I look up and see her watching me. "Are you telling me the truth?" she asks.

"Yes," I say simply.

She sighs and sits back against the booth. She taps her fingers on the table. "What you did to Alexis was really rotten, you know? Like lowlife, bottom-of-the-barrel, snake-in-the-grass rotten."

"I know," I say.

"She's not the only one, either."

I shake my head.

"Why do you do it?" Her question is quiet, but the answer is not. The answer is loud, roaring into my nightmares every night, waiting for me at home every day, never far from my mind. I can't answer her, so I just shrug.

"I guess . . ." she begins, then stops. She seems to be thinking as she examines the condensation on the side of her glass. She brings her gaze to mine. "Are you trying to do the same thing to me, Benjamin? Trying to get me to date you so you can hurt me?"

My jaw clenches at the thought of seeing the same pain in Charlie's eyes that I saw in Alexis's. My stomach tightens at the thought of being the person who would *cause* that pain in her eyes. When in the world did I begin to give an ounce of caring about someone besides myself? *I don't!* I think fiercely. *I don't care.*

"No," I finally say. She lifts a dubious brow. "Okay, maybe at first. I mean, have you seen yourself? You're gorgeous. What guy wouldn't want to date you? But you flat-out turned me down. That was rough for me." The tiniest smile touches the corner of her mouth. "But no, Charlie, not now. I think you're the first real friend I've had in a long time."

Her brows furrow. "What about Daniel and the rest of the guys you hang out with?"

I think about her words. Are they truly my friends?

"My first real *girl*friend," I say. At her look I correct myself. "Female friend, how about that?" She smiles and I add, "Although I like the idea of girlfriend better."

She tosses a roll at me, which I catch neatly, a smile on her face. "Just when I thought there was hope for you." She sighs. "Jury's out on this one, Nefer. Not that I don't believe you, but . . . I'll be watching you."

Her words are quiet, serious. "Of course you'll be watching me," I joke, flexing my arms. She rolls her eyes, but not before I see that she definitely notices the guns.

Nefer, she called me. Guess things are back to normal.

TWENTY-FOUR
CHARLIE

I begin watching Daniel, and realize he spends a lot of his time watching Alexis. I can't blame the guy. Alexis has the prettiest eyes I've seen—big, green—and an infectious smile. She likes to laugh, and is constantly cracking jokes and doing funny accents. And when she thinks no one is looking, she's watching Daniel.

I think about playing matchmaker for them, but since I don't know Daniel all that well, and since I don't want to see Alexis hurt, I stay out of it. If they're going to be together, they'll do it on their own.

Plus, I don't have the energy to play matchmaker. I thought that having a car would make my life easier, but since I've insisted on picking my mom up each night, due to my stupid pride and all, I'm emotionally exhausted. Every night, she wants to stay at Dayspring. She's moved from throwing tantrums to wailing to a pitiful crying that wrenches my heart. Naomi has offered to pick her up, but I can't let her know how much it's getting to me. You know, stupid pride and all.

Instead, I lie in bed every night and cry myself to sleep that my mom prefers her friends at Dayspring over her own daughter. Me. I'm not enough for her. I thought that as time went on she'd maybe tire a little of Dayspring and its day-in, day-out monotony. Instead, she becomes more and more enamored of it.

I'm jealous of an adult care center, and a woman named Josie who's never been anything but sweet and guileless in her life.

Things have gone back to mostly normal between Benjamin and me, though I admit to a little hesitancy with him now. I keep remembering Alexis's story. I can't put it out of my mind.

A knock on my bedroom door rouses me from my musings. I glance at the clock. Only an hour until I have to pick Mom up. My shoulders slump at the thought.

"Come in," I call.

Naomi comes in, standing just inside the door. "Can I talk to you?" she asks.

"If this is about picking Mom up—" I begin.

"It's not," she says. She indicates the chair at the vanity and I nod. Like I could keep her out anyway. This is *her* house.

"I just thought maybe it's time I told you the truth," she says. "About me."

Great, confession time for Naomi.

"I'm younger than your mom by two years," she says, and I nod. I know she is, but sometimes I forget because mentally my mom is so much younger than even me. "And when I was about twelve or so, I became clearly aware that not everyone had a sister like mine."

"It took you that long?" I'm surprised. I don't remember when I knew my mom wasn't like other moms, because it seems I've *always* known.

She smiles. "Yes, it took me that long. I loved my sister, you see. She was always fun to play with, always happy to see me. Like she is now. And she always called me Mimi." Her grin widens. Then suddenly it falls and she covers her mouth with her hand.

"I'm so ashamed," she says. "To the depths of my soul I'm ashamed." Tears glimmer in her eyes and I'm taken aback. "They sent her away because of me."

"What?" I gasp. I knew this to a degree, knew part of the story. But I'm shocked to hear her admit it.

"I was embarrassed by her. I didn't want my friends to see her. I threw quite a fit, for a long time. Then I threatened to leave home, run away, go live with *any*one else. So they acquiesced and put her in that wretched place."

I'm frozen in place with astonishment and a mounting fury as tears spill down her cheeks.

"And, selfish girl that I was, I was happy about it. I rarely went to see her, and I didn't care about anything regarding her. Out of sight, out of mind, right? I didn't care that she was lonely. I didn't care that my parents missed her desperately or that they struggled to pay the bill, causing my dad to have to work a second job and my mom to pick up overtime where she could. I didn't care that Cora hated it there and cried to come home every day."

I shove up from the bed, pacing away from her to the window, glaring out. My jaw's clenched so tight I don't know if I can speak. This is definitely more detail than I've heard before.

"It's my fault," she says, her voice anguished. "What happened to her . . . that man . . . that orderly who—"

"How *could* you?" I explode, swinging her way. "How could you put her there? Do you know *what* he did to her?"

Naomi lifts guilt-filled eyes to me.

"I *read* the reports," I shout. "Grandma didn't know I saw them. She thought she hid them. Have *you* read them?" I'm shaking with fury, fists clenched. I can see by her face that she *hasn't* read them. *She* did this. She placed my mom in the position to be at the mercy of that monster, so she should have to share the burden of knowledge with me.

"It wasn't *once*, Naomi," I bite out. "He didn't force himself on her one time only. It went on for *months*. For months that pig violated her—" My voice catches on a sob as I picture my poor, innocent, helpless mom as his nightly prey, unable to tell, not having the words needed to explain, crying to come home to escape her nightmare while her *sister* kept her a captive. "In the shower, Naomi. In the shower! That's why she refuses to shower now. Did you know that? The things he did to her . . ." I groan in remembrance of the report, of the sick, horrific, vile things he subjected her to once they were able to pull the story from her. As much as I think Naomi deserves to be subjected to the knowledge, I can't bring myself to say the words aloud.

"They might not have ever known if someone didn't finally realize she was pregnant. And it was too late then, Naomi, too late for *your sister*. Her nightmare continued when she was pregnant and had to suffer labor, never knowing or understanding exactly what was happening to her!"

I feel like throwing something, screaming, raging at the heavens that allowed a damaged, childlike woman such as my mom to be subjected to such horror—a girl, really. She was only eighteen at the time.

Naomi is pale. She looks as sick as I feel. "I knew some of that, Charlotte. Some, but not all. I wish I could convey to you how incredibly guilty I feel about everything."

"Yeah," I scoff, shoving tears from my cheeks. "So guilty that as soon as you graduated you left home and never looked back. How often did you visit over the years? She asked for you all the time. Did you know that? That your sister, who you caused so much pain, still cried for you and asked when you were coming."

Naomi drops her face into her hands. Sobs wrack her body. Finally, she looks up. "Words can't . . . I'll never be able to . . . I thought I was doing what was best for her by going away."

"*How?*" I ask incredulously.

"Because I felt so shameful that I'd been the reason . . . and that she was at *that* particular place because it was all they could afford . . ." She shudders a deep sigh. "I went to college so that I could get the kind of job that would support her for the rest of her life. But then when I graduated . . . it wasn't enough. It was never enough."

I flinch in realization as I glance around the room, the room that sits in the middle of a really large, expensive house. "Your husband . . . ?"

She nods. "I married him knowing that he could easily provide what I needed for Cora. He was . . . quite a bit older than me. He had no children or siblings who would claim his money when he was gone."

I swallow, disgust and pity warring in my chest. "You married an old dude so you could have his money?"

She lifts her hands in supplication, asking for what? Understanding?

"I did," she admits. "Don't get me wrong, there was plenty in the marriage for Ronald. He liked having a young, pretty woman on his arm. Underneath everything, he had to know I only married him for his money."

"That's sick," I mutter.

"Yes," she agrees. "It was—is. But he and I grew very close, became good friends, and eventually we loved each other. Maybe not with the passionate kind of love that many newlyweds have, but we had a good marriage, I think. And I told him, when he got cancer and we knew he wouldn't survive. I told him the whole sordid truth."

"Why?" The word was out before I could stop it.

"Because I wanted him to have the final decision on where his money went."

"He left it to you," I say flatly.

"He left it to me."

"And yet, you still stayed away."

"Charlotte," she says, "How do you think your grandma could afford to stay at home and take care of both you and Cora?"

"I don't kn—" I begin, then stop. Because I do know. "You?"

"Me. And Ronald for the time he was with me. He was happy to provide for you all."

"But you still didn't come."

"I couldn't," she says miserably. "I couldn't look at her and know what I'd done." She looks at me. "I couldn't look at you."

I can't decide which emotion to settle on with the roiling maelstrom that surges through me. Anger seems to be the overriding emotion, but beneath that, beneath the disgust and disdain for her, there's the smallest flicker of understanding. I douse it.

"Why would you want to send her back to someplace like that after everything? Why would you even consider having her spend one single minute at Dayspring?"

She hesitates, as if she isn't sure how much more she wants to say. But finally she takes a deep breath, lifts her eyes to mine, and says, "I know it's safe because I own it."

TWENTY-FIVE
CHARLIE

I'm stunned into silence. Even my thoughts are quiet, unable to process this bit of information and understand her words. I drop onto the window seat, staring at her. Finally the words swirl down into sense.

She *owns* Dayspring? *Owns* it? *Naomi* owns Dayspring. Owns it . . .

I snap my sagging jaw closed. "Own it," I repeat, my voice quiet in the room. I try to decide what this means. "Did you . . . did you buy it so you'd have somewhere to *put* my mom?"

"Of course not," she says, her response quick and firm. "I've never, I mean, since then, I've never had a single thought of 'putting' Cora somewhere. Other than here, with me."

"Here?" I ask. "But we didn't come until Grandma . . ." I can't say it. She was the one who raised me. She was more of a mom than my own mom is. I miss her desperately.

"Grandma wouldn't come," she says with an ironical smile. "I tried to get her to come, but she didn't want to upset Cora's routine."

"Why didn't you come while Grandma was sick?"

"She didn't tell me," Naomi says, lips thinned. Anger lines her voice. "She kept it from me. I could have gotten her better doctors, paid for better treatment . . . maybe it wouldn't have helped, but maybe it would have."

Pride, I think. Something I suffer from. Something apparently my grandma and Naomi also have too much of.

"I bought Dayspring," she continues, "as a sort of repentance. I wanted to create someplace where people like Cora could live and *not* have such a . . . *loathsome* thing happen to them. I've worked very hard to make sure it's as safe as humanly possible. Over the years, I've seen how much the residents flourish.

"When you first came here," she says, shrugging, "I didn't intend for Cora to go to Dayspring at all. I thought she might have some memory of . . . before. But I quickly saw how bored she got sitting here all day, waiting for you to come home. And all I could think was how much she'd enjoy being with the others at Dayspring."

I clench my jaw against the fresh pain of knowing my mom preferred to be there than here with me. "Is that why you wanted me to pick her up?"

She looks down, threading her hands together. "Sort of." She looks up as if to gauge my reaction. "I knew if you could see for yourself how much she loves it, you might forgive me for suggesting she spend more time there."

"More time?" I come to my feet, the action coming before the thought of it. "How much more?"

Naomi shrugs. "I thought maybe she could stay there during the week, and come home on the weekends."

I'm already shaking my head before she's even finished speaking. "No."

"Charlotte, she's safe there. All employees have to pass a rigorous background check, and if anyone enters a room at night, a security camera is automatically turned on until the person has left the room. We have security officers always watching the rooms. She'd be safe." I'm still shaking my head. "She'd be happy," she says quietly.

I glance at the clock, refusing to acknowledge her comment. "I have to go pick her up."

"Charlotte," she says, catching my arm as I pass her. I stop, but don't look at her. "Just think about it, okay? That's all I'm asking: consideration. Whatever you decide I promise to abide by."

I want to shove away from her and tell her to go jump off a cliff, but then I remember the whole pride thing. I nod once and leave.

☙

I walk into the dayroom. It's quiet, only my mom and two aides doing a simple puzzle, the aides giving her the pieces and gently guiding her where to place them without making it too obvious that they are. I'm late, and apparently all of the other residents have gone to bed. I stand silently, observing. Even with everyone in bed, she's content—happy, even.

One of the aides looks up and notices me. She says something to my mom and points. My mom glances back at me and disappointment marks her face as I cross the room to them. My heart crumbles beneath the look. I try not to take it personally, understanding that she's childlike in her desires, and her desire is to play, not come with me to go home and go to bed.

"Hi, Mom," I say, waving.

"Hi," she mumbles, dropping her head sullenly, then scooting the puzzle pieces back into the box with jerky movements, upset she has to quit. "Everyone in bed?" I ask the aide.

"Yes," she says. "Bedtime is nine o'clock on weeknights."

"Sorry I'm late."

"It's okay," she says with a smile. "Naomi called and said you were on your way. We just thought we'd do a puzzle while we waited, right, Cora?"

My mom nods, still unhappy about leaving. Resigned, she stands and turns to me. I open my arms and she steps forward, hugging me around the waist somewhat listlessly.

"Mimi and I have a surprise for you," I suddenly say, a little shocked at the decision that comes into my head.

"Where?" she asks, brightening, looking behind me.

"We'll tell you when we get home, okay?"

That puts a spring in her step, and she willingly follows me to the car.

TWENTY-SIX
BENJAMIN

S o, other than when I work, it looks like my weeknights will be pretty free," Charlie says at lunch. "You can decide when you have time available to work on our report and let me know."

"Why the sudden free time?" I ask.

"Um, well, I had a . . . babysitting thing I was doing that I'll only have on the weekends now."

I wonder at her hesitation over the word *babysitting* but decide to let it slide. If there's anything I understand, it's keeping secrets.

"You have a babysitting job but you don't have money to make good on your bet?" I tease.

"It's more of a volunteer thing," she says, and I can swear she's blushing a little. "But, um, yeah, I have a little money now, so next time we both have a night off together, and we don't have homework, I promise to take you to a movie."

"How about Thursday?" I press. I know her schedule because I've fallen into the slightly stalkerish habit of checking hers when I check mine to see if we'll be working together.

"What about our report?"

I grimace. "Seriously? You can't take a night off to do something interesting? You really need to learn how to have fun, new girl."

She wrinkles her nose at me. "I know how to have fun."

"Prove it," I say. "I dare you to make good on your bet *and* skip doing homework for one night."

She laughs. "Wow, I don't know. That's a pretty tough challenge," she says sarcastically. "But okay, you're on."

"My choice?" I ask.

"Of course. What kind of bet would it be if I chose?"

"Huh," I say, watching her from the corner of my eye. "New girl is a low-maintenance date."

"Not a date, Nefer," she says, standing to return her tray. But she's smiling. That's something, right?

❦

Somehow we end up going to the movie with a large group of people. Daniel, Cozi, Alexis, Phoebe, and Mario all showed up in a separate car. I'd picked Charlie up over her protests that that was too date-like. But it made sense since she lives on the way, and the others came from the opposite direction.

When we arrive at the theater, and purchase our tickets and popcorn, I manage to stay close enough to Charlie to sit next to her. And oddly, she wrangles it so Daniel and Alexis are sitting together. I look at her with lifted brow and she flashes me an exaggeratedly innocent look.

As the lights go down, I glance over at Charlie. She seems content, more than I've seen her look since I met her. I wonder what changed. She looks at me, and catching me watching, she holds the popcorn bucket my way, I suppose assuming that's what I want. I take a handful and turn toward the screen.

The previews begin and my mind wanders—I've seen them all already. My mind wanders to Charlie. I've never wanted a girlfriend, knew it was impossible for me. I didn't want to have to pretend to like a girl for any extended amount of time. It isn't that I don't admire a pretty girl, and want to spend a little time with her, but I don't think it'd be fair to make her think there was a chance for more than I can offer.

With Charlie, though, I think I might be able to do it. I have fun when I'm with her. It's never a drag—other than when she's mad at me, but I suppose she's had good reason. She's amusing to tease, and gives it right back. She's easier to hang out with than even Daniel sometimes. Plus, she's reserved with me. I don't think she'd be clingy in the slightest, and I have the feeling she wouldn't expect much from me. She doesn't seem to expect much from anyone. I know she has plans after graduation, and she knows I plan to leave for college, so there shouldn't be a long, protracted, tear-filled good-bye on her part. She seems practical enough to simply say good-bye and go on her way.

The more I consider it, the more I think it's a perfect plan. A girlfriend who's only the *appearance* of a girlfriend, without any expectation of love from me. Now I just have to figure out how to convince her.

But what if she's not into guys? She hasn't come out to say one way or another, so maybe she's still trying to keep it secret. Or maybe I'm wrong.

In the car on the way home, I come up with the beginning of my brilliant plan.

"Can I ask you something?"

Distractedly, she says, "Sure."

"Are you . . . I mean, if, say, Mario or Jake or someone asked you out on a date, would you say yes?"

She stares at me. "Are you trying to set me up?" Her voice is incredulous.

"No, I mean . . . I just wondered . . . would you? Or would you rather go out with, say, Cozi or Phoebe?"

She just looks at me for long moments, clearly trying to figure out what I'm getting at. "I guess it depends," she finally says.

"On?"

"On where we were going. I'm confused, Nefer. What are you asking me?"

"Not that it's my business, or anything, and it won't change our friendship or whatever, but I wondered if you, you know . . . are into guys, or . . ."

Her brows pull together in confusion, then suddenly her face clears and she gasps out an astonished sound. "Nefer, are you asking me if I'm *gay?*"

I shrug. "It's none of my business, like I said. I just thought maybe you'd like to know that—"

She bursts out laughing, leaning over and burying her face in her hands. When she finally gets control, she turns to me. "Why do you care?" The question wars with the humor still dancing in her eyes.

"I don't," I say defensively. "I just . . . wondered."

"Wait a minute," she says. "Are you . . . do you think that's the reason I won't date you?"

I can feel a flush steal up my cheeks. I shrug.

"You seriously thought the only way I wouldn't fall at your feet was if I preferred girls over guys?"

Well, when she puts it that way, it sounds rather egotistical. "It occurred to me," I admit, and she laughs again.

"Oh, Nefer, you're something else, you know that?"

"So I've been told," I say, waggling my eyebrows, trying to regain my nonchalance. I admit it—it was really stupid of me to assume such a thing. I decide to change the subject.

"Hey, new girl, I was wondering if you'd do me a favor."

She narrows her eyes at me. "Last time you asked a favor of me, it nearly cost me a friend."

I give her my most apologetic look. "I know. I'm still sorry about that. I promise it has nothing to do with setting anyone up together. In fact, it's to do the opposite."

Wariness steals into her expression. "What's the favor?"

I laugh at her expression. "Nothing painful, I promise. Fall Formal is coming up in a couple of weeks. I'm asking—no, I'm *begging* you to go with me so I don't have to ask someone else who'll read more into it than a simple dance."

"Thought you said it wasn't anything painful," she says.

"Ouch," I say, grinning.

"Kinda sounds like a date," she says, not apologizing for her comment, which makes me wonder how much truth was in her teasing.

"It's *so* not a date," I say. "It's rescuing me from some smitten female."

She chokes out a laugh. "*Smitten*, Nefer? Ego a bit large, is it?"

I lift one side of my mouth in a smile that usually charms the girls. "I only speak the truth." She shakes her head, but she's still grinning. "C'mon, new girl, do me a solid. Go with me. You can even shout from the rooftops that it's not a date, just two friends having a good time together."

"What makes you think I haven't already been asked? Maybe I'm going with a girl."

Okay, I deserve that. Then my smile falls. I hadn't considered that someone might have asked her. "Who asked you?" I say, more sharply than I intended.

She glances out her side window, folding her hands together in her lap. "Well . . . no one. Yet. I just wondered why you thought I hadn't been."

Her meek voice makes me smile. "That's not true."

She looks at me, confusion in her eyes.

"You have been asked. By me." She still hesitates. "Please," I say. "Please, please, please, please, ple—"

"Okay," she says loudly over my intonation. "Sheesh, Nefer, are you always this annoyingly persistent?"

"I can be," I say. I grab her hand and pull it to my mouth, quickly kissing her palm and then releasing it before she can protest. "Thank you, new girl. You have no idea the pain you just saved me."

"How romantic," she says, rolling her eyes. "I always dreamed my Fall Formal invitation would be for nothing more than saving some guy from pain."

"So you're saying I just made one of your dreams come true? Go me."

After dropping her off, I think about my plan. The dance is only the beginning. She'll have to dance with me at least a few times, which means she'll have to allow herself to be held by me. Dating all the girls I have gives me a bit of an advantage. Charlie's different from anyone I've dated, true, but still I think I can convince her before she knows she's being convinced. It'll save me *tons* of trouble if I have a "steady" girlfriend, especially one like her.

No expectations.

I repeat the words I'd thought of earlier. That's the key.

No expectations.

When I get home, my dad is surprisingly already in bed, snoring loudly. Relief drains the tension from my shoulders. I didn't have to fight Charlie too hard to convince her to come to the dance with me, and I won't have to fight my dad at all.

All in all, a good night for me.

TWENTY-SEVEN
CHARLIE

Naomi gives me money to buy a dress for the dance. I didn't ask; she offered. I justify it as letting her ease her guilt a little. She's been übernice since her confession—and since I came home that night with the offer of letting my mom stay at Dayspring through the week and coming home on weekends. It's made a big difference in all our lives.

Phoebe and Alexis come with me to the mall to pick out dresses. I was surprised when Alexis told me she's agreed to go with Daniel. Cozi doesn't go with us since, though she isn't against dancing itself, some of the music and current dance moves aren't in line with her religious beliefs. I admire her for sticking to it and not giving in to peer pressure.

I'm still stunned by Benjamin thinking the only reason a girl could possibly not fall at his feet is if she's gay. I mean, seriously. I open my mouth to tell Alexis and Phoebe about it, but then I don't. Neither one of them have much affection for Benjamin, with good cause, and I don't think they'll find it amusing in the same way I do. They're already not exactly thrilled that I'm going to the dance with him.

The dance is on a Saturday, which takes away from time I can spend with my mom, but Naomi is going to take her to a movie so

I can at least not feel quite so guilty over not being with her on one of her two nights home. Today's Friday, and I'm half-tempted to go pick my mom up tonight rather than in the morning, but I happen to know they're having a game night and she'd never forgive me. So instead I'm going to the football game with Alexis.

We get there just as the football team is heading off the field after their warm-up. Alexis and I stop to let them jog past. Benjamin is at the back of the pack. He pulls his helmet off, his dark hair matted with sweat.

"New girl!" he exclaims, a grin lighting his face. Just that. Nothing else. So why do I feel like he's given me a shout-out, marking my presence here as something special?

I sit in the stands with a bunch of friends, cheering on our football team, watching Alexis watch Daniel.

Watching Benjamin.

He's good. No, that's not right, he's really, *really* good. No wonder he has such an ego. I have no doubt he'll get a scholarship for football, and maybe even play professionally. I guess it's hard to gauge when he's playing a bunch of high school guys, but still. I know a little about football because my grandpa watched all the time when I was a kid, and after he died, my grandma and I kept watching in his memory, though neither of us knew the teams or players. So I can recognize talent when I see it.

Benjamin was definitely born under a lucky star, as my grandma would've said. Tall, good-looking, built like an Adonis, talented in sports, smart in school . . . too bad he has no idea how to treat his girlfriends. That thought reminds me of Alexis's story, and I turn to her during a timeout.

"Just curious," I say. "What made you say yes to going to Fall Formal with Daniel? I thought he was on the 'no-way' list."

She shrugs, seemingly embarrassed by the question. "I guess I just figured, you know, that I'd give him a chance. It wasn't fair of me to judge him based on Benjamin. So I'm dating him—but with caution. I don't want to be used again."

Impulsively I hug her. "I'm so sorry for what you suffered," I say. "And if Daniel hurts you, I promise to . . . beat him up, or something."

She looks at me slantwise. "What's the story with you and Benjamin? I'm a little shocked that after what I told you about him you're going on a date with him."

"It's not a date," I say quickly. She lifts her eyebrows and I explain. "He asked me if I'd go with him, as a *friend*, because he says that way he won't . . . uh . . . he won't have to ask a girl who thinks it's a real date." I'm not sure why I hesitate to tell her everything.

She looks skeptical. "Are you sure this isn't just his way of getting you to go on a date with him by making you think it's not a real date?"

I shrug. "Doesn't matter, really, because it's *not* a real date to me."

"Okay," she says, still sounding uncertain. "Just be careful, Charlie."

∾

Alexis refuses to double-date to the dance, which I don't blame her for. We meet her, Daniel, Phoebe, and Phoebe's date at the dance. We all share a table. Alexis is fine with that, and I think maybe she's okay with it so she can keep an eye on me, make sure I don't fall for any of Benjamin's tricks.

Benjamin looks amazingly hot. He's wearing a black tuxedo with a black shirt and silver vest. His eyes look greener than ever, and his skin goes well with the color. I know it's just part of Benjamin's persona, part of the "date" so to speak, but he's very attentive, keeping his attention almost exclusively on me, smiling at me with a wide grin when others are watching, and with a private little upturn of the corners of his mouth when no one is. Maybe it's a good thing Alexis is here to keep an eye on me. I can see why all the others fell for him so easily. I probably would, too, if I hadn't been forewarned.

Fall formal is held in an old, historic building that was once a church, and over the years through its various incarnations has been completely gutted and redone. All that remains of the original church is the shell, which luckily historians stepped in and saved before it could be razed to the ground. Benjamin gave me the history of it on the drive over. It's a really cool building, but I wish I could have seen it when it was still a church.

A buffet is set up in the back, and after we've gorged ourselves on chicken fettuccini, garlic asparagus, salad, and gooey brownies, Benjamin asks me to dance. I follow him out to the floor and we dance several songs, joined by a group of friends. Everyone just sort of dances all together, so it feels okay, not like I'm really dancing with Benjamin exclusively. I discover that amazing dancer can be added to his list of talents.

Suddenly the music slows, and people begin either drifting off the floor, or melding together in couples. I begin to walk away, but Benjamin catches my arm and pulls me back. I think of arguing with him, but he's looking at me guilelessly, not even grinning his usual flirty grin, just pulling me lightly into his arms for a dance, holding me close, but not too close.

His hands on my back, touching gently without trying to pull me against him.

Nothing dangerous in that, nothing to make my heart pound faster, or to make me lightheaded.

Nothing at all.

TWENTY-EIGHT
BENJAMIN

I look down at Charlie as we dance, keeping my face carefully neutral. I don't want to startle her, or have her think I'm trying to press her into anything she's firmly told me she doesn't want. I want her to come to the conclusion on her own that we should be together.

She's wearing a strapless gold dress, unusual and different from most girls, who wear either black or pink. Her hair is curled into ringlets and held back with a sparkling headband that gives the impression of a tiara. Her insulin pump is hidden somewhere beneath the dress, though I can see the faint pinprick scars on her bare arms. I forget sometimes that she deals with her diabetes every day because she doesn't make a big deal of it. Her face is flushed from dancing—and she won't look me in the eye.

"Having fun?" I ask.

She looks up at me and away again. "Yeah, I am."

"You look great," I say, the first time I've told her tonight. She looks up at me, suspicion in her eyes. "That's an awesome dress."

She relaxes. "Yeah, thanks, I really like it." She hesitates then says, "You clean up pretty good yourself, Nefer."

"Thank you," I say, ducking my head a little toward her as I say it.

She lifts one eyebrow. "Wow, you're not going to say that you know you do, or anything about how good-looking you are? How girls always fall at your feet? You're slipping."

I shrug. "Not *all* girls fall at my feet," I say meaningfully.

She blushes and looks down again. I slide my hands up her back a little, bringing her closer to me. She doesn't resist, and I bite back my smile.

TWENTY-NINE
CHARLIE

My mind is a riot of confusion. Benjamin is clearly and firmly in the friend zone. He uses girls. He hurts them. He humiliated Alexis. His arms pulling me closer. His unique smell, something I realize with a jolt that I know already because of our time spent together: clean, musky, masculine. His chin resting lightly on the top of my head, a touch barely felt . . . possessive.

He's Benjamin, Benjamin Nefer, the guy all of my friends warned me about. The guy who, on my first day here, tried to ensnare me. Who would use me and dump me at a moment's notice. Who tried to use me to set Daniel and Alexis up when he knew she'd already said no. The guy who makes me laugh, who somehow always calls when I need a friend the most. The guy who smiles at me in a way that makes my heart thump.

The guy who agreed to be my friend, nothing more.

The song changes and Benjamin hugs me lightly, then runs his hands down my arms before releasing me. He immediately begins dancing to the new song, and soon we're surrounded by our friends again, nothing intimate in the way we're dancing now. So why do I feel so flustered?

After a while, Benjamin places a hand on my arm and leans near. "I'll be right back," he says over the music. I nod. He walks away, and I look around for Alexis. I need her to talk some sense into me. She's not too far away, but she's dancing with Daniel, her face alight as she laughs at something he said. I don't want to interrupt her because she looks happier than I've seen her for a while. Phoebe is nowhere to be found. I consider calling Cozi, but before I can Benjamin comes back with a sly smile.

"What's up with you?" I ask suspiciously, teasing but a little serious, too.

"You'll see," he says.

Three songs later, I do. The music slows again, but it's not just any ballad. Def Leppard. I look at Benjamin, and he grins, opening his arms. Shaking my head in mock exasperation, I go into them.

He holds me closer this time, his cheek against the side of my head. I know I should move back. I don't.

He begins singing the lyrics, "'Walk away . . .'"

Lyrics I know as well as he does. Lyrics that haven't meant the same thing they mean now as he sings them. Lyrics about walking away, running away, but being unable to hide.

I pull back at the words and look up at him, wondering if he's trying to give me a message. He smiles and says, "Your turn."

I swallow, gathering my scrambled thoughts and sing the next few lines. Then he sings again.

"'I'll be two steps behind you . . .'"

I sing the rest of the chorus, then he picks it up, singing not playfully as he usually does, but with a seriousness beneath his tone. More words, about not fighting it, about the fire burning inside. Just words. But at his emphasis of specific lyrics, I realize he might not be teasing at all.

I think he picked this song purposely. I don't sing the next lines when he stops, and he doesn't say anything. We've stopped moving, and are just standing in the middle of the crowded dance floor, my arms around his neck, his hands pressing against my back, his gaze intense on mine. There's something in his eyes I haven't seen before. He looks as confused as I feel.

"Benjamin, I—" I begin at the same time he says, "Charlie—"

We both stop, and then suddenly he grins. The strange spell is broken and we both laugh.

THIRTY
BENJAMIN

I win," I say.

"What?" she asks, teasing back in her voice. "How do you figure?"

"You didn't know the words," I say, putting finality into my tone.

"You're crazy," she says. "I know the words. *All* of them. What kind of fan would I be if I didn't know the words to 'Two Steps Behind'?"

"Not a very good one," I say, "because you stopped singing. You didn't know them."

We're moving again, and she's stepped a little back from me. I let her do it, too, with some relief. Something weird just happened, when I was playing my game, trying to charm her in one of the ways I thought might work on her. As I sang those words to her, and she looked at me with something different in her eyes, something happened to me. Something I can't name. A strange tightening in the middle of my chest, a feeling in my lungs like I'd just done fifty pushups, my head whirling like I'd been on a spinning ride. I almost felt physically ill, like I needed to run away, or just . . . run.

Then we'd both spoken, and I suddenly remembered where I was, *who* I was. As soon as we'd laughed, the strangeness went away—or maybe not away, exactly, but at least it eased up. I don't try any more moves on her the rest of the night, and in fact when the next slow song comes on I suggest we take a break and get a drink. She agrees, relief and disappointment in her face. I worry that the same is in mine.

As it turns out, it's a good thing, since her blood sugar is a little low and she needs some juice before dancing again. I keep watching her, waiting for signs of a seizure, as if I have any idea what to look for, until she finally tells me to quit staring at her, that she's okay.

Later, as we pull up in front of her house, she moves to get out of the car.

"Wait," I say, jumping out and hurrying around to open her door for her. She gives me a strange look. "I know you're not calling it a date, but still, it was a dance, so there are certain rules that should be followed, right?"

"Says who?" she asks.

"Me."

"Whatever," she murmurs, though she sounds anything but flippant. "Good night, then."

"Oh, no," I say. "I'm walking you to the door."

She glances nervously at her door. "Um . . ."

"I'm not asking to come in," I say. "Just to your door."

She looks ready to argue again, but finally nods, arms folded tightly against herself. I follow her to the door, where a porch light provides a small amount of illumination. She turns toward me, and looks down at her feet, shuffling them. This I'm familiar with—a girl who isn't sure if she wants to be kissed or not, but really does.

"I had a really good time tonight," I say.

"Me, too," she says, still not looking up.

146

"Guess we should get together soon to do our next observation for school."

"Oh, yeah." She's still shuffling around, not looking at me. "Any ideas for that?"

"How about the bus station?"

She finally looks up at me. I'm suddenly, overwhelmingly filled with the desire to kiss her. I'm not sure where the idea comes from, but my eyes drop to her lips at the thought. Time freezes as she seems to catch my mood. Conscious of me looking at her mouth, she nervously licks her lips. I can't wait any longer. So I do something really stupid—I lean down and kiss her.

She stills as my hands come up to lightly rest on her waist. I keep the kiss soft, nothing demanding in it, no matter how much I want to press her against me, slant my mouth, deepen—her lips move beneath mine, just the tiniest amount. It's as if a thousand pricks of the brightest light shower down on my head, shivering into my brain, lighting me up. At the same time, we both jerk back.

She stares at me, eyes wide, mouth slightly open, shocked. Finally she finds her voice. "Benjamin," she says warningly.

I take a step backward. "I . . . that was just supposed to be a peck, you know, between friends. A sort of good-night kiss."

"Benjamin, I—"

"I think I should go," I say, cutting her off. "Before you say something that *I'll* regret."

I step off the porch backward, watching her. She's just gazing at me now, not saying anything over my babbling.

"It's nothing to worry about, okay? No biggie." That's a lie. "I'll talk to you tomorrow, we can decide when to do the next assignment."

I reach my car, and she still hasn't spoken. She turns as if to go into the house.

"Hey, Charlie," I call. She turns back, hand on the knob. "I'm not sorry."

Before she can react to that little piece of information, I duck into my car. She watches me a moment longer as I turn the ignition. I put it into drive and flip a U-turn. By the time I'm facing the opposite direction, she's disappeared into her house.

When I arrive home, my stomach sinks. The old man is here. And with the lights blazing, he's still up. I sit in the car a few minutes, thinking about Charlie . . . about that kiss. I've kissed a lot of girls, it's true. But I've never felt anything like that before. Maybe because it's Charlie, and she's been so resistant to me. Maybe I wanted it to be something special to make my quest to convince her to be my girlfriend easier. Even as I make excuses, I know they're lame. Something strange happened—again. Every time I touch her something inside of me shifts. Maybe I should give up this quest and find someone else.

With a sigh, I climb out of the car. Right in the driveway I change out of the tux and back into my regular clothes, folding the tux back into the rental box to return on Monday. I can't afford for it to get ripped in what I know is coming. Once finished, I close the trunk and head for the door.

Suddenly I'm exhausted. I lean against the side of the house, dropping my head into my hands. I really, *really* don't want to go inside. I don't want to fight anymore. I just want to be *done*. I hear him bellow my name from inside and, resigned, I open the door.

THIRTY-ONE
CHARLIE

Lying in bed, I press my fingers against my mouth. Benjamin kissed me. The refrain runs through my mind over and over. I can't make sense of it. Or maybe I can. One thing I know about him is what a player he is. He was relentless with me for a while until I told him we could be friends and nothing more, and he seemed to accept it. Now, I wonder if it was all part of his plan.

I roll onto my side, hugging my pillow. Closing my eyes, I see it again, Benjamin leaning closer, eyes on my mouth, pressing his lips to mine. The jolt that ran through me. I haven't kissed many boys, only three in fact, so I realize my scope of comparison isn't that great. And yet, it wasn't like that with any of the others.

He knows what he's doing. The thought slices into my head without consciously thinking it. Of course he knows what he's doing. Who knows how many girls he's kissed? Probably quite a few, enough to know how to make a girl's toes curl.

"I'm not sorry," he'd said. Not in his usual cocky, egotistical way. But simply, honestly. I curl up into a ball. I can't fall for Benjamin Nefer, I just can't. But even as sleep claims me, my hand still pressed to my mouth as if to hold his kiss there, my heart cracks just the tiniest bit.

❧

"Wake up! Wake up!"

I'm jarred awake by both my mom's singsong voice, and my bed being bounced by her as she says it.

"Mom," I mutter. "What time is it?"

"Time for *pancakes*," she says happily.

I groan. I'm still tired, feeling like I did a workout the day before and am paying for it now. I sit up and almost immediately I'm assailed by the remembrance of Benjamin's kiss. I bring my fingers to my lips.

"C'mon," my mom says, grabbing said hand and pulling it away from my mouth to get me to stand. I shove the covers back and get my feet beneath me before she can tumble me from the bed onto the floor. She holds my hand all the way to the top of the stairs before releasing it to make her way down.

"I'll be right there," I say to her. "I'm just going to use the bathroom first."

She glances at me, but it's a legit excuse, so she goes on her way and I turn back to the bathroom. Inside, I lock the door and walk over to the mirror. I stare at myself to see . . . what? If I look any different? If somehow he branded me with his kiss and everyone is going to know? I look like the same Charlie, curls mussed from sleep, tired eyes, and my mouth . . . my mouth looks exactly the same. I laugh. What did I expect? I turn away and go join my mom and Naomi for breakfast.

When I near the kitchen, I see Naomi first. She's smiling broadly at my mom, playing some kind of hand game. I feel a ping of jealousy. My mom's never played anything like that with me. I don't know any of the hand games. Then I notice that there's something different about Naomi. I watch her, unobserved, trying to figure it out.

She's relaxed, I realize with a start. None of the usual stiffness or hesitancy in her. With it gone, I see the resemblance between me and her. And my mom to a degree as well, though I definitely look more like Naomi. Watching her with my mom like this, it's clear how much they love each other. It's a little surprising to me, I guess, that she genuinely does love her sister.

I move forward, catching her attention. "Well, hi, Charlie," Naomi says.

I lift my brows at her use of my nickname, but don't remark on it. I mumble a greeting and sit at the counter, checking my blood sugar as she serves my mom and me pancake smiley faces. My heart wrenches. My grandma used to do that, every Sunday. I glance up at Naomi and understand my grandma must have done it for Naomi and my mom when they were girls. I wonder if she kept doing it for Naomi after she caused my mom to be sent to the home.

"Guess what, Charlie?" my mom asks brightly. Without waiting for an answer, she says, "Tomorrow I get to see Josie again."

"I know," I say, trying to keep the jealousy from my voice. "Are you excited to see her?"

She nods, her mouth full of pancake. As soon as she swallows, she says, "Can I go today? Can I go see Josie today, Charlie?" Her voice is plaintive, and it strikes me, not for the first time, how odd it is that I parent my mom.

"Not today," I say. "Do you want to do something fun today? Go to the park?"

Her face shadows disappointment, but she nods anyway, digging back into her pancakes. I ignore the look of pity that Naomi gives me.

151

As much as I desperately miss my mom all week while she's at Dayspring, I see her every day. I usually go over after school to spend some time with her, or if I have to work I stop by on my way home and tuck her into bed, reading to her as she falls asleep.

I have to admit, she's exuberantly happy there. She loves having her own room, as if she doesn't have her own room here. But it feels different to her. I think she feels like she belongs there, as if it's a place made just for her. And I guess in a way it is. She loves her friends, and the nurses and aides, and honestly, everyone there.

Naomi took me over to see the security room, and showed me how the cameras work. She even offered to hire someone who would sleep in my mom's room every night to protect her, and though I considered it, I decided that was probably overkill. But I feel like she's safe there, or as safe as can be. I really don't have a good reason to hate dropping her off there every Monday morning.

After I shower and get dressed, my phone rings. I glance at it and see that it's Benjamin. Immediately a flush steals up my throat and I feel like I can't breathe. I drop to my bed, clutching my phone against my chest. I debate whether to answer or not, and finally, just before it goes to voice mail, I answer.

"Hello?"

"Oh, hey, new girl." His voice is casual, the same Benjamin who's only been my friend these last weeks. "I didn't think you were going to answer. I was just getting ready to leave a message."

"Sorry, I was . . . getting dressed," I finish lamely.

"No worries," he says. "I just wanted to call and tell you again how much fun I had last night. I'm glad you went with me."

His voice is still light, nothing in it reflective of the storm inside my chest. "I had fun, too," I say. "I was surprised at how well you can dance."

"Wha—?" he sputters indignantly, making me laugh. "How could you not know that I, Benjamin Nefer, can do *any*thing?"

"Oh, brother," I say. "You mean anything except retain some shred of humility."

"Okay, fine, tell me one thing I can't do well."

"I haven't seen you try everything, Nefer."

"Of the things you have seen me try, name one."

"Other than the humility thing?" I ask. "Hmm, let me think. Well, I'd say you don't know how to box very well since you're constantly getting beat up."

There's a pause, not a long one, but obvious, and I wonder if I've hit a nerve. Then he laughs. "*Everyone* gets beat up in a boxing ring, new girl. You haven't seen me box, so how would you know whether I'm good or not?"

"Just going by the evidence," I say.

"Okay, I'll make you a deal. You come down and watch me, and then you can pass judgment."

"Watch two guys purposely hit each other for the fun of it? No thanks."

"C'mon, you're passing judgment again without any true knowledge."

"I've seen boxing on TV," I say.

"Not the same," he says. "We wear protective gear."

"And yet you still get beat up. Seems mindlessly brutal to me."

"How about a bet then? You tell me something you're good at, and if I can do it better than you, you have to come watch me box."

I swear, my cheeks ache from smiling so much since he called. "And what do I get if you can't?"

"Then you don't have to come watch," he says.

"That hardly seems fair. Because if I don't bet you, then I *still* don't have to go."

"Okay, fine, what do you want?"

Another kiss. The unexpected thought jars me and I quickly push it away. "Ummm," I say, tapping my lip as I think. Unfortunately that brings to mind the kiss again, so I immediately stop the action. "Let's see. How about if I win then you have to . . ." A thought suddenly comes to me. "Same bet as last time. You have to show me your house."

"What?" His tone is heavy. Silence, and then, "Why do you want to see my house so bad?"

"Because no one ever has," I say. "It's one of the great mysteries of Jefferson High—where does Benjamin Nefer live?"

"Something else," he says. "Pick something else." The teasing has gone out of his voice.

"Afraid you'll lose?" I ask, trying to keep my tone light.

He sighs loudly. I have a feeling it's not a put-on. He's quiet so long I actually pull my phone from my ear to see if the call was lost. Just when I'm about to tell him I'll choose something else, he says, "You're on, new girl."

"Really?"

"You sound surprised," he says.

"I genuinely thought you'd refuse and I'd have to pick something else."

"I decided it doesn't matter, because there's no way you're going to win."

"But you don't even know what it is that I think I can do better than you."

"I'm not worried," he says, his voice full of laughter again. "So, when are we doing this thing?"

I laugh. "Let's 'do this thing' on Tuesday after school, if you're off."

"I don't have work but I have practice until four." He pauses, then, "You could come watch, and when I'm done we'll go from there."

I think about pointing out that I have my own car. Instead, I say, "Okay, sure. Sounds like a plan."

"And, new girl," he says, before hanging up. His voice drops into a deep, cheesy, gravelly imitation of a sports announcer. "Prepare to be humiliated."

I laugh as I hang up, but then remember Alexis's story of being humiliated by Benjamin.

"What am I doing?" I say to the empty room. Not surprisingly, there's no answer.

THIRTY-TWO
BENJAMIN

My dad's at home all day, so I decide to leave. Daniel's doing some family thing, and I already know Charlie isn't available because of her babysitting job. I really don't feel like hanging out with anyone else, so I get in my car and start driving without any real destination in mind.

I almost stop at the gym to get in a workout, but don't feel like getting pummeled today after the pummeling I got last night. So I drive past. As I'm passing the park, I see Charlie's car—or at least a car just like hers. Remembering she has a babysitting job, I decide to stop and meet the kids she watches.

Parking next to her, I get out and see her walking across the grass alone. I jog to catch up to her.

"Hey, new girl," I say. She freezes, then slowly turns to face me. Her face is stricken, as if something horrible has happened. I catch up to her, worried. "You okay?"

"What are you doing here?" she asks urgently. She sounds a little angry that I'm here.

"I was driving by and saw your car."

"You have to go." She takes my arm, turning me back toward the parking lot. Now I think her stricken look is either because she's doing something she shouldn't—or she's in trouble.

I dig my feet in and stop walking. "What's going on, Charlie? Is everything okay?"

"No. Yes. You just . . . you shouldn't be here."

"Charlie!" I glance up at the sound of her name being called. A woman is running toward us, and at first I think she's worried I'm harassing Charlie. Then I realize there's something different about the way she looks, about how she's smiling, like she's retarded or something.

"Go!" Charlie hisses at me.

"Charlie, look what I found." The woman holds out a seeded dandelion. I can see why she's so excited; those are rare this time of year.

Charlie's cheeks are bright pink. She closes her eyes, swallows, and turns to the woman. Strange reaction since she clearly knows her.

"Yes, that's really pretty, huh?" she says, her voice sounding strangled.

Her aunt comes jogging up. "I'm sorry, she got away from—oh, hi, Benjamin," she says, seeing me.

"Hello, Naomi. How're you doing?"

"I'm fine, thanks. I didn't know you'd be here today."

"I'm not supposed to be," I say, glancing at Charlie. "I mean, I was just driving by and saw Charlie's car and thought I'd stop to say hi."

"That's nice," she says, sounding genuine. There's something different about her than the last time I saw her. She seems less uptight, happier. "How was the dance?"

"A lot of fun," I say, noticing that Charlie is getting more tense by the moment. She's squeezing her hands, agitated, rocking from foot to foot.

"Yes, that's what Charlie said."

"Who are you?" the strange woman asks. She sticks a hand out to me. "I'm Cora."

I take her hand as Charlie groans. "Hi, Cora. I'm Benjamin. I'm Charlie's friend."

"Cora is . . . Naomi's sister . . ." Charlie jumps in quickly, the last half trailing off as if she's miserable sharing the information.

"Mimi is my sissy," Cora says. She holds up the dandelion. "Look what I found."

"That's very lucky," I say. "Do you know if you make a wish, then blow the seeds off, your wish will come true?"

"Really?" Cora's eyes are wide. She looks at Charlie. "Can I?"

"Of course," Charlie says, still looking uncomfortable.

A wide grin splits Cora's face and she scrunches her eyes tightly closed before taking a deep breath and blowing the seeds into the air. Her eyes fly open and she laughs as the seeds scatter. "I want to look for more!"

"First we need to eat," Naomi says. "We're having a picnic. Would you like to join us, Benjamin? We have plenty."

I look at Charlie, who's glaring down her feet as if they've offended her.

"I don't know," I say slowly. "Maybe I should go."

"No," Cora says. "Don't go. We're having a picnic. Come have a picnic on the blanket."

I look at Charlie, trying to read her. She finally looks at me and shrugs with a halfhearted smile.

"Come," Cora says, taking my hand, pulling me with her. I don't want to jerk away and make her feel bad, so I follow.

Beneath a tree they have a red checkered blanket. I smile at how traditional it is. They even have a big wicker basket. Cora doesn't let go until we near the blanket, then she plops herself down and pats the space next to her. Charlie moans miserably and I glance at her.

"You don't have to do this," she says.

"I know," I say, moving to sit by Cora. Charlie plops down on my other side, and Naomi on the opposite side of Cora.

As Naomi is pulling out sandwiches and chips, I turn to Charlie. "So, is this your mysterious babysitting job?"

Her eyes flick to Naomi. I follow her gaze. Naomi is still pulling items out, seeming to ignore us, and yet there's a sort of stillness about her, as if waiting for Charlie's answer.

"Yes," Charlie mutters, playing with a blade of grass.

"Well, I think it's cool," I say, thinking to put her mind at rest about not needing to be embarrassed by the fact that she takes care of a disabled adult.

Instead, she doesn't even look at me, just nods slightly in acknowledgement of my words, still looking unhappy.

"I get to go see Josie tomorrow," Cora pipes up, reclaiming my attention.

"Oh yeah?" I ask. "Is that your mom?"

"No, my mom is in heaven," Cora says sadly. Then she smiles. "Josie is my friend at Day Ring."

"Dayspring," Charlie corrects.

"Dayspring," Cora parrots, taking a big bite of her sandwich.

"Is that where you live?" I ask. I'm familiar with the place. She nods enthusiastically. I accept the sandwich Naomi hands to me. "Are you sure you have enough?"

"I'm positive. We always bring extra in case Cora changes her mind about what she wants, or in case Charlotte needs something more to eat."

"Right . . . *Charlotte*. She needs to eat," I say, grinning.

Charlie pulls a handful of grass and throws it at me. "Shush," she says. "I don't make fun of your name, *Nefer*."

"Nefer?" Naomi asks, looking at me with a funny expression. Only her voice isn't teasing, it almost sounds like she knows the name. My stomach tightens as I realize she might know my dad, and somehow know my home situation.

"Yeah, why?" I ask suspiciously.

"No reason," she says, suddenly very interested in her sandwich. "Just an unusual name, I guess."

"It's Egyptian," Charlie says. I'm surprised she remembers that.

"As in Nefertiti?" Naomi asks.

I shrug. "Not sure. I'm not really into genealogy, so I don't know a lot about my family's origins."

"You should look into it," Charlie says. "Might be interesting. How many people do you know with an Egyptian heritage?"

"Well, at least all of the Egyptians," I say.

Charlie laughs, the first time I've seen her smile today. "You know what I mean."

"Can I swing?" Cora asks Charlie. I'm surprised she keeps directing her questions to Charlie instead of Naomi since she's the adult here, but I guess if Charlie's the one who takes care of her, then it makes sense.

"Not right now, M—Cora," she says. "You have to finish your lunch first."

Cora crosses her arms. Charlie sighs, and so I say, "Tell you what, Cora. If you finish your sandwich, I'll push you on the swing."

"You will?" she asks.

"Yes," I say at the same time that Charlie once again says, "You don't have to."

Cora picks up her sandwich and begins eating. I look at Charlie with a smile and lift my brows at her to say, *See?* She shakes her head, but doesn't say any more on the subject.

After Cora finishes her sandwich, I take her to the swings and make good on my promise. Charlie comes along while Naomi leans back on the blanket, pulling a novel and cigarette out. I don't miss Charlie's eyes narrowing as Naomi lights up.

Charlie leans against one of the swing-set bars, hands in pockets, watching me while I push a laughing Cora. "Why are you doing this?" she finally asks.

"Because I promised," I say.

"Not just this," she waves a hand toward the swing. "I mean all of it, stopping by, then staying when . . ."

"When?" I prompt.

She glances at Cora, and then drops her eyes. "When you don't have to," she says.

"I'm not all bad, Charlie."

She looks at me. "I didn't say you were."

"You're my friend, right?"

A blush steals up her cheek. I have a feeling she's remembering the kiss. So am I. She nods.

"Well, I had nothing to do today, and didn't want to hang out at home. I was driving around, saw my friend's car, and thought I'd see if she wanted to help alleviate my boredom. And what I found was that she has this great friend named Cora that I could also hang out with."

A strange look crosses her face, one I can't read.

"Higher!" Cora calls. I push a little more, but not too much. I don't want to be responsible for her getting hurt.

I look at Charlie. "If Cora is Naomi's sister, wouldn't that make her your aunt also?" And then, before she can answer, I say, "Oh, wait. Is Naomi one of your parents' sister-in-law? Is that how you're related? I guess that would make Cora a distant relative by marriage, but not by blood." Charlie doesn't answer. "I don't know much about your family. How can we spend as much time together as we do and I've only met Naomi, and don't even know which of your parents you live with, or if you live with both? I don't even know if you have siblings."

"I don't know anything about your family, either," Charlie says. "Do we really need to know that much?"

An odd answer, but since I definitely *don't* want to talk about my "family," I drop the subject.

"I guess not," I say. She looks surprised by my easy capitulation. I can see curiosity in her face. "So, what are you doing after this?"

"After what?"

"The park," I say, as if it should be obvious. "Do you want to go for a drive in the canyon or something? There's this really great overlook where you can see the whole city."

"Are you asking me to go parking with you?" she asks, then immediately looks away, cheeks reddening. She's thinking about the kiss again, I can tell.

"Parking?" I repeat. "What is this, the fifties? No, new girl, I'm just asking if you want to hang out."

She shakes her head. "I can't. I have to . . . watch Cora all night."

"You want to come over and watch SpongeBob?" Cora asks, surprising me that she was paying any attention at all to our conversation.

"Sure," I say, then look at Charlie. "If it's okay with Charlie."

"Charlie, please-please-please-please-please," Cora says as she swings back and forth.

"Great, thanks a lot," Charlie says. "Now I look like the bad guy if I say no."

"So don't say no."

It's manipulative, I know. But I'll take it anyway as Charlie sighs again, which I take to mean yes.

THIRTY-THREE
CHARLIE

I sit on the couch, watching Benjamin dance with my mom. It's strange and surreal, this day. When we got home, my mom took a nap for about an hour while Benjamin sat and charmed Naomi, asking her about Dayspring once he somehow got her to tell him she owns it. Then he talked to her about gardening, something I vaguely know she has some interest in, but had no idea how passionate she is about it. After that he watched cartoons with my mom, patiently, for a couple of hours before suggesting an impromptu dance.

He picks one of my Def Leppard CDs, of course, laughing when he discovers my mom knows many of the lyrics, not correcting her when she gets them wrong. For a minute I thought he'd figure it out, who she is, by that alone. When he doesn't seem suspicious, I finally relax. Naomi invites him to stay for dinner, and to my consternation he agrees.

I've nearly called Cora "Mom" several times. It's exhausting, this pretending. Yet I don't want him to know who she is—and I'm ashamed of that. I'm also worried that if he finds out, he'll go from being amused by this somewhat eccentric "aunt" I have and become repulsed that she's my birth mother.

When I'm checking my blood sugar before dinner, he comes close to watch. After I'm finished, he says, "Can I try that?"

"You want to check your blood sugar?" I ask.

"Yeah. I'm just curious how it feels."

"It hurts if you're not used to it," I say. Still, I change the needle in the lancet and put a new strip in the monitor. "Squeeze your finger a little to get some blood into the end. Okay, now just cock the lancet like this"—I show him how—"and hold it against the tip of your finger and push the trigger."

He pushes it, then jerks his hand back when it pierces his skin. "Ouch!"

"Told you," I say. "Now quit being a baby and squeeze it a little to get a drop of blood. Put it against this." I point to the area on the test strip. He does, and it starts counting down. He pops his finger into his mouth.

"Does it ever get any better or does it always hurt?" he asks around his finger.

"Being diabetic doesn't make me automatically immune to pain," I say. "It used to hurt, but I didn't have a choice, so what could I do? I'm used to it now." The monitor beeps and I look down. "It's 78," I say.

"Is that good?"

"For you," I say. "For me it would mean I probably need to get some carbs in me."

"What was your blood sugar?" he asks.

"Mine was 139."

"Oh. Is that good?"

I laugh. "Good enough. I'm supposed to try to stay between 80 and 130, but if I'm below 150, then it's okay."

He shakes his head. "How do you remember all this?"

I shrug. "I've been dealing with it since I was nine. It just seems, I don't know, normal, I guess."

"Does it scare you sometimes?"

"I get really tired of it sometimes," I admit. "It'd be nice to have just one day where I didn't have to think about it, where I didn't have to poke myself, or fill up my insulin pump, or worry about what I was or wasn't eating. I try not to think too much about the other things that can happen, the things that are scary, or I'd just be depressed all the time."

"Like having a seizure?" he asks.

"That, and all the other things that can go wrong. I figure, why live in fear? All I can do is take care of myself the best I can, and if other things happen, then I'll deal with it."

"Wow," he says. "You're like a superhero, or something. And here I thought I was pretty great."

I shake my head. "Classic Nefer," I say.

"I am classy, aren't I?"

"I didn't say classy, and you know it."

"It's true nonetheless," he says, making me laugh again. "Can I see your pump?"

I pull it out of my pocket, explaining to him how it works, pulling out the cartridge for him to see where the insulin is, and show him the site in my arm.

"Does that stay there all the time?" He lightly fingers the site, and my skin breaks out in goose bumps. He glances up at me knowingly, his green eyes hooded by his long, dark lashes.

I pull my arm away. "I have to change it every three days. Sometimes I have it in my arm, sometimes in my belly."

"Change it how?"

So I pull out a site and show him how it works. He grimaces when he sees the needle.

"Okay, you're even more of a hero now," he says.

"Well, then I should get me a cape," I say.

"And a tight spandex outfit," he says, waggling his eyebrows.

165

I feel heat stealing up my cheeks again. Luckily that's when Naomi comes to tell us dinner is done. We walk into the kitchen, and I pray my mom can manage to eat with a minimum amount of mess while Benjamin is here.

Later, when I walk Benjamin out to the front porch, he says, "Does Cora live here?"

"During the week she stays at Dayspring, and she stays here on the weekends. She's only been doing that a couple of weeks. Before that she was here every day."

"Ah," he says. "That explains it."

"What?"

"Up until a couple weeks ago, you were never available, and now suddenly you're free most of the time except weekends. Is she the babysitting job you had?"

I can't look him in the eyes as I lie. "Yes."

"Why didn't you just say something?"

I bite my lip. How can I possibly explain what I don't understand myself? I shrug.

"Well, I think she's cool," Benjamin says. "I had a lot of fun with you guys today."

I look at him then to see if he's telling the truth or if he's being facetious. He *looks* sincere, anyway. Suddenly his eyes drop to my mouth again, and I remember clearly what happened the last time he looked at me like this. I should back away, twist the door handle, and go inside. I really, *really* should. Instead I tip my face up, just a little, not enough to be an outright invitation, but also a movement that might be easily misconstrued as one. He leans toward me, the smallest amount, and I meet him halfway.

His lips. On mine. Benjamin Nefer kissing me. Not the gentle, unassuming kiss of last night, but a full on, toe-curling, shiver-inducing, mind-blowing slant of his mouth across mine, showing me that I can pretend all I want that he's just my friend when in

166

reality he's much, much more. His arms around my waist, pulling me close, two spots of heat against the chill of the night. My own arms around his shoulders, holding him just as tight.

Finally, when I think I may never be able to breathe normally again, he pulls back. I stare at him, speechless. His hand comes up, resting alongside my jaw, his thumb stroking my cheek lightly. His eyes are dark with emotion, intense, an expression I can't interpret. One corner of his mouth upturns just the smallest amount before he leans and kisses me softly on the corner of my mouth. Without a word, he turns away, walking to his car. He looks back once before climbing in and driving away.

I slump against the door, my mind reeling. What just happened?

THIRTY-FOUR
BENJAMIN

I'm purposely not early to school Monday morning. I want to retreat a bit, give Charlie time to process. I'll see her at lunch. I slip into first period, sliding into my seat just as the bell rings.

I think about our two kisses. I'm still shocked Charlie let me kiss her once, let alone twice. And the second time . . . It might have been me who initiated the kiss, but it was Charlie who closed the deal. Her response was fervent, better than I could have imagined.

Seems my plan is working. If she kissed me twice over the weekend, that pretty much makes her my girlfriend, even if it isn't official. I debate about whether to say anything to her, to clarify in words what's between us. I'm not sure if that's a good idea, or if it'll only chase her off.

As the teacher drones on about chemistry, my thoughts wander to Charlie. I remember the day she had her seizure, how freaked out I was. Even now my stomach clenches in response to nothing more than the memory. Charlie, sitting in her windowsill, talking on the phone, afraid to admit her real "babysitting" job is caretaking her aunt. Charlie at the park, looking at her aunt with the kind of love that I haven't felt since . . . well, since *her*. I quickly pull my mind from that path. Charlie, singing Def Leppard songs, dancing with a wide smile on her face. Charlie, leaning toward me, asking for a kiss.

A sharp pain sears through my chest, and I push a fist against it. Panic races through me. I look around to see if anyone notices, but everyone is either pushing buttons on their cell phones or doodling on paper. No one looks my way. I think I'm having a heart attack and wonder if I'll die right here, among my classmates, without anyone looking my way.

I push out of my chair, not stopping when I knock my books to the floor, and, ignoring my teacher calling my name, I rush from the room. It's a short walk to the restroom, but it feels like three football-field lengths. Once there, I'm thankful to find it empty. I crash into a stall, slam the door, and drop to the commode. I can't catch a breath, and my hands feel numb, curling involuntarily into fists. The room spins dizzyingly as I gasp. From miles away I hear my name being called. It sounds not quite real, so I ignore it. I'm dying.

Suddenly Daniel is in front of me, shaking me, calling my name.

"You've gotta calm down, man," he's saying urgently. His words slowly filter past the panic, and I focus on him. "Take some deep breaths—slow," he urges when I begin gasping again. I concentrate on breathing as he is doing.

"I think I'm having a heart attack," I say when I'm finally able to form words.

"Nah," he says, standing and locking fists with me, pulling me upright. "You're too young for that."

"It happens," I say, following him out of the stall. "You hear about it all the time—young, healthy athletes just dropping dead."

He shakes his head and pounds me on the back. "You're not dead. Here, splash some water on your face."

I lean over the sink and do as he says. The semi-cold water helps calm me. I toss a few handfuls into my mouth and swallow. I stand up and look at him in the mirror, standing a few feet behind me.

"What's wrong with me?" I ask.

"Panic attack," he says, shrugging like it's no big deal. "My sister gets them. She's not as bad as she used to be, but we've all had to learn tricks to help her calm down and get past them."

I turn to face him. "Your sister has panic attacks?" How did I not know this?

"Yeah." He's talking down to his shoes, leaning against the corner of the stall, his legs crossed at the ankles. He shrugs again. "No biggie."

I lean against the sink, the realization of what just happened sinking in. I'm flooded with embarrassment that Daniel saw me like that, having a *panic attack*, of all things.

"Thanks," I mumble. I wave a vague hand. "You know, for that."

He shrugs yet again and stands up, eyeing me. "Feel better?"

"Feel stupid," I say. "Listen, Daniel, can we . . . can we just keep this between us?"

"Sure, of course," he says. He makes an *X* on his chest with his finger. "Scout's honor and all that."

I chuckle, then glance at the stall door. I tip my head at him. "I thought I locked the stall door."

He grins widely. "I might've had to kick it in."

I laugh outright at that, walking past him to look at the door. Sure enough, the metal piece inside that holds the catch dangles uselessly.

Daniel looks at it as well, then hitches like a sheriff from the Wild West, pretending to straighten his holster and tip his hat. "Are you sure I can't tell the pretty ladies about my act of heroism and brute strength?" He's dropped his voice into a John Wayne drawl.

I shake my head. "Sorry, you already promised using the Scout oath."

He straightens, back to the usual Daniel. "I doubt that was the Scout oath, but since I have no idea what the Scout oath is, I'll have to take your word for it."

"Thanks, man," I say, bumping his fist with mine. "I appreciate it . . . everything, I mean."

"No problem. What do you think brought it on?"

I have no idea. I'd only been thinking about Charlie when it happened. "I don't know," I say honestly.

"Well, next time just try to slow your breath, deep, even breaths. Sometimes it helps to either count, or to draw an imaginary box in the air over and over and concentrate on it." I raise my brows skeptically. "Works for my sister," he says. "Worth a try, right?"

The bell rings, startling us both. "Guess I better go explain why I ran out in the middle of class."

"I'm witness to the fact that you just got sick," Daniel says, following me from the restroom.

That's the excuse I give the teacher, and since I ran out the way I did he seems to believe it. I try to keep my mind off Charlie and keep calm—at least until lunch, when I'll see her again.

෧ඹ

When I get to the lunchroom, Charlie is already surrounded by Cozi, Alexis, and Phoebe. Daniel's there, sitting near Alexis, and several other guys crowd around. I grunt and take the open seat at the end of the table, not very close to Charlie.

"Are you guys coming to the game on Friday?" I hear Daniel ask.

"Maybe," Phoebe says. Cozi shrugs and Charlie says nothing.

"I can't," Alexis says. "I have a date."

All eyes turn to her, most stunned—especially Daniel's.

"You have a date?" he asks.

"Yeah." Her answer is simple, and I can tell Daniel wants to probe for more info but doesn't want to sound jealous. I usually stay out of stuff like this, couldn't care less about it, but since he helped me earlier I figure I owe him.

"With who?" I ask loudly to be heard at their end.

Alexis shoots me a glare that should wither me. Guess she still hates me. She answers, but she's looking at Phoebe when she does. "With Brad Felton."

"*Felton?*" Daniel echoes. I can understand his disbelief. Felton is as opposite from Daniel as you can get. He doesn't play sports, is captain of the debate team, and I think he might even be on some math competition team or something. He's a nerd.

"Yes, with Brad Felton," Alexis says firmly. "He's a nice guy. He asked me out, and I said yes. Do you have a problem with that?" She's looking directly at Daniel, daring him to say anything.

"No, it's just . . . *Felton?*" Daniel says.

"I'll go to the game if you're going," Charlie pipes into the awkward silence, speaking to Phoebe.

"You don't have to work?" Cozi asks.

"No, not Friday."

"I'll come, too, then," Cozi says. "We'll make a night of it. The game, then pizza at Tony's."

"Sounds fun," Phoebe says. "Anyone else want to come?"

Everyone chimes in that they'll be there. I want to groan, wishing they'd pick somewhere other than Tony's for once, but if Charlie's planning to be there, so will I.

THIRTY-FIVE
CHARLIE

I've been in a quandary since Benjamin kissed me—twice. I really want to talk to one of my friends about it, but since they all hate Benjamin, I don't think they'd be much help.

There haven't been many times in my life when I've wished for a mom who I could talk to about these things. When I went through the horror that's puberty, I had my grandma. And though I imagined it might be better to discuss them with my mom, well, that was impossible in my particular situation. When I had my first crush, my grandma thought it was "cute," and I wished I had a mom who could objectively look at the situation and help me know what to do. I don't *know* that a mom would do that, but I *imagine* she would.

Now I don't even have my grandma to talk to. I miss her desperately. I can't even go to the cemetery and talk to her there because she's buried in Idaho, too far away.

After school I go see my mom at Dayspring and play with her and Josie for a while. I can't deny how happy my mom is here. She's positively beaming each time she gets to come back, and sullen when first she comes home for the weekend, though she's usually fine after a few hours.

When I get home, I go to my room and pull out my homework. I grumble at the math page in front of me, as if that will somehow cause the numbers to suddenly make sense. While I'm trying to figure out a problem, Naomi knocks on my door.

"Come in," I yell angrily.

She opens the door, hesitance on her face. "Everything okay?"

I sigh loudly. "Sorry. Just doing math."

She enters the room and sits on the chair. "Math was never my strong point, either," she says. "I don't think I ever advanced past Algebra II while in high school, which made college math that much more challenging."

I toss my pen down. "There's gotta be an easier way to do this."

"Maybe some tutoring?"

I grimace. Like I can afford that. "Not unless you can find some free tutoring."

"I'll ask around," she says, surprising me. I thought she'd offer to pay and then I'd have to fight her on that. She already pays for too much, giving me a burden of guilt that's heavier each day.

"Thanks," I say.

"So, how's everything else going?"

"Okay," I say. "Most of the classes are the same as I would've had in Idaho, so they're not too hard. Except math, but that'd be hard anywhere."

"You've made friends?" she asks. "I mean, besides Benjamin. He's the only one I've met."

"Yeah, I have friends. I just haven't . . . brought them over."

She nods in understanding, which only makes me feel worse. "You're welcome to have them over anytime you like. I can be pretty good about staying out of the way. Why don't you have them over Friday night?"

"We're going to the football game at school, then going to Tony's after. It's kind of the local hangout."

"Oh, okay. Well, anytime you want." She pauses, and I can tell she wants something else. "Listen, Charlotte, I know you have certain . . . I know there are things about me that you don't particularly like, and that's okay. But I also want you to remember I was your age once, and I remember what life was like." She looks at me. "If you ever have anything you want to talk about, like you and Benjamin—"

"There *is* no me and Benjamin," I interrupt. "He's just my friend. I mean, yeah, he tried to get me to date him at first, but I told him no. I knew his reputation. So he agreed to be just friends." I shove off of my bed and pace to the window. "He *agreed*. So why did he kiss me?"

"He kissed you?"

I turn toward Naomi, dropping onto the window seat. I hadn't meant to say that aloud.

"Twice," I admit. "And the first time I might have thought it was just . . . but then, the second time." I cross my ankles and lean on my fists. "He shouldn't have done that. I shouldn't have kissed him back."

"You don't like him in that way?" she asks.

I stare at her, thinking about her question. Benjamin is just my friend, right? He's fun to hang out with, and makes me laugh. He was really cool with my mom. He's absolutely gorgeous. And his kisses . . .

But he humiliated Alexis, and she wasn't the first. He even admits that he's not exactly boyfriend material. Like him like that? "I shouldn't," I say.

"You shouldn't, but clearly you do." She hits it right on the head, and I lean back against the window.

"How did it happen?" I ask, as if she'll have any clue. "I was determined not to let him get to me. I really thought he was just my friend. He's a complete player."

"He seems nice," she says. "He was really great with Cora."

I swallow. "He doesn't know she's my mom," I admit shamefully.

"I figured as much," she says. "And that's your right to not tell him. But if you think there might be any kind of real relationship with him, you have to be honest. It's not fair to keep secrets."

Secrets. Benjamin is full of secrets. Doesn't that give me the right to keep my own?

"I don't know if he's capable of having a relationship," I say. "He's never had a girlfriend. He just uses girls and then tosses them aside."

"He hasn't done that to you," she points out.

"Yet," I add.

"Fair enough. Don't sell yourself short, Charlie. You might just be what he's been waiting for."

I grin. "That's so cheesy."

She smiles. "Maybe. But it could be true." She leans forward in her chair. "I can see in your eyes how much you care about him. So maybe this advice is already too late, but be careful. It's easy enough to fall for someone who will break your heart. Trust me, I know. If you already know there's a chance of that, take it slowly, carefully, until you're sure of whether your heart is safe with him before you fall completely in love with him."

I lean forward also. "The thing is, he's different with me, different than he is at school with other girls or even with his friends. He could just be fooling me, you know, trying to break me down just because I *did* resist him at first."

"Do you think he's doing that?"

"I just don't know. If he truly is the person who he is when he's with me, then no. But how can I know that for sure? The only way to know is to give in, and then see if he breaks my heart or not."

She looks at me for long moments. "You're more mature than most girls your age. You've had to be, with the kind of life you have.

I think you'll do what's right. All I can tell you is to be careful, step easily. If you're going to offer your heart for him to break, just make sure it's worth it."

"Thanks," I say. "I mean it. I can't really talk to my friends about this because they all hate him."

She stands. "While you shouldn't sell yourself short, you shouldn't sell your friends short, either, Charlie. They just might surprise you." She walks to the door. As she steps into the hallway, I call her.

"Naomi?"

She looks back in. "Yes?"

"You called me Charlie."

She smiles. "I guess people can change, huh?"

❦

On Tuesday as promised I show up to Benjamin's football practice after school. He grins when he sees me sitting in the stands, and I suddenly feel like being here was worth that one smile. I shake my head. I've really gotta get a grip on this thing.

The band isn't far from me, practicing loudly. Keeps me from thinking too much, so I welcome the noise. I watch Benjamin and his teammates as they go through all their drills. Looks like a lot of hard work. They're all drenched in sweat before long in spite of the fact that there's a cool breeze. I'm amazed that Benjamin has any energy to get into a boxing ring after this kind of workout every day.

Without knowing much about the exercises they're doing, I can still tell that Benjamin is the top athlete on the team. He works harder than the others, and also encourages them when they flag a little. They all seem to look to him for guidance. No wonder he's the captain. He definitely has leadership qualities.

An hour later the coach dismisses them, and Benjamin jogs my way. I stand and walk to the bottom of the stands. Benjamin's hair is matted with sweat, his shirt drenched, smiling at me as I make my way to him. He's never looked better.

"You came," he says as I near.

"Told you I would. Were you hoping I'd let you out of the bet?"

He laughs. "Not a chance. I'm still curious as to what this hidden talent is that you have that you think you can do better than me."

I stop, just in front of him, separated by the low cement wall between the stands and the field. "After watching you work out like that, it almost seems unfair now."

"Something physical?" he asks. "You think there's something *physical* you can do better than me?"

I narrow my eyes at his arrogance, which only makes him laugh again. "No, smarty, not physical . . . exactly."

"Now I'm *really* curious."

"Okay," I say. "I can hold my breath underwater for a long time."

He shakes his head. "That's your bet? Breath holding?"

"You don't understand," I say. "I can hold my breath a *really* long time."

"You know I swim, right? The only reason I'm not on the swim team is it overlaps football."

I shrug. "Well, then I guess it'll be a real contest." I crinkle my nose at him. "You're really sweaty, Nefer, and kind of stinky."

"Yeah, that happens when you work your butt off for an hour straight."

I think about telling him how much I admire his athleticism, how he was with the other players. Instead I say, "You're gonna shower, right?"

"Anything for you, new girl." He takes a step back. "Where am I meeting you?"

"My house," I say. "Naomi has a pool we can use. I turned the temp up so we won't freeze to death."

He glances up at the overcast sky. "Good day for a swim, huh?"

"We won't be long," I say. "It'll be easy to kick your butt."

"Ha, ha," he mocks. "I'll run home and get my suit after I shower and meet you then."

"Prepare to lose for once in your life, Nefer."

"Lose? To a girl?" he says as he backs away. "Not today, new girl." He turns and jogs across the field.

Half an hour later he's at my door. I let him in, self-conscious in my swimsuit cover-up. He's wearing swim shorts and a T-shirt, carrying his backpack as he follows me through the house and out back.

"Ready to be schooled, Nefer?" I ask.

He drops his backpack and peels his T-shirt off. I try to keep my eyes away, I swear I do. I fail. I'm shocked to see some bruising around his ribs and on his back. It looks really painful, especially when I remember the hard physical workout he just had.

"Not a chance," he says, turning and diving cleanly into the pool, swimming with long strokes to the other side. When he emerges, he turns my way. "It's almost as warm as bath water."

"I hate cold water," I say, removing my cover-up and jumping in. He swims back over to me.

"Baby," he says, splashing me.

"I'm not a baby, I just like warm water."

"All right, whatever. What are the rules?"

"No rules," I say. "We just go under, and the first one up loses."

"You mean *you*," he says. "When you come up first, you lose."

"Oh, you are so going to eat crow," I say, pushing his shoulder. "Okay, on the count of three. One. Two. Three."

I suck in a lungful of air and dip beneath the surface at the same time as Benjamin. I keep my eyes open, watching him. His eyes are also open. I calm my nerves, not allowing panic to set in when first my lungs crave oxygen. I can see when it happens for Benjamin, when he begins to get to that point that he feels his lungs are going to explode. His eyes widen and suddenly he thrusts up out of the water. I slowly follow.

He's gasping, trying to replace lost oxygen. I grin at him.

"Don't you have something to say?" I ask.

"Best two out of three?"

I shrug. "Okay."

After I beat him three times in a row, and his chest is heaving with exertion while my breathing is normal, he finally concedes.

"You win," he says breathlessly.

"I'm sorry, what did you say?" I turn my head his way, hand behind my ear, leaning in.

He grimaces. "I said you win. I lose. You beat me. Happy now?"

"I really am," I say. "It does my heart good to see you brought down."

He laughs and pulls me into a hug, surprising me. I need to tell him to stop. And then his hug becomes tossing me into the air so I land in the water five feet from him. I come up spluttering to his laughter.

"Butthead," I say, splashing him. "Wanna get in the hot tub?"

"We're in the hot tub," he says.

"Ha-ha," I say sarcastically. "C'mon."

THIRTY-SIX
BENJAMIN

Sitting in the hot tub across from Charlie is more relaxing than anything I've done in . . . I don't know how long. Maybe ever. I'm frustrated, though, that she won—not so much that she won, but because I lost, and now I'm going to have to make good on my end of the bet and take her to my house. I'm not sure how I'm going to pull that off since I never know with absolute certainty when my dad will be there and when he won't.

Charlie's long hair is floating in the water. "You have curly hair," I say.

She self-consciously raises her hands and pushes her hair back from her forehead. "Yeah. Sometimes it's nice, sometimes it's a pain," she says, trapping it in a bun using a hair band she has around her wrist. "It's not naturally blonde."

"It's not?" I'm surprised. I mean, I guess probably most girls dye their hair, but how can I know who does and who doesn't? "What color is it?"

"Dark brown," she says. "I've only been blonde since . . . not long before we moved here."

"What made you decide to do that?" I can't imagine her as anything but blonde, probably because that's all I've known her as.

"You know, new place, new start, new . . . hair." She grins at me, her dimples more prominent with her wet, slicked-back hair. I also notice how long her lashes really are. Clearly they aren't fake, as I'd once thought.

"So what's your secret?" I say.

Panic crosses her face. "What do you mean?"

"For holding your breath so long."

"Oh." Her shoulders slump, almost as if she's relieved at my question. "When I was little, I used to lie in the tub and hold my breath underwater. After doing that for so many years, I learned tricks to fill my lungs with more air. Then I studied it."

"You *studied* it?"

"Yeah. I wanted to know who'd done it the longest, so I read about it and how they managed it. Then I practiced until I could last for nearly three minutes."

"Why?"

"Well, Nefer, three minutes is a pretty long time. I didn't—"

"No, I mean, why did you hold your breath in the tub?"

"Oh," she says, blushing. She seems to think for a minute whether to answer before she does. "Um, well, I guess . . . there were just some things in my life I was dealing with, and beneath the water there was quiet, calm, peace in the warmth. I can't honestly say why it ever occurred to me to see how long I could hold my breath other than I wanted to stay under as long as possible."

I think about asking her what those things were that she was dealing with. Instead I say, "Three minutes, huh? What's the record?"

She laughs. "Something like twenty-two minutes, though most people would die long before that. That takes some serious training."

"Wow. Okay, so could you beat me in a swim race?" Hoping she'll say yes so we can make another bet and I can get out of taking her to my house.

"I doubt it. Holding your breath for a long time doesn't make you swim any faster. I'm not much of a swimmer."

Bummer. I'm trying to figure out another way out of it when she says, "So when do I get to see your house?"

So much for my grand plan. I look at her. "Are you sure there's nothing else you'd rather have? It's just a house, nothing too exciting."

"It's the mystery of it, Nefer. Why is it such a secret? Do you live in a cave or something?"

"No way. If I did, I wouldn't hide it. That'd be cool."

She watches me for a minute, making me uncomfortable as I try to figure out what she's thinking. Then she says, "I understand about secrets, about wanting to keep some parts of your life private, and deciding who you can trust with information. Whatever the reason is you keep your house secret, it will never be told by me." Not sure how to react to that, I stay silent. Then she surprises me by saying, "You don't have to take me to your house."

"What?" I wonder if my gaping jaw reflects the amount of astonishment I'm feeling.

"I'm serious," she says. "It was a stupid thing for me to ask. You don't have to take me. In fact, I'll even come watch you box—once."

"No way," I hear myself saying. "You won fair and square."

"Not really," she says. "I didn't tell you that I've had years of practice, and I didn't give you any warning to practice yourself."

Is she for real? What girl—what *person*—gives up their win and claims the loser's prize? I slide across the hot tub until I'm sitting right next to her. Her eyes widen, a mixture of alarm and expectation. I tuck a loose strand of hair behind her ear, then leave my hand resting on her jaw, stroking with my thumb.

"I'll make you a deal," I say.

"What's that?" Her response is barely above a whisper.

"I promise not to tell anyone that you've fallen for a loser like me."

"You're not a—"

I cut her protest off with my mouth on hers. That strange feeling comes again, a tightening in my chest, lightheadedness. Afraid a panic attack is about to hit, I concentrate on Charlie, the feel of her lips, her hand coming up to rest lightly on my cheek. The panic recedes until there's nothing but her.

❧

Later, after my dad finishes with me and is snoring in his room, I lock myself in the bathroom. Filling the tub, I sink beneath the warm water, feeling not a little foolish. I can't stay under longer than thirty seconds at the most, but I begin to understand what she means. Even when I slide under far enough to keep my mouth and nose above the waterline, but my ears beneath, I feel the peace, the quiet . . . the pretending the world has gone away and can't touch me here.

Beneath the water, I think about Charlie. About her fully kissing me back. About her smile and her laugh. About those long lashes. About her saying I don't have to bring her here and expose my greatest shame. About the fact that she didn't let my ego destroy what's been my most carefully guarded secret.

Long after the water's gone cold, I stay with my ears beneath the water, listening to the sweet nothingness, and using thoughts of Charlie to push away other, more disturbing thoughts that try to intrude.

❧

Two nights later, the night before the game, Charlie makes good on her word. She follows me in her car to the gym after practice. On one hand I'm nervous about having her watch me box. On the other hand, at least now I have another eyewitness to why I'm usually bruised.

Daniel came with me once, a few years ago. Of course everyone at the gym goaded him into getting into the ring. After a few hits, he left and never asked to come back, which is why I'd let them goad him in the first place. I couldn't let him understand that for the most part, I *don't* get bruised here. Then how would I explain all the black eyes, split lips, swollen jaws?

I don't enjoy getting hit, but getting hit by a gloved hand while wearing protective headgear is a walk in the park compared to the brutal, meaty, bare-knuckled swings of my dad.

Charlie follows me into the gym, looking a little pale. She crosses her arms tightly around herself, her mouth rigid, eyes wide. I stop just inside the doors trying to see it from her eyes. It's a busy place, some guys working the punching bags, others on speed bags. Some are jumping rope or running. A few are sparring. And overall it smells like rancid socks.

"You don't have to do this," I tell her.

She ignores that and says, "There're girls here."

"Yeah, of course. Do you think girls don't box?"

She shrugs. "I don't know. I didn't really consider . . . it just seems so . . ."

"Violent?" I provide. "Brutal? Cruel? Sadistic?" She's smiling now. "Hostile? Foolish?"

"Okay, okay," she laughs, holding her hands up in surrender.

I put my arm around her shoulder, wondering if she'll allow it. She does.

"I'll take it easy on you, okay? No sparring. I'll just show you some of the workouts I do."

She nods and follows me as I go through the paces, first running, then some jump roping, which I admit I show off a bit with since I'm pretty good at that. I do some of the speed bags and the

185

punching bags but can't help but notice how her eyes keep returning to those sparring, as if she can't keep her eyes away.

After we've been here about an hour, I begin removing my gloves. She walks over and helps unlace them. I can do it much faster with my teeth than she does, but there's no way I'm going to tell her that. I watch her, smiling, as she works the laces.

Once the gloves are off, I go speak to the coach before picking up my bag and leading her to the parking lot. She still hasn't said much.

"Everything okay?" I ask.

She nods, and then shakes her head. "I just keep imagining you in the ring with those men. Hitting you. I just . . . I don't get it."

We arrive at her car, and I set my bag down. She leans against her door, making no move to get in her car.

"Remember the other day when you told me how you used holding your breath under water as an escape?" She nods. I wave toward the gym. "This is my escape. It's a great stress reliever, and helps me deal with . . . stuff."

She sighs. "I guess I can understand that." Her fingers lightly brush my brow, which is still tender and swollen. She watches her fingers, a strange look on her face I can't decipher. I'd never tell her the injury is not from the gym. "Doesn't it hurt?"

"Not right now," I say.

Her eyes drop to mine and subconsciously she licks her lips. "Benjamin, there's something I need to tell you."

"Must be serious," I say. "You called me Benjamin. Are you breaking up with me?"

"How can I break up with you? We're not . . . you know."

"Aren't we?"

She swallows visibly. "You scare me."

"I'm not going to hurt you," I say, knowing the words are a lie. For the first time in my life I want the words to be true. It's just not possible for me to not hurt her—not because I want to, but because it's inevitable. I can't feel, therefore I can't care. I can't love.

"Have you said that to other girls?" she asks, dropping her hand.

"Yes," I admit.

"So why should I believe you?"

"You're different," I say. That, at least, is the truth. "You're my friend." Or at least as close to a friend as what I'm capable of having.

"I'm not really good girlfriend material," she says. "I have a lot of baggage."

"Cora?" I ask. She nods. "Cora isn't baggage. She's a sweet lady. I don't know why you feel like you have to hide her—"

"She's my mom," she blurts.

THIRTY-SEVEN
BENJAMIN

I stare at her, speechless. Her eyes are locked firmly on the ground. Cora's her *mom*? As in, gave birth to Charlie? Something must have happened to make her how she is. Maybe that's why they moved in with Naomi.

"What happened to her?" I ask. "I mean, to make her the way she is?"

Charlie shrugs, still watching her feet. "She was born that way. The cord was wrapped around her neck in the uterus, and she was without oxygen for too long."

"Wait," I say, confused. "She's always been . . . but then, how could she have a baby?" She doesn't answer or look at me. "Is your dad . . . is he like Cora?" She shakes her head. I'm more confused than ever. "Then who? What kind of man would . . ." Suddenly I realize what kind of man as Charlie's arms cross around herself again and her head drops.

Her voice is tortured as she says, "A man who's a pig, who's the lowest of all lowlifes. A man who turned my mom's life into a living hell for months. A man who—" Her voice catches and she stops speaking, still not looking at me.

Anger surges through me, fury ripping through my gut as horrific images slaughter my mind. A picture of sweet, innocent Cora comes to me and I have the sudden desire to hunt this man down and pummel him until he no longer has the breath of life in him.

I swing away from Charlie, not wanting her to see my unexpected rage. I grit my teeth against the explosion of cursing fighting to get out and shove my hands in my pockets to keep from hitting something. My anger amazes me—I haven't felt anger since I realized *she* wasn't coming back for me all those years ago.

"I'm sorry," I hear Charlie say. "I shouldn't have told you."

Something in her tone forces me to turn her way. Tears on her face are reflected by the dim light that proposes to keep the parking lot safe. She's fumbling her keys into her hand, turning toward her door. As quickly as my anger came, it drains.

I cross over to her hurriedly and place my hand on her shaking one that tries to unlock the door. She must be upset if she's trying to use her key to unlock the door rather than pressing the button on the fob. She stills beneath my touch, but doesn't look up. I gently take her keys from her, then urge her face toward mine.

"Charlie," I say quietly. "If he were here, I'd rip him from limb to limb. In fact, if you know where he is, I'll gladly go do it right now."

She shakes her head. "He's in prison."

"Good," I say vehemently. "That's where he deserves to be."

"He's not there because of what he did to her. He's there because of some other things he did, later. She couldn't . . . she wasn't able to testify clearly, so even though they had DNA evidence, she couldn't reliably say . . ." A sob escapes her and I pull her into my arms. She holds on tightly to me, her body quaking. A few minutes later, she says, "You must hate me."

I push back from her so I can see her face. "Are you crazy? Why would I hate you?"

"Because I'm his daughter. I have his DNA."

I give her a light shake. "Charlie, if there's one thing I know without any shred of doubt, it's that DNA means nothing. There isn't anything that says whatever makes our parents do the things they do, that we'll do the same." Her face clears a little.

"Do you think I'm . . . I mean, I've had my IQ checked and everything, they did that a lot when I was little, to make sure, you know?"

"You're one of the smartest people I know," I say honestly.

"You don't know me that well," she says.

"I know you well enough," I say. "Why didn't you tell me before, when I met her?"

Charlie is still encircled in my arms. She frees her hands and places them on my arms. "I was ashamed. And I'm *beyond* ashamed that I was ashamed. I was also afraid."

"Afraid I'd make fun of you?"

"Yes, I was afraid you'd make fun of me. I was even more afraid you'd make fun of her."

"Why would I do that?"

She smiles sadly. "You'd be surprised how many people do. They seem to think because she has the intellect of a child that somehow she can't have her feelings hurt." She glances toward the gym. "Maybe I should learn to box so that when they do, I can give them a good pounding."

I chuckle. "I'll do it for you." She looks up at me, a real smile—small, but real—upturning her mouth. "Your mom is great, Charlie. I think you're underestimating people by hiding her."

"I am? How?"

"There are some jerks out there who'd probably be mean, but I don't think Alexis or Phoebe would be, and I *know* Cozi wouldn't be."

She nods. "You're right. I know you're right. It's just . . . it seemed like a good idea to keep it secret when I first moved here since no one knew. Then I wouldn't have to explain how I came to be. That's the part that's hardest because then people know that I only exist because my mom was the victim of horrible violence." She pauses. "It's really selfish of me, to hide her, to be *ashamed* of her just because I don't want to have to admit . . . everything."

I make a sudden, probably reckless, decision. "I want to show you something," I say, leading her to my car.

"I can just follow," she says.

"No, not for this. We'll come back and get your car soon."

She climbs in, and I can only hope I'm not making a really horrible mistake.

THIRTY-EIGHT
CHARLIE

I watch Benjamin as he drives. His response to finding out Cora is my mom wasn't what I expected. When he first turned away from me, I thought he was disgusted by my parentage. Then I realized he was just angry on her behalf, and somehow that made me feel better, almost as if he could share in some small way the burden of what happened to her.

I'm still not sure why I told him. Alexis's story keeps flashing in my mind. Benjamin isn't trustworthy, and could very possibly use what he now knows to hurt me, to humiliate me.

After we drive for a short time, he pulls up across the street from a rundown trailer, cutting the engine and staring at the place.

"What is this?" I ask.

He takes a breath then says, "It's where I live."

My eyes jump to his face, then back to the trailer. It's a little more than rundown, actually. Siding is falling off the trailer in several places, the roof is drooping. The front porch sags precariously. Weeds grow out of control against the trailer, the rest of the ground nearly bare. I can see that the window coverings are sheets or towels. There's even a broken window covered with a large piece of cardboard duct-taped into place.

I turn to see he watches me as I examine the trailer. "Well, I guess it's better than living in a cardboard box," I say.

He stares at me, and I wonder if I've completely offended him. Suddenly he bursts out laughing. I grin back.

"Barely, new girl," he says through his laughter. "It's *barely* better."

"No, come on, think about it, Nefer. A cardboard box would crumble at the first rain. And trying to shower in one . . . well, that would be a nightmare. They don't make them tall enough for someone like you to stand upright in."

"Not to mention a complete lack of privacy," he adds. "And the annoyance of having to find a new home each time a good, strong wind came up."

"That would be horrible. Though there are some positives to a cardboard box over your house."

"Like what?" He's smiling broadly.

"Easy to add onto for minimal cost. In just a few short months you could positively be living in a mansion—sans wind and rain, that is."

"It'd have to be a one-level mansion."

"Not necessarily," I say. "You could have as many levels as you wanted—you just couldn't actually use them."

He reaches over and takes my hand. "Thanks," he says.

I shrug. "I could say the same."

We sit in silence, looking at each other. My phone buzzes and I pull it from my pocket. It's a text from Cozi, but that isn't what alarms me.

"Oh, no," I say, looking at Benjamin wide-eyed. "I need to go, fast."

"What's up?" he asks, peering at my phone as if to find the answer there.

"My mom," I begin.

"Is she okay?"

"She's fine," I say, trying to force myself to relax. "It's just . . . since I didn't get to see her after school today, I told her I'd be there to tuck her into bed. It's almost nine."

"I can take you," he offers.

"I have to get my car."

He turns the ignition. "It's safe at the gym. There're people there until late, so no one will bother it. I'll take you to get it after we see Cora."

"*We?*"

He looks at me. "If that's okay."

"It's okay," I say, buckling my belt, wondering if he's really this person, or the one everyone else has told me he is.

❦

We arrive at Dayspring just before nine. Nancy, the front desk nurse, greets me, lifting her eyebrows when she sees Benjamin behind me. I introduce them and she says, "Ah, the mysterious Benjamin. Cora told us about you. We wondered if you really existed."

"She talks about me?" he asks.

"All the time. Calls you Prince Benjamin, in fact," she says with a grin.

He looks at me with lifted brows and I shrug. "She's on a *Cinderella* kick right now, and she's quite taken with the prince in the movie."

"Well, I've been called worse things," he says.

"No doubt," I say, leading the way to my mom's room, ignoring his look of astonishment.

"Charlie!" my mom cries when I step into her room, rushing over and hugging me. Then she spies Benjamin and she pulls back shyly.

"Look, Mom, I brought Benjamin with me tonight."

She places her arms behind her back, glancing at the floor, twisting her body back and forth. "Hi," she says quietly. This is odd—my mom's never been like this with anyone before. I take her into the bathroom and help her into her nightgown. She brushes her teeth and I brush her hair out. When we go back into the room, Benjamin is sitting in a chair, waiting.

"What book do you want to read tonight, Mom?" I ask.

She goes to her bookshelf, still abnormally quiet as she watches Benjamin. It occurs to me that she might be nervous having a male in her room. The last time she had a male in her room . . . I shake the thought away. As she climbs into bed and I pull the covers up, I lean near and whisper, "Do you want me to ask Benjamin to leave?"

She shakes her head and smiles. "I like him," she whispers back—loudly enough for Benjamin to clearly hear. I glance at him and he lifts his brows at me, grinning as if to say, *See, all the girls like me.* I grimace at him and turn back to my mom. I glance down at the book she chose and grimace in earnest. This book requires me singing to her in certain parts, like my grandma used to read it to us.

"Are you sure you don't want to read something different?" I ask.

"I want this," she says, poking a finger at the book.

I begin reading and when I get to the part where I usually sing, I just say the words.

"No, Charlie," my mom whines. "Do it right."

I clear my throat and turn so my back's facing Benjamin, and then I begin to sing quietly.

"I can't hear you," she complains, reaching up to play with a strand of my hair.

Face flaming, I clear my throat once again and sing louder, praying that Benjamin has fallen asleep or something so he can't hear me. I finish the book, and my mom sighs contentedly. She tucks one hand beneath her cheek as she turns her head to the side, an indication she's about to sleep. I lean down to kiss her on the forehead.

"I love you, Charlie," she says.

"I love you, too, Mom."

I stand and face Benjamin, wondering just how much teasing I'll be getting for the singing. Instead, he's looking at my mom with a strange, tight look on his face, as if a torrent of emotion struggles to break free—not one of those emotions humor.

"Ready?" I say quietly.

Without looking at me, he nods and stands. His whole body is taut, almost as if he's afraid of exploding. I can't figure him out. As I study him, my mom timidly says, "Charlie, can Prince Bennamin give me a kiss?"

Oh, man. Benjamin shoots a glance at my mom so I quickly intercede to save him having to say no. "Mom, I don't think—"

Benjamin holds a hand toward me and I stop speaking. He walks over to my mom, leans down and places a kiss on her forehead where I did. "Goodnight, princess," he whispers. My mom giggles.

And my heart tumbles.

THIRTY-NINE
BENJAMIN

"Nine-forty, two-seventy, seven-hut."

The ball is snapped and I run backward. I can see the defensive end coming toward me, ready for a sack. Not gonna happen, not on my watch. Instead of looking for the receiver and risking the sack, I barrel forward. My guard sees the change and makes a path for me. Between my bulk and the speed I've gained from boxing, I manage to shove past two more defenders. I run full bore down the field, crossing into the end zone, ensuring our win.

I turn back to my team, tempted to spike the ball but not willing to risk the penalty for doing so. Several of the guys barrel into me, sweeping me along in their cheering. I glance toward the stands and see Charlie cheering with Cozi and Phoebe. She sees me looking and gives me a thumbs-up. I return the gesture.

After the game, we all head for Tony's, as usual. I see Charlie there, sitting at the table, and make my way over amid the cheering. I really want to lean down and plant a kiss on her, but have the feeling that just might be the one thing that'll chase her away immediately.

I slide into the booth next to her, the overcrowding forcing a close proximity. She can't complain about that, right? It's just physics. The crowding forces me to place an arm on the back of the booth behind her in order to fit on the bench. She glances at me, eyes narrowing just the slightest. I give her my best innocent look and shrug. She answers by elbowing me in the ribs—lightly, but it just happens to be where the old man got a good hit in a couple of nights ago, and was exacerbated by the game tonight. I wince, then hope no one notices.

I should have known Charlie would. "Are you okay?" she asks, her eyes dropping to my ribs.

I lean down, grinning. "Just kidding."

Her expression says she doesn't believe me, but she lets it go. "Hey, are you working tomorrow?" she asks.

"Nope. Day off." I happen to know she also has the day off, just as she does every Saturday.

"Me, too," she says. "I mean, like, around noon?"

"Why? Are you asking me on a date?" I put teasing into my voice, but I'd actually like to know.

"No," she says, deflating the ego a bit. "I thought we'd better work on our assignment. Do another observation."

"You have an idea?"

"Um, yeah," she says. Her hesitance intrigues me.

"Do you want to share or is it a surprise?"

"No, not a surprise. I'm just not sure how you'll feel about it."

I look up and realize that while most of the people around us are oblivious to our conversation, caught up in their own, there's one person watching and listening. The one person who I know will be the wrench in my plan to make Charlie my temporary girlfriend: Cozi.

Charlie follows my gaze, and smiles at Cozi. "It's just home-work, Coz," she says, as if Cozi had spoken.

"Uh-huh," Cozi replies, voice heavy with doubt.

"So, what is it?" I ask, pulling Charlie's attention back to me.

"I . . . I'll tell you about it later."

"Don't you have to, um, babysit?"

"Well, it has to do with that, with observing how others are around . . . the . . . kids."

I sigh. I'd hoped she'd have told her friends about her mom by now, but it seems she's still keeping the secret.

"I think that's a good idea," I say. "Let's do it."

"You're taking the kids you babysit somewhere to see how people react around them?" Cozi asks.

"Yeah," Charlie says. "In fact, I was going to ask if you'd come along."

"Me?" Cozi looks at me as if I'm to blame for this.

"You, and Phoebe, and Alexis, too. I've already talked to Alexis and she's available. I just need you and Phoebe."

"Count me in," Phoebe says, apparently having been listening closer than I'd thought.

"You need more help?" Daniel pipes in.

Charlie glances at me to see what I think of that. "Sure, why not?" I say, holding her gaze. She gets a slightly sick look, but nods.

"How awful are these kids that you need so many people to help?" Cozi asks. "I'm not the best person to help around little people."

Charlie's mouth tightens, but she says, "It's only one person that I babysit."

"Must be a holy terror," Cozi says before biting into the pizza that's been delivered to our table.

Charlie glances at me again, panic in her eyes. I drop my arm from the back of the bench to her shoulder and squeeze her. "It'll be good," I say, trying to infuse a positive tone into my voice. Truthfully I'm as worried as her—I don't want to see Charlie or Cora ridiculed.

"Thanks," she says quietly.

Cozi glances over at my arm, and I'm glad she doesn't have the power to burn me with her eyes. I remove my arm from Charlie's shoulder and put it back up on the bench.

❧

My phone buzzes two hours later when I'm lying in bed. It's a text from Charlie.

Is this a bad idea?

I know exactly what she's asking.

No. It'll be fine. Of course I have no way of knowing if that's true.

Will you still be my friend if no one else is?

I stare at my phone. There was a time when the easy answer to that was no, absolutely not. I'm not outright cruel to others, haven't bullied anyone since I gave up fighting others to contain it to the ring and my dad. Helps with the popularity thing. But I've never befriended anyone who couldn't help my social status.

Don't worry, they aren't that shallow.

It's not an answer, but an avoidance.

Should I pretend you don't know her?

She's giving me an out, a way to save face and go with however the crowd feels. But of course Cora knows me, and I doubt she knows how to pretend. Besides, she might need someone else in her corner.

No. Cora won't know how to pretend.

I can talk to her.

I think about Charlie sitting on Cora's bed, reading a book, singing to her during certain parts, telling her mom she loves her and receiving the same sentiment back. Charlie worrying about being there in time to tuck her mom into bed, a reversal of traditional roles. As if I'd know anything about that.

I said no. It's fine.

K. See you tomorrow.

See ya.

I tuck my phone beneath the mattress—the only place I've found to keep it safe from Dad. Why he never thinks to look in the most obvious place is beyond me, but whatever. I close my eyes, ready to drift into sleep when the door to the trailer slams open. He's bellowing my name. Guess it would have been too much to ask for a Friday night off. I keep my eyes closed, hoping he'll come in, see I'm asleep, and leave. Fat chance.

My bedroom door slams open as loudly as the trailer door previously. I hold still, waiting. And then he's on me. This time, I don't wait for the invitation to fight back.

FORTY
CHARLIE

My mom is contentedly playing on the playground. There are a few kids with her, but they seem to accept her easily enough. Now if only my friends will, too. I'm sitting on a bench where usually it's parents waiting for their kids. I breathe a sigh of relief when I see Benjamin coming across the expanse of lawn from the parking lot.

"Hey, new girl," he says when he nears.

"I'm not really new anymore," I say as he sits next to me.

"True. I'll have to think of something else to call you, then." He looks up. "Where's Cora?"

I point. "She's playing over there." He looks where I indicate. "She hasn't seen you yet or she'd be over here. I told her you were coming and it's all she could talk about all morning."

Instead of his usual flippant remark about how all the girls love him, he instead looks at my hands. Weird, but whatever. Then he reaches over and takes them, prying them apart.

"Been wringing your hands?" he asks.

"What? No, why?" I look down and see how bright red they are. "Maybe," I concede.

"Charlie, you don't need to be so nervous. You were worried about how they'd react to your diabetes, and it was no big deal. This is going to be the same."

"It's just . . . you don't understand."

"Understand what?"

"Okay, it's bad enough being a child born of, you know, a pig who did violence to your mom."

He tips his head. "Why do you have such a hard time calling it what it is?"

I shake my head, "Because if I put a name to it, it brings up an image that I can't deal with. I imagine my mom . . . and him . . . I just can't."

"Okay, no worries." He squeezes my hands lightly. "I won't say it then, either. Do you think anyone is going to care about that? You had nothing to do with it."

"I know that. It doesn't change that he's my biological . . . whatever." I refuse to give him the name *dad*. "But, you know, that would be enough to not want people to know. But then my mom . . . and it's horrible, Benjamin. Horrible that I feel this way. My aunt felt this way and because of her, my mom was sent away where he was able to do that . . . and I judge her for it, always have. But I'm no different, because I hide her, too."

"What about at your other school? Didn't people know?"

"No. From the time I was little my grandma told me she was Cora to others, but I could call her Mom at home. It didn't occur to me to think it was strange, I just did it. I remember by the time I realized the reason I called her Mom at home was because she *was* my mom, I knew enough to know how people felt about others like her. We had some kids at school from special ed. Kids could be cruel, say mean things to them and about them. It didn't take that long for me to figure it out, that I couldn't say she was my mom. I hated that. I hated who I was, the lie I felt I had to live."

Benjamin's jaw tightens and a look of understanding floods his eyes. "So why now?"

I sigh. "I guess I just . . . I don't want to turn out bitter like my aunt. I don't want to live with the guilt of not doing everything I can for her, to make up for . . ."

"Charlie," he says, turning toward me. "*You* don't have to make up for your dad—your biological donor." He changes his words when I open my mouth to protest. "You have *no* responsibility in that. As for your aunt, she seems like she's trying to make things right. And you, Charlie, *you* take care of your mom, you love her, you sing to her when she asks you to, you bring her to the park. You're *not* like your aunt in that way. So even though it sucks that she had to deal with . . . that . . . I'd guess that she wouldn't change it if she had the power to because she wouldn't want you gone from her life."

Tears threaten and I blink them back. I'm *not* going to cry. Then Benjamin pulls me into his arms, and I can't stop a few from falling.

"Let me ask you something," he says, his voice rumbling through his chest that my ear is pressed against. "Are you worried more about what your friends will think of you, or her?"

I push back to look at him. He smiles and wipes my cheeks with his thumbs.

"Her," I say. "She's already been hurt . . . I don't want her to be hurt again."

"Well, if they say anything mean, then they're just jerks who don't deserve to be your friend."

"Easy for you to say. You get to keep your secret."

His face changes, becomes hooded at my words. "What do you mean?"

"I mean, no one still knows where you live."

His face clears. "I'm not as brave as you," he says. His eyes lift and he glances over my shoulder. "They're here."

I quickly scrub the rest of my tears away and turn to look. Clearly all four of them rode together since they're walking together. I stand and wait for them to come.

Cozi reaches me first. She turns to look at the playground. "So which kid is yours?"

"Wait," Phoebe says. "You have a kid?"

"No, she just babysits . . . right?" Alexis asks, and I realize they thought maybe they were coming to meet *my* child. They must have discussed it after I left Tony's last night.

"I don't have a kid of my own," I say, rolling my eyes.

"Then why are we here?" Phoebe asks.

"Because she babysits some demon kid and she wants to see how we deal with it for her psychology report," Cozi says with a grin.

"That's also not true," I say.

"Prince Benjamin!"

All heads turn toward the voice calling from the playground. I wonder how Benjamin will react as the adult-size child bounds across the playground toward us.

"Princess!" he yells back, waving a hand.

I sneak a quick glance at the others and stifle a laugh at their expressions. They aren't looking at my mom at all, but at Benjamin, as if he's grown a second head. Daniel's look is probably the most stunned, his jaw gaping the most.

My mom stops just short of Benjamin, shyness suddenly suffusing her body. She crosses her hands and ducks her head. Benjamin steps forward, puts his arm around her and kisses her forehead.

"Hi, Princess Cora," he says.

She looks at me with a wide smile. She thinks she's whispering even though she's saying quite loudly, "Charlie, he called me *princess.*"

"I heard," I say. I turn toward my friends again. "Guys, this is Cora. She's . . . my mom."

Now their eyes are drawn from their gape-jawed staring at Benjamin to gape-jaw stare at me. Cozi is the first to recover. She steps forward and holds out a hand. "Hi, Cora. My name is Cozi."

My mom takes her hand, though her grip is more like a handhold than a handshake. "Cozi isn't a name," she says. "It's what happens when you're all cuddled on the couch with a blanket getting warm."

Cozi laughs, as do the others. But not cruelly, not like I worried.

"That's true," Cozi says. "But it's also my name."

"You have black hair and brown skin," my mom says. Jeez, I forgot she could be so blunt. I should have told her about Cozi. She doesn't see many black people. Then she says, "My friend Jemmy has skin like your color."

"Does he?" Cozi says.

"Not really," I say. "He's Indian."

"Close enough," Cozi says.

"Your hair is pretty," my mom says. Well, she's not lying there. Cozi has amazing hair.

"That's only because she has extensions put in every month," Phoebe says, stepping forward to take Cozi's place.

"What?" I'm surprised. Somehow I didn't think a Jehovah's Witness . . . I stop myself. I shouldn't judge what I don't know.

My mom holds hands with all of them, calling them by slightly different names: Bebe, Lexus, Dan-Dan. And she decides to call Cozi "Blanket." With relief I watch as they all laugh with her, not making fun, but rather having fun. Somehow it's decided we should all play on the playground with her. My mom's in an absolute frenzy of happiness having so many new friends.

And not once do any of them say anything mean, not even Daniel. I watch to see if any of them are pretending, but they seem to be genuine. It should make me feel better, I know, but instead

I feel guiltier that I spent all those years hiding her when I didn't need to.

"Can they come to our house and play?" my mom asks when I tell her it's time to go. I was at the park with her an hour before they arrived, and it's been another hour. Two hours at the park is about as long as my mom can handle.

"You need to take a nap, Mom," I tell her.

"What if we come over when you wake up and we can have pizza or something?" Alexis offers.

Benjamin and I both groan loudly. "Please, no pizza," I say.

"Well, something else then," she says.

"You don't have to do that," I say.

"She knows that," Cozi says, hooking her arm through Alexis's. "Neither do we, but we're still coming."

We all pile back into our cars and drive to my house. I finally convince my mom to take a nap by threatening to send everyone home if she doesn't. If she skips a nap, she'll fall asleep by seven tonight, and then she'll be awake at three in the morning. Once I convince her, she lies down and falls asleep rather quickly, just like always. I wish I had that ability instead of lying in bed and worrying about everything.

I close her door and go onto the back patio where they're all sitting in a circle, talking about the football game the night before. I take the empty seat, which happens to be right next to Benjamin. I'm not sure if it's because Benjamin made sure I had a seat next to him, or if it's because none of the others want to sit by him, except Daniel, who's on his other side.

"Why didn't you tell us?" Alexis asks when there's a lull in the conversation. She's looking directly at me.

I shrug. "I wasn't sure how you'd react."

"I like to think I'm not so shallow I wouldn't be your friend because of your mom," Phoebe says.

"I don't think you're shallow," I say. "I just . . . I don't know. I don't know my reasons anymore."

"Kind of like the diabetes thing," Alexis says. "Why didn't you tell us about that, either?"

"It just seems like a strange conversation starter," I say. I lower my voice. "'Hi, I'm Charlie. I'm diabetic and my mom has the mental capacity of a six-year-old.'" There's silence, so I say, "Sorry. I should've trusted you."

"No, you shouldn't have." I glance at Daniel, surprised by his words. "I mean, you'd just met everyone, how could you know enough to trust any of us?"

"Yeah, he's right," Alexis says. "Sorry."

"You obviously have met her," Cozi says to Benjamin, who's sat silently throughout.

"Yeah, I have. I showed up at the park one day and Charlie was there with Cora and Naomi."

"Who's Naomi?" Phoebe asks.

"My aunt that we live with."

"You live with your aunt?" Phoebe says.

I blow out a breath. "Hi, my name is Charlie. I just moved here from Idaho, because my grandma, who raised me, passed away. And I can't take care of my mom alone. They won't let me since I'm not eighteen yet, so we're living with my aunt, who smokes by the way, which drives me crazy. And she owns Dayspring, the care center where my mom now lives during the week. And before you ask, no, I don't have a father—not one I want to claim anyway. He's in prison, not for what he did to my mom, but for something else, which really ticks me off. He should be there for what he did to her. And I think I'm dating . . ." I glance over at Benjamin. He smiles and reaches for my hand. "I think, anyway."

"You might've just decided you're dating me, but I've been dating you for a while," he says.

"No way!" Phoebe says.

"Way," I say sarcastically. "And I know you guys think I'm crazy, and maybe I am," Benjamin lifts his brows at that, "but I'm dating him anyway."

Silence greets my pronouncement, but Benjamin just keeps smiling at me, leaning back on two legs of the chair.

"Hi, my name is Cozi, and I'm a Jehovah's Witness." At Cozi's words laughter breaks the awkward silence.

"Hi, Cozi," a few of the others say, as if we're at an AA meeting. This brings more laughter.

"Hi. I'm Phoebe, and I do think you're crazy." She pauses, then shrugs. "But maybe it'll be okay." She turns a dark look on Benjamin. "I swear, though, if you hurt her, I'll poke your eyes out."

"You should leave his eyes," Daniel says. "The girls love his big, green eyes—actually, you might be on to something. That's a good threat."

Everyone laughs again, including Benjamin. "Glad I can be here for your entertainment."

"Hi, I'm Daniel, and I really wish Alexis would date me." He leans toward me. "Any advice?"

Alexis blushes, and I lean toward Daniel. "Just be a nice guy. Kinda like this one," I say, thumbing toward Benjamin.

"Nice?" Daniel asks, one brow lifted. "Benjamin? That's what worked for him? Being *nice?*"

Everyone laughs again, and Benjamin drops the front legs of his chair with a thud. "Ha, ha," he says, voice dripping with sarcasm.

"Hey, having a party?"

I glance up at Naomi's voice. She stands in the doorway.

"Oh, um, hi," I say. "These are my friends." I introduce everyone to Naomi, except Benjamin, of course, who smiles charmingly at her, asking her about her day, winning her over just as he always does. She offers to pick up Chinese for dinner, and since everyone seems to agree that Chinese from Wong's Café is just what they were craving, I don't argue.

I worry a little about what they'll think when they see my mom eat. She might have the mental capacity of a six-year-old, but she has the eating manners of a two-year-old. But as I glance around at the group, laughing and talking easily, making jokes at one another's expense, I begin to think I really have nothing to worry about.

I look at Benjamin. Maybe he needs to realize he doesn't have anything to worry about, either.

FORTY-ONE
BENJAMIN

It's after ten when everyone finally leaves Charlie's house. I think they would've stayed longer, but Cozi's mom called for her to come home, and since Alexis was everyone's ride, they all left. Cora went to bed at nine, and Naomi, who'd eaten dinner with us, disappeared around the same time. The last hour has been torture. I just want everyone to go so I can talk to Charlie.

When we're alone, Charlie refuses to look at me. She starts stacking the chairs we'd been sitting on, and picking up empty soda cans. Busy work, so she can avoid the subject I'm sure she knows I want to talk about.

"Charlie," I say, taking her hand and removing the crushed can from it. I set the can down without relinquishing her hand. "That can wait."

She freezes, still not looking at me. The silence extends, and she says, "I'm sorry, Benjamin. I know I shouldn't have . . . I mean, I know how you feel about—"

I place a finger beneath her chin and gently force her head up, though she keeps her eyes downcast. "If you know how I feel, then you'd know I'm glad you said it."

Her eyes lift to mine. "But I thought you had this rule about two dates."

"Guess I've broken that. How many dates have we been on?"

"None, really," she says.

I hold up one hand, and hold a finger to tick the dates off. "There was the movie—"

"That was paying a bet," she says.

"And the restaurant," I add, ignoring her argument.

"Homework," she says.

"And the park—twice."

"Once an accident, the second, homework."

"Then there was our first date, watching the traffic."

"Homework," she refutes. "Followed by a seizure."

"Oh yeah, and the hospital," I add. "Plus the gym—"

"Another paid bet," she says.

"Nope. I lost the bet, you didn't have to go. That makes . . ." I glance up as if doing the math then bring my gaze back to her. "More than two."

"You're crazy, Nefer," she mutters.

"Maybe," I say. "Maybe we both are. *Maybe* we should quit arguing about what's a date and what isn't, and just kiss."

She smiles. "I like the way you think."

I lean down, pressing my mouth to hers. This time, maybe because she's decided it's official, she doesn't hold back. Her arms come up around my shoulders, her fingers threading in my hair. I pull her close, amazed at the sensation that riots through me whenever I kiss her. Heat swirls through my gut, my chest tightens almost painfully, my head feels so light I think it might just bob away like a balloon.

It's unlike anything I've ever experienced with any of the other girls. With them it was all about my enjoyment. With Charlie, it's all about her. My chest continues to tighten to the point where it begins to feel like a panic attack, so I pull back.

"Wow," she breathes. I grin at her and she smacks me lightly on the chest. "You're pretty proud of yourself, aren't you?" she teases.

"Oh yeah," I say, sounding like the Kool-Aid dude. She laughs and bends to pick up the soda can I set down. I help her clean up, and then we watch some corny eighties movie. Charlie sits next to me, leaning into my side with my arms around her. I guess the movie's not so bad.

When I'm leaving, I kiss her again. She stands on the porch while I make my way to my car. Just before I get in, I yell, "Hey, new girl?"

"Yeah?"

"I agree. Wow."

She grins as I climb into my car. It sputters to life, and I pull away from the curb, away from Charlie and the little fantasy bubble we created, back to my reality.

❦

"Nefer, get in here when you're dressed!"

I glance at Coach, who stands in the doorway to his office.

"Sure thing, Coach," I say, drying off from my shower. I pull on gym shorts and an oversize tank, slipping my feet into my flip-flops. I sniff my jersey. Not too bad; it can wait for a few more days. I avoid washing my uniform whenever I can because it's not exactly a joy with our occasionally working washing machine and rarely working dryer.

I shove my equipment into the locker, and grab my duffel before heading to Coach's office. I knock and enter when he calls me in.

"What's up, Coach?"

"Have a seat," he says distractedly, waving his hand toward a chair that's stacked with books. He doesn't often call people in. I'm curious about why he called me, but not worried. I know there's no way he's cutting me, and my grades are still top-notch. I grab the books and set them on the floor next to the chair while he continues to scribble away in his playbook.

Finally, he looks up. "Good game Friday."

"Thanks." I doubt that's why he called me in.

"You played extra hard. Any reason why?"

Charlie's face flashes in my mind. I admit I was showing off a little for her. No way am I going to admit that here.

"No reason, just wanted to win."

Coach leans back in his chair, folding his hands across his deceivingly rounded belly. I know that his belly is a solid mass of muscle. "No one there you wanted to impress?"

I freeze. How could he . . . there's not a chance he could know. "No, sir."

"You didn't see the scout in the stands?"

I sit up straight. "Scout?"

"That's right, Nefer. The University of Florida scout came to watch you."

"Me?" I squeak, then clear my throat. "Me, Coach?"

"He's not the only one interested, either."

I'm stunned. Scouts. That means there's a very real chance I can go to a *real* university rather than the local community college.

"I thought maybe you'd heard and that's the reason for the hard playing."

I huff out a laugh, slumping back in the chair. "No, sir, I had no idea."

He leans forward, placing his elbows on his desk. "Here's a bit of advice for you, son. Don't take the first offer. Play them against one another to get the best deal you can. Don't accept anything less than full ride with room and board."

I stare at him, unable to process his words. "You think . . . you think I'll have offers? Plural?"

"I do. You're a great player, Nefer. I've never coached anyone better. Have you thought about what school you'd like to attend?"

I look at him and grin. "Whichever one is farthest from here."

FORTY-TWO
BENJAMIN

A re you sure about this?" Charlie asks.

"No," I answer honestly, dropping my head onto my hands, which clench the steering wheel.

"You don't have to," she says, lightly touching my back.

I suck in a deep breath. "Yeah, I know."

I'm still not really sure how I came to this, why I felt the need to bring her here. I glance up at my house—my trailer, I should say. I know the old man won't be home for several hours because he's working in Springville, which is a two-hour drive away. It's three now, and if he gets off at five, he won't be home until seven.

I glance toward the sky. *Please, God. If you exist, keep him away for a little longer.*

"Let's go." I get out and walk around to open her door. She looks at me nervously. I don't blame her. I'm a wreck, and I'm sure she's picking up on my vibes. I still have no idea why we're here, other than I think if I'm going to fake the whole boyfriend thing, it seems that bringing your girlfriend to your house should be something you do.

We enter through the side door. As usual, it's not locked. It doesn't need to be. We have nothing of value, and any crook worth his salt would know that by looking at the outside of the house. When we step inside, I try seeing it through Charlie's eyes.

I cleaned up this morning before school, washing the dishes and wiping the counter and table. It's shabby, no doubt about that. And it's as opposite as Charlie's living conditions as possible. She stands inside the door, looking around. I step past her, taking her hand.

"C'mon, I'll give you a tour. Kitchen," I say, waving my hand around.

I lead her through the kitchen into the small living room with its tattered couch and old console TV. "Living room." Without pausing, we head down the narrow hall past the scrawny bathroom—laundry room combo, into my small room. Once inside, I step back and lean against the wall to watch her reaction. "My room."

My bed is nothing more than a lumpy mattress on a rickety bed frame and box springs, covered with a plain, dark-brown blanket. I have a small table next to my bed that holds an alarm clock and flashlight. My dresser is trashed, probably older than even my dad, if I had to guess. Nothing is on top of it.

Charlie steps over to the dresser, then turns to face me. I can see she's trying to avoid looking pityingly at me, but she's losing that particular battle.

"It's a little different from where you live, huh?"

She smiles thinly. "A little." She glances around again and says, "It's not what I imagined."

"Worse than you imagined?" I guess.

"No, not worse. It's just . . . I guess I expected your room to be filled with shelves of trophies and framed awards. Maybe posters on the wall—at least a Def Leppard one." She smiles. "I'm just surprised that everything is so . . . empty."

I look around the room. She's right, it's definitely empty. Kinda like me. I walk over to my closet and, pulling a key from my pocket, unlock the padlock that holds it closed.

"You lock your closet?" she asks, sounding as if the words are pulled from her against her will.

"Everything I have of value is in here," I say. I don't tell her that the threat of having my stuff taken or destroyed doesn't come from an outsider, but rather from the thing I call Dad.

I open the door and Charlie steps up to me, curiosity in her eyes. I pull the string beneath the bare light bulb, throwing minimal illumination into the corners. I push my shirts to the side, revealing a set of shelves against the back wall.

"Those are all I have," I say, pointing to the six trophies there. She steps into the closet and squats, looking closely at them. "Move the one on the middle shelf and look behind it."

She sets it gently on the floor and I smile. The trophies are hardly fragile, and don't hold any value, sentimental or otherwise. She reaches back and pulls out my iPod. She begins scrolling through it, reading the names.

"Taking Back Sunday, Fallout Boy, Brand New, the Used, My Chemical Romance . . . Do you have anything *good* on here?" She looks up at me with a wide smile.

"Hey, those are all good."

She turns back to the iPod with a laugh. "I know. Wait, here we go. Linkin Park, Paramore, the Cranberries, Evanescence, Aerosmith, Heart, Poison, Guns N' Roses, Queen, Josh Grobin—*Josh Grobin?*" Her eyes fly to mine, mocking shock blaring up at me.

I swipe the iPod from her. "That's not something I listen to regularly. It's only for—" I clamp my mouth shut and she laughs.

"Oh, I get it. It's to help with the *lo-o-ove* life." She turns and flops down onto her butt, still in the closet.

I grimace. She's right. How lame is that?

"So where's your Def Leppard music?"

"On its own playlist," I say, scrolling back to the home page and showing her.

"Had me worried for a minute, Nefer." She glances behind her at the shelf. "Anything else I should see in here?"

"Not unless you're interested in dust bunnies."

She places the iPod where she got it, then picks up the trophy and sets it back on the shelf. Suddenly she moves the trophy next to it and pulls out the picture frame.

"Who's this?" she asks, turning it to the light. She grins. "Is this you, Nefer?"

She glances up long enough to see me nod. I watch as she traces my six-year-old face with a finger. "I assume this is your mom," she says, pointing to the dark-haired woman who is indeed my mother. "You have her eyes. But who's this? Do you have a sister?"

She's touching the photo over the image of the little girl who can't be mistaken for anything but my sibling since we look so similar. When I don't answer she looks at me.

"I did," I say shortly, turning away from her. "We should go."

I can hear movement as she replaces the photo and trophy, then she's up on her feet and out of the closet, closing it behind her. She moves behind me and snakes her arms around my middle, leaning her head against my back. The gesture is somehow more intimate than the kisses we've shared. I rub my hands lightly on her arms. My chest tightens and I quickly step away, not wanting to have a panic attack in front of her.

"We should go," I repeat, leading the way out of the room. My chest still feels tight and I take deep, inconspicuous breaths, trying to control it.

"We can hang out here for a while," she says as we reenter the kitchen. "It's not as bad as you think."

Yeah, well, that's because the old man isn't home yet. Of course I don't say the words.

"It's not that good, either," I say. "I'd rather not stay here."

She shrugs. "Okay. Do you want to go back to Naomi's?"

"Don't you mean your place?" She shrugs again. Once we're back in the car, I say, "Why don't you ever talk about your grandma? She raised you, right?"

Charlie looks out her window, silent for a few minutes. I wait.

"It's still too raw," she finally says. "Why don't you ever talk about your sister? Or any of your family, for that matter?"

Touché.

"I live with my dad," I say. "No one else."

She looks at me. I don't meet her gaze. Thankfully, she lets it drop.

"Why do you do that?" she says a few minutes later.

I glance at her, thinking she's going to ask about my family again. "Do what?"

"Rub your chest like that, like you're in pain."

I drop my hand. I hadn't realized I was doing it.

"I don't know," I say. "I just had a little . . . indigestion, I guess."

"Indigestion? You're seventeen. You're not exactly an old man."

"Maybe it's an ulcer or something."

"Well," she says, "you should probably go to a doctor then. You're a little young for that."

"You wanna go see Cora?" I ask. Anything to change the subject.

She smiles. "Yeah, I do. It'll make her day to have her prince show up."

"That's me," I say. "Prince Benjamin of the trailer park."

FORTY-THREE
CHARLIE

I lie in bed, listening to Def Leppard with my headphones, staring at the ceiling. I can't get Benjamin's place out of my mind. It's not the trailer he lives in, which is falling down as much inside as out. I mean, I'm aware that there are poor people who live differently than I ever have. I know how blessed I am to have what I do. It doesn't bother me that he lives in basically a hovel, because it's beyond his control. I feel bad that he does, but I don't judge him by it.

It's his *room*. That big, blank, empty space that should be the place he uses as a refuge. It's the place that should reflect who he is. But there was nothing—no posters, pictures, clothes scattered on the floor, anything at all that would give insight into who Benjamin Nefer is. He has everything important to him locked up in the closet. Again, not that big of a deal. He lives in a rough neighborhood, so it makes sense he'd lock up his valuables.

It's the fact that the items in his closet that mean enough to be locked up could fit in a small box. A few trophies and his iPod. Only one photo, which he keeps hidden in his closet rather than out on a shelf where he can see it. And a small pile of papers that caught my curiosity as much as the picture, but that I didn't think were any of my business. Still doesn't curb my curiosity about what they were. Otherwise, the whole room was stark, barren, looking more like a ghost town or something than a teenage boy's room.

His reaction to the photo has me wondering as well. Did his mom and sister die? Or did they leave? Whichever, it seems too painful for him to talk about. I have to admit, I'm extremely curious.

I roll onto my belly, propping my chin on my hands. There's so much about Benjamin that just seems . . . not quite right. Little things. He's the most popular guy in school, athletic, honor student, always dressed like he lives in Naomi's house more than his own. Then he goes to the boxing gym to get pounded on a regular basis. I totally don't understand that. He works at a pizza joint, lives in a rundown trailer with only his dad, and doesn't date girls for more than two dates—present company excluded—leaving a trail of broken hearts in his wake.

I stand and move to the window, plopping onto the window seat. That last thought opens a whole new set of questions, the biggest of which is: why me? Why am I the one he breaks the pattern for? There's nothing particularly special about me. Alexis is much funnier than I am. Phoebe is prettier. Cozi wouldn't give him the time of day no matter what unless he converted to Jehovah's, and even then she probably wouldn't, so I know he wouldn't even try with her. The school is full of girls who are cuter, smarter, funnier, and more fun than me. So . . . why me?

That's the million-dollar question, isn't it?

෬ඁ

"So, how're things going with Daniel?"

Alexis and I are sitting in my room, listening to music. Not Def Leppard, since she claims to hate all eighties music. Whatever.

She glances up at me from the magazine she's flipping through on the bed. "Not really *going*, per se."

"Oh. You don't like him?"

She slaps the magazine closed then flops back on the bed. "I *do* like him. That's the problem."

Sitting in the window seat, I pull my legs up, wrapping my arms around them as I scrunch my face at her. "Okay, I'm confused. You like him so you don't want to date him?"

"Yes," she groans, pulling a pillow over her face. She throws the pillow violently to the side and sits up, all in one motion. "It's because I like him that I don't want to date him."

"Well, that makes complete sense now," I say.

Alexis grins. "I know, it doesn't make sense. But because of *who* he's friends with, I'm a little worried that—" She stops speaking and shoots me an apologetic look.

"It's fine," I say, lifting a hand. "I'm aware of the history."

"Anyway," she continues. "What if it's all another game? I can't . . . I mean, I don't want to risk it again. So I think I'm just going to date a bunch of guys and not get serious with anyone."

I stand and walk to the bed, sitting next to her. "That's gonna *kill* Daniel." I look at her and we both burst out laughing. I shake my head. "But, honestly, it's probably pretty smart."

She shrugs. "Maybe. Maybe not. But it's what I'm gonna do." She blows out a breath. "What about you? What's the story there?"

Now it's my turn to shrug. "I know what you think of him, and if I were in your shoes I'd probably think the same. But, I don't know, with me he seems different . . ." I trail off, realizing how lame my words are, as if I'm so special I could change him.

"He *is* different with you," she agrees. "I mean, at first I think it was just because you wouldn't date him. But then, something changed. He doesn't treat you like he treats other girls."

"What do you mean?"

"I mean, he always treats girls like they're trophies or something." The vision of trophies hidden in his closet flashes through my mind. She continues, "He's not really genuine with them, you know? Super attentive and all, but it somehow feels forced. But with you, he's just more . . . natural. It's like he really cares about what you're saying or what you think. And when I saw him with your mom . . . honestly, you could've knocked me over with a feather. Who knew Benjamin had compassion in him?"

I smile when I think of him having a tea party with my mom and some of her friends at Dayspring. I'll never tell anyone about it, promised him I wouldn't, but still, the memory warms my heart.

"I worry sometimes, though," I say.

"About what?" she asks distractedly, paging through the magazine again.

"That this is just some grand scheme of his to prove that he *can* get me, before he, you know, does the same thing he did to you."

She tosses the magazine aside again and turns her attention to me.

"I mean," I continue, "when he smiles, there's just something . . . I don't even know how to explain it. It's like the smile never quite reaches his eyes. He smiles a lot, and laughs, but his eyes almost seem . . . empty. Or maybe not empty, maybe just—"

"No, you're right," Alexis says. "Empty describes them perfectly. I've noticed it before, but didn't quite know how to describe it. Wonder why?"

"Maybe it's all those poundings he takes at the boxing gym." I laugh, but wonder how much of it's the truth.

"Have you ever watched him? Box, I mean."

"No. I went with him once, but he just worked out."

"Showed off, you mean," she says.

I shrug. Maybe he was. I feel like I know a lot about Benjamin, and that he's probably shown more of himself to me than anyone else. But I also think there's a *lot* I don't know, things he keeps to himself. When we were at his place he didn't want to stay long, as if he didn't want to be there when his dad came home. Maybe his dad has some kind of "no friends" rule and that's why no one else has been to his house.

"Why does he do it?" she asks.

"Boxing? I don't know. Seems like he gets plenty of exercise with football. I don't understand the appeal of having someone hit you hard enough to leave bruises. Wouldn't that hurt?"

"Maybe he's a masochist," she says.

"That's sick," I say, tossing a pillow at her.

"You're the one dating him," she teases, flopping back onto the pillow.

❧

"Wanna do some deliveries tonight?" Benjamin asks. It's nice of him to offer since he's told me that's where you make the most money on tips. Serving pizza inside doesn't even pay as well because it's mostly kids from school who come in, and they're not exactly the best tippers. We're crazy busy tonight, though, so it's probably best to get the new girl out of the restaurant and let the more experienced workers keep the flow.

"Sure," I say, a little nervous about finding addresses.

"There are two deliveries to do right now. Don't break any laws or anything, but try to get them there as fast as possible. Better tips that way. The addresses should be on the receipts over there." He points to another counter.

I get the slips of paper and look at them, sure that I can find them both. Luckily the city is laid out in a block pattern, streets mostly running north-south and east-west, with coordinating numbers. Shouldn't be too hard to find.

I take the two insulated bags, double checking that everything is inside. Chelsea gives me two magnetic signs to stick on the sides of my car. I suppose that's less humiliating than a lighted sign on top. After making the first drop—and getting a nice eight-dollar tip—I begin searching for the next address.

When I stop directly across from Benjamin's place, I double check the address against the receipt. Definitely the right place. I look over at Benjamin's and see that it's dark. Guess his dad isn't home. I also doubt I'll get much of a tip at this place.

I carry the pizza to the door and, after failing to find a door-bell, knock. Thirty seconds later an extremely overweight woman answers the door. I give her the total, then wait while she moves back inside to get her wallet—as if she didn't know she had a pizza coming. While waiting, a car comes slowly down the road and makes a wide turn into Benjamin's driveway. Curious, I watch the occupant exit the car.

It's a man and I wonder if it's Benjamin's dad. Hard to tell from this distance. He's tall, at least as tall as Benjamin, I think, if not taller. He has messy, dark hair, though it's not curly like Benjamin's. His skin looks like it might be even darker than Benjamin's, but in the shadows it's impossible to tell. He stumbles, and with a shock I realize he's drunk. Drunk and yet clearly he'd been driving his car. He stumbles against the side of the trailer as he makes two attempts at opening the door before finally getting it on the third.

"Shame, isn't it?"

I jump at the sound of the woman's voice behind me. She's watching the man and shaking her head.

"Is he like that often?" I hear myself ask.

Her eyes come to me as the man enters the house. "More often than not. How he hasn't killed anyone in that car yet is a mystery to me."

"Have you ever . . . called the cops on him or anything?"

"Not for that," she says. "By the time they'd get here he'd be out of his car and there's no proof he was driving. But I've called them a few times when the fighting gets too loud."

I swallow the knot that suddenly forms in my throat. "The fighting?"

"Wife finally left him after too much of it, I heard. That was, oh, probably a decade ago. Left them two kids there. Then one day she came back and got the girl."

"She—" I have to swallow the dread again. "She only took one of the kids?"

"Left the boy. Guess she figured he was big enough to take care of himself. He's a handsome one, that boy. Seems like a good kid. I only hope he escapes without turning into his daddy. Not likely, though. Kids tend to follow in their parent's footsteps, right?"

Do they still fight? I think the question but don't voice it. I don't want to know. It seems like an intrusion, already knowing what this woman told me.

"Here's your pizza," I say, passing the boxes to her, accepting the payment and two-dollar tip. Walking back to my car, I'm shaky. I think about all the bruises I see on Benjamin, and wonder how many of them come from the boxing gym, and how many of them don't.

FORTY-FOUR
BENJAMIN

Sitting in Charlie's kitchen doing homework has become almost normal. Last night after Charlie came back from delivering pizza, she was especially quiet. I wondered if something had gone wrong on one of the deliveries, but she assured me all was well, and then did deliveries for the rest of the night, which didn't give me much time to talk to her.

"Big game Friday, huh?" she asks.

I haven't told her about the scout that Coach told me is coming—one from Notre Dame, where I'd really like to play. The game is against our rival. I'm not sure why I haven't told her—or anyone—about the scout. It's enough pressure knowing he's coming, I guess, without having others scrutinize my playing. So other than Coach, no one knows.

"You gonna be there?"

"Of course," she says, snuggling next to me. She's still for a few minutes while I absently rub her arm. Then she sits up. "I want to come to the gym with you again."

"Why?" I can't figure out any reason she'd want to. She hated it last time.

"I want to watch you actually box."

"Thought you didn't like it. Thought it was too violent and all."

"It is," she says, dropping her gaze to her hands. "But I just thought if I actually see you doing it I might understand better."

"Let's go now," I say, fully expecting her to back out.

"Okay." She surprises me.

"You wanna change and spar with me?"

"No way," she laughs.

"Chicken?" I ask.

"I'm intelligent," she says.

"Are you saying I'm not?"

She kisses me. "You're one of the smartest people I know . . . except in that part of your brain that avoids danger."

"Ha, ha," I mock, unable to suppress my grin at her laughter. "Fine. No sparring with me. You could work out with me, though, while I warm up."

She runs upstairs to change and we leave for the gym. It's pretty dead at the gym, but that's usual for this time of the day. Most of the people who'd come to the gym are working now and will start filing in within the next hour or two.

She checks her blood sugar, then unclips her pump, wrapping the tubing around it and putting it in her bag.

"Isn't that bad? To have that off?" I ask.

"No, not for the short time we'll be here. Plus, exercise drops my levels, so it's better to not have it on for a while so I don't get too low. I'll check myself again soon to make sure I'm okay."

It worries me for her to take it off, since I know it's the thing that keeps her alive. But I guess I don't really know enough about it to have much of an opinion. I'll just have to trust she knows what she's doing.

Charlie shadows me through my warm-up and she even goes after the punching bag for a bit, and though she's a little clumsy, she manages pretty well. The speed ball punches her back in the face

229

so she gives up on that piece of equipment quickly. I slowly lead her around the gym until we're next to the ring. I look around me overdramatically.

"No one to spar with," I say.

"I'm not getting in there," she says, holding her gloved hands out to me to unlace.

I lift my own gloves and shrug. "Sorry, my hands seem to be full."

She wrinkles her nose at me. "You had that guy over there put them on you." She lifts a hand toward the office, where one of the trainers talks on the phone. "Have him take them off."

I ignore her and climb into the ring. I begin hopping from side to side, and then weaving as if avoiding punches. Charlie laughs.

"Do I look ridiculous?" I ask.

"Yes," she affirms with a nod.

"Then get in here with me so I don't."

"I'm not going to hit you, Benjamin."

"Of course not. I'm too quick." I throw a few quick jabs, still performing footwork around the ring.

"And I'm not going to let you hit me, either."

I stop moving and drop my hands. I'm sickened by her suggestion that I would hit her as visions of my dad laying into my mom try to creep in. I shove them away. "I would never do that, Charlie."

Her eyes drop, and then, as if my words decide her, she climbs up next to the ring. I hustle over and hold the ropes for her to climb through.

"I'll just show you how it works," I say. "Do what I do."

I begin moving again and she shadows me, though ungracefully, which makes me grin. After a few minutes she catches on so I begin circling the ring, facing her. She does the same, staying on the opposite side. I throw some punches into the air in front of me.

Charlie does likewise, but they're weak, and would probably hit below her opponent's belt. I grimace.

"What?" she asks defensively.

"That's a low blow," I say. Not understanding, her eyebrows scrunch. "Let me show you."

I move behind her. "Okay, put your arms against the inside of mine." When she does, I moan loudly and she immediately moves away from me. I burst out laughing, "Sorry, just kidding. Couldn't resist. Come back."

She narrows her eyes at me but then moves back. I show her the level at which she should keep her hands and how to throw a somewhat effective punch. Then I move opposite her again.

"Okay, now throw a punch right here," I say, hitting my chest with my gloves.

"No!" She pales. "I'm not going to hit you, Benjamin. I told you that."

"Relax," I say, winking at her, trying to diffuse her panic. "I'm going to show you how to block. You won't actually hit me. I promise."

She stares at me as if trying to decide if I tease her. Suddenly she brings her hands up and swings clumsily at me. I easily avoid it by feinting back. With a grin, I begin dancing again, circling her. She throws a few more weak punches.

"C'mon, Charlie, give it some effort. I *know* you can hit harder than that."

"And how would you know that?" she asks.

"Because I've seen how strong you are at work. You lift things that give some of the guys trouble."

"But not you, right?" she mocks.

I lift my arm to the side and flex my muscle. "Nope, have you seen these guns?" I kiss my bicep as she throws a harder punch.

I block it at the last second. "See what I said? You don't stand a chance."

"You're so arrogant, Benjamin," she accuses, though her eyes sparkle in spite of her refusal to smile.

"I have reason to be, don't you think?"

The more I goad her, the harder she tries. She begins swinging harder, faster, and I show her some blocking moves, explaining as I block her punches. That only makes her try harder. Finally she lands a punch against my shoulder.

"Ugh!" I groan, dropping to the mat.

"Oh, no!" she cries, dropping next to me. "I'm so sorry, Benjamin. Are you okay?"

"Come closer," I groan, waving her in. She leans down and I quickly wrap my arms around her, rolling so she's beneath me, laughing.

"You're such a jerk," she mutters.

"Yeah, yeah," I say, kissing her willing mouth. I love the way Charlie melts beneath me.

"Well, you never thank me like that for hitting you." We both jerk at the masculine voice, and I look up to see one of my regular sparring partners standing outside the ring. Bowman looks like a boxer—flat nose, drooping lip on one side. A little like Rocky, to be honest.

"All you have to do is ask, Bowman, and I'll be glad to accommodate." I grin at him and he throws his head back and laughs. Charlie struggles beneath me, her cheeks pink, and I let her up, standing as well.

"You wanna spar with me now?" Bowman asks her.

"You couldn't take her punches," I say. "She knocked me right down."

"That's not exactly hard to do," Bowman returns.

"Says the guys who hasn't learned how to cover his face."

"Hey, I figure getting hit a few times makes me look more manly for the ladies," he says, placing his gloved hand beneath his chin and turning his head side to side.

Charlie shakes her head as she ducks beneath the ropes. "There's something wrong with you guys."

"Come on in and let's show Charlie how it's done right," I say to Bowman.

"Only if you promise not to kiss me."

He joins me in the ring and we spar for a while. Bowman tries extra hard, showing off for Charlie, I'm sure. Of course, I'm doing the same, so I can't blame the guy. Then I make the mistake of glancing at Charlie and see how pale she is watching us. All it takes is that one second of distraction for Bowman to get in an extra quick jab at my face. I feel my lip split beneath his glove.

A worried look flits through Bowman's eyes. I can see he's about to apologize, so I quickly smile and say, "How about that? First time you've actually landed a punch."

"Dude, I'm . . ." I flick my eyes toward Charlie. I can't have him letting her know that it's unusual to get this kind of injury when sparring. Thankfully, he shrugs. "First time in the last thirty seconds, you mean."

I look at Charlie, see that she doesn't look too happy. I wipe the blood from my lip with my glove. "Guess I'm done for tonight," I tell Bowman.

"Until next time," he says, holding his gloves toward me. I hit them with mine and grin at him.

"Next time you won't get so lucky."

"No luck, friend. It's all skill."

I roll my eyes and exit the ring. Using my teeth, I unlace my gloves and grab a towel. Charlie's silent while I unlace her gloves, refusing to look at me.

"Charlie," I say, still kneeling in front of her. I wait for her eyes to lift to mine. "It's nothing. Doesn't even hurt."

Her gaze drops to my lips. "Looks like it does."

"It doesn't, I promise." I could tell her what pain really is, that a split lip is nothing in the scope of damage that can be done by a pair of fists.

"You're bleeding."

"Does it make me look tough?"

She huffs out a laugh against her will and pulls the towel from my hand, dabbing it lightly against my lip. "Makes you look like an idiot who just willingly got punched." Her words have no venom behind them. I close my eyes to the feel of her gentle touch across my mouth. Almost immediately my chest begins to ache and I realize I'm on the verge of a panic attack. I quickly open my eyes.

"Wanna kiss my ouchy?" I tease, pushing the claustrophobic feeling away.

"Your ouchy?" She laughs. "Are we three?" But then, without waiting for an answer, she leans down and lightly presses her lips against mine, kissing the edge where the wound is.

"You're something else, Charlie," I say.

"Yeah, well, I like you."

"Lucky me," I murmur, lifting one corner of my mouth before giving her a kiss that should obliterate any idea of my lip hurting.

FORTY-FIVE
BENJAMIN

Dread fills my stomach as I pull up outside my house and see the lights on and my dad's car in the driveway. Him home this early—before midnight—is never a good thing, and almost always means I can count on excessive anger. I've had an amazing day with Charlie. I *really* don't want a run-in with him to ruin that. Maybe I can sneak in without him seeing me.

Maybe pigs can fly.

I glance at my face in my rearview mirror. My lip is a little swollen but not bad. If my dad wants to get into it tonight, I'll have to protect my face. Charlie was with me at the gym, so she knows how minimal the damage is. I blow out a breath, and open my door. I glance across the street and see Mrs. Davis slowly carrying a trash bag out to the curb. She stops when she sees me, staring. I lift a hand and wave at the obese woman. She doesn't return the gesture, simply continues to stare so I turn away.

Up the three steps, I place a hand on the trailer next to the door, leaning my head against it. I'm tired of this. Beyond tired. Exhausted by facing him more often than not, of having to take a beating until he commands me to fight back . . . and then having to fight back, knowing I can't win, knowing there's no end until he decides there is.

I draw in a deep breath, lift my head, and open the door, stepping across the threshold. I'm met immediately with a fist to the face, reopening my lip, blood spurting from the fresh wound as my head jerks back. Before I can recover, his other fist lands a hard blow to the side of my head, making my head spin a little. I throw my fists up to block him and he gets in a hard kidney blow, taking my breath away.

"Fight, you spineless coward," he bellows. His breath reeks of alcohol, worse than usual, and I know I'm in trouble. I manage to land a fist to his jaw before he does something he hasn't done before. He fists his hands in the front of my shirt and, lifting me from my feet, flings me back out the door, crashing through the screen. My legs hit the low railing, which doesn't stop or slow my flight but serves to flip me feet over head so that I land on the gravel drive headfirst.

The world wavers and for a moment I'm unable to move. Then I hear him stumble out the door and I scramble to my feet. I don't quite make it upright but I do manage to get high enough to tackle him. Together we smash to the ground, but his bulk wins and I find myself beneath him as he pummels my face over and over. I bring my arms up, trying to protect myself, but it's a lost cause. I give up and try to find an opening to hit back. Clenching my fists together I jab upward and catch him beneath the chin. Instead of knocking him over as I'd hoped, it enrages him and he barrels to a stand, using his feet as weapons against my stomach and ribs. I curl in a ball and hear screaming. Is it me? No, not me. I can't draw a breath deep enough to scream.

It's the neighbor, Mrs. Davis, holding her phone and screaming about the police. That catches his attention, and with one final vicious kick at my head that causes darkness to swirl at the edges of my vision, he heads for his car, slamming the door and peeling out of the driveway, nearly taking out the mailbox.

"Sweetie, are you okay?" Mrs. Davis's bulk squats next to me, her hand rubbing my arm, phone pressed against her ear. "We need an ambulance, quick," she says into the phone.

"No," I say, lifting a hand. I cough and blood gurgles from my mouth. "No ambulance." It's too late, she's already spouting her address into the phone. For one wild second I hope they won't be able to find me since she gives her address, as if they couldn't just look across the street and see us. I try to push to a sitting position, but another coughing fit grips me and I collapse back to the hard ground.

FORTY-SIX
CHARLIE

As I stare at Benjamin, another tear slides down my cheek, joining the rest that wet my face. Benjamin's own face is nearly unrecognizable. Swollen, blackened, his lips bleeding . . . there isn't anything there that is Benjamin. I'm used to looking at him with some bruising and occasionally a fat lip, but this is something different.

Daniel called me as soon as he heard. By the time I got to the hospital after school, Benjamin had been moved from the ER to a regular room and was sleeping. They drugged him up pretty good so he hasn't woken up at all since I've been here.

His dad did this to him. His neighbor, Mrs. Davis, the one I delivered the pizza to, called for help. I remember her words about all the fighting. I stroke a finger lightly along his swollen cheek. How often does this happen? My stomach twists at the thought of Benjamin having to live with someone who beats him up regularly. All his injuries aren't from the gym. Some of them, maybe, but not all. Probably not most.

I stand and walk to the window, but unable to stay away I return to his side, taking his hand in mine. I rub my thumb lightly across his injured knuckles and notice the scars that mar his hands beneath the fresh cuts. How often have I held hands with Benjamin? Not once did I notice the scars. Even if I had, I would have thought they came from boxing, even though he wears gloves to do that. It would never have occurred to me to think they came from fighting with his dad.

I remember his dad, the one time I saw him, drunk and stumbling up the driveway. Mrs. Davis had said something then about it being a common thing. A tremor runs through me at the thought of what Benjamin's life must be like. I guess I'm not the only one with a monster for a father.

Benjamin's hand squeezes mine and I gasp, looking at him. His eyes are still closed so I quickly swipe my face dry. "Benjamin?" I ask softly.

He groans and his eyes slowly open. He looks confused about where he is. Then memory seems to return and a hardness enters his expression. Only now do I realize how often I see that hard, closed-off expression on his face. I've gotten so used to it, it seems almost normal.

"Hey, new girl," he says wryly, his tone at odds with the anger that flashes through his eyes.

"Hey, Nefer." I pause, not sure how to proceed. I decide to go for flippant. "You look like crap."

Benjamin smiles at that, grimacing a little as the action causes him pain. "Now you're just lying. That's not possible."

"Well, at least your ego isn't broken."

Panic crosses his face and he pulls his hand from mine, a painful breath escaping him. "Do I have something broken?" He begins moving various parts of his body.

"Relax, you're still intact." I place a calming hand on his arm and he stops moving. "They said you're lucky."

He chokes out a cynical laugh. "You call this lucky?"

I shrug. "No, of course not. But it could be worse, they said. Your ribs are really bruised, and Daniel said they told him you're lucky they aren't broken. And according to your neighbor, Mrs. Davis . . ." I swallow quickly, forcing a sob to stay down. "She said he was—" Another swallow. "—he was kicking you and you're lucky he didn't break your arm, and he threw you off the porch and you're lucky you didn't break a leg." I shake my head. "So I guess they think you're lucky. I don't."

Benjamin's eyes stay firmly on me through my words, eyes blank. Then he turns away and stares out the window. His jaw ticks a few times before he speaks. "If he screwed up my game this week, I'll kill him."

His words send a chill through me—he sounds as if he means it. I ignore the last part of his sentence, not wanting to know if he *does* mean it, and say, "You can't play this week, Benjamin. I mean, look at you, you're all beat up—"

His head jerks toward me, his words biting. "I *will* play this week, and I *will* impress the scouts who are there! I won't let him win, Charlie. Do you get that? Do you get how important this week's game is?" He's halfway risen from the pillow, wincing in intense pain.

I clench my teeth, not wanting to give in to the emotion that threatens to overwhelm me. Benjamin is a little frightening in his anger—and yet, I get it. I would do anything to make sure my mom was safe. Benjamin will do anything to get out of his situation.

"I get it, Benjamin," I finally say. "Then you better take it easy and do anything and everything your doctors tell you so you can be in the best shape possible."

He relaxes back against the pillow and nods once.

"Benjamin, do you . . ." His eyes come to me and, chicken that I am, I glance down at my hands. "Do you have somewhere you can go?" When the silence becomes uncomfortable I finally dare a peek at him. He's watching me expressionlessly.

"I'm going home."

"What?"

"I'm going home."

"But, you can't—"

"Why can't I? This was a . . . an anomaly. Not normal. It's not going to happen again. He's going to feel bad, apologize, then go overboard trying to make it up to me. And in a few months, I graduate, leave for college, and never look back. Simple."

I'm at a loss for words. I can't believe he'd even entertain the idea of going back home, but his words tell me this isn't the first time this has happened to him, being put in the hospital—or at least being badly beaten. I try to find words to argue, to try to persuade him to leave, but he's looking at me with such certainty that I can't think of anything that doesn't sound trite.

"Charlie," he says, taking my hand and bringing it to his mouth, almost managing to not wince as he presses his battered lips to my skin. "Don't worry about me, okay? I swear this is not a big deal."

"Don't worry?" I repeat. Like I'm not going to lay awake nights worrying for his safety.

He squeezes my hand and his voice drops, almost warningly. "Don't worry. I'm fine now, and I'll be fine later."

I stare at him, wondering not for the first time just how well I really know Benjamin Nefer.

FORTY-SEVEN
BENJAMIN

Sitting on the edge of my bed, I push a hand through my hair, ignoring the twinge of pain it causes across the top of my head. Charlie finally left after I convinced her I was going to survive without her here—and after I made her believe my lies about my father's regret. I really just need some time alone to regroup.

The cops came after she left. My dad was arrested and is sitting in jail, waiting for me to press charges. I refused. They assured me he'd be out within a day if I didn't. I kept my mouth closed. They were frustrated, pleading and badgering, but finally left when I still refused to say anything. I'm smart enough to know that even if I press charges, he won't be in for that long. And I'm not so dumb that I don't know how much worse it will be once he gets out if I *do* say anything. It's already going to be bad enough just based on the fact that he was arrested.

This is not a part of my life I ever thought Charlie would be privy to—or anyone, for that matter. I now know that Daniel is the one who called Charlie in the first place, and I wonder how many people at school know. Anger rushes through me at the thought of facing all their pitying faces, anger I usually reserve for *him*. There isn't that much time left at school in the whole scheme of things, but enough time that it could be miserable with their sympathy, enough time that I might not be able to hold it together long enough to escape before I explode.

Just when I think things can't get worse, Coach walks in. I groan inwardly, dropping my head and taking a bracing breath. Then I meet his gaze unwaveringly. "Coach."

"Nefer." He thrusts his hands into his pockets and shuffles a bit. Great, that means I'm not going to like what he has to say. Coach is *never* unsure. "I'm sorry about . . ." He waves his hand up and down at my battered body.

I try to think of a flippant response but can't. Instead I say, "Sorry I missed practice today."

He makes a low sound in his throat, dropping his eyes. "Nothing to be sorry for, Nefer." He clears his throat, shuffles some more, and finally looks at me again. "Obviously you don't need to worry about the game Friday. I'll just have Ashford play—"

I push quickly to my feet and he stares, gaping. "Coach, no, I—I'm fine. I'll be there. I won't let you down."

"Nefer, I'm not worried about you letting me down. But, son, you can barely walk. Your ribs are bruised. One hit and you'll be out."

"I won't run the ball, I'll only pass. I can do this, Coach. Please. There are going to be scouts there. They can't watch me play if I'm not playing."

"Nefer, you're hurt."

"I'm okay. I'll *be* even more okay by Friday." I blow out a breath. "Look, if it's too much, I'll take myself out of the game. This isn't . . . it won't be the first time I've played when I'm hurt, Coach."

I watch as my words sink in, their meaning become clear to him, and then see the hated sympathy enter his eyes. But I'll bear it because it's that important to me to play for the scouts. I can't lose my ticket out of this hell. I watch until I see the beginnings of wavering in his eyes, and force my own to tear up. The tears don't mean anything, they're just the means to an end that I can use. My begging, however, that's genuine. "*Please.*"

"Okay, son, I'll let you play as long as the doctors say it's not a danger to you, and as long as I feel it's safe. But the second I feel it's not, I'm pulling you."

I nod, my shoulders relaxing. "Fair enough."

He nears and lands a heavy hand on my shoulder. I force myself not to wince. He gives a little squeeze, his mouth tightening. "Take care of yourself until then, Nefer. Maybe you should consider staying somewhere other than home."

I nod in agreement. "You're right, Coach, I'll see what I can do. Thanks."

After he goes, I call Daniel. He already knows I'm here, so there's no worry about having to explain why I am. He'll take me home without trying to talk me into staying somewhere else.

∾

"Wrap it tighter."

Daniel lifts a brow and smirks at me. "Any tighter and you're not going to be able to breathe, bro."

"It feels better when it's tight," I argue. "I won't be able to breathe if you don't make it tight as possible."

Daniel pulls the wrap on my ribs tighter. I don't want to show up for the game and have Coach see the black and purple of my entire right ribcage. I'm sure he'd prefer the team doc wrap me, but if it's already done what can he say? He won't know it wasn't done by one of the docs at the hospital. I'm already worried about my lightheadedness; don't want to give him any reason at all to pull me today.

I can see in Daniel's eyes that he doesn't think I should play today, either, but he won't say it. He's got my back, same as he always has. I don't deserve it, but I know I can count on him. I stand, tightly bound, which makes it bearable. Forcing myself not to limp, I follow Daniel out of his house.

When we arrive at the school, Coach takes me aside and offers to let me take it easy on warm-ups, but I refuse. I'm not sure what exactly the scout will watch for, and he might or might not be here. I'm not taking any chances. I won't risk anything that might keep me from getting out of here.

When finally we huddle for the first play, I feel like I've been beaten again. If the warm-ups can make me feel like this, I can hardly wait to see how the game goes. So much for college. I glance at the offensive coach. A passing play. Good. I can handle that.

Halftime comes eons later, and I drag my sorry butt into the dressing room, struggling to seem the normal amount of tired rather than showing I feel like I've just been hit by a truck. Leaning back against the locker, I take the time to catch my breath. My ribs are on fire. My cheek and eye throb from the pressure of my helmet. My head feels like it's going to explode.

"Doing okay, man?" Daniel asks as he slides down next to me.

I give him my best carefree grin and a thumbs-up. I don't make the effort to speak, saving myself for the second half. When Coach finishes half-yelling, half-encouraging us, Daniel jumps up and turns back, offering a hand to pull me up. I lock fists with him and let him do most of the work getting me upright. A look flashes through his eyes when he notices, but again, credit to Daniel, he doesn't say anything.

We run back out onto the field. The other team has the ball first, so I take the time to look up into the stands, searching out Charlie. She's been here since the beginning of the game, watching me intently. I know she's worried, another reason for me to make sure no one knows the pain I'm in. I raise a hand and she smiles, but beneath the smile her worry resonates across the distance, almost a physical touch. My chest tightens and, afraid I'm going to have a panic attack right here, I turn away from her.

An eternity later I glance up at the clock from the huddle. Seven seconds left in the game. We're on the twenty-one-yard line, down by four. A field goal isn't going to do it—we need a touchdown. I glance over at the offensive coach for the play and see the understandable frustration on his face. Normally we'd be well in the comfort zone of an easy win, but after the first half the other team seemed to realize how much my guys are protecting me. They know I'm the weak link, so they aren't even bothering to try to sack me. They concentrate solely on my runners and receivers. The best way to win is for me to run the ball—something they won't expect. But Coach has clearly given instructions to avoid that, if his short argument with the offensive coach is any indication. My own frustration ratchets up to anger.

I watch as the offensive coach's shoulders droop and then he gives the signal. A passing play. Of course. It's a guaranteed loss. I turn back to the team, and reluctantly give the play. We line up and I examine the defensive line in front of us. They know exactly what we're going to do. If my ribs weren't to the point of extreme pain, I'd draw a deep breath and blow it out in frustration. I have to be satisfied with a head shake.

I line up for the snap, and as I'm making the call, I do something I've rarely done before. I call an audible. Daniel, standing to my left, whips his head toward me, but before he can do anything, the ball is in my hands. I back up as if to pass, then when I see the path, I tuck and run. Ten steps and my lungs are on fire, my ribs feeling as if they'll explode past the tight wrapping. Thirty steps and my vision swims. I focus intense concentration on the goal line.

Memories of my father's meaty fists pounding me, his feet contacting with my body violently enough to cause me to be in this position, flood my mind. I use the rage that streams through me to keep me going, to keep me upright. From my peripheral I can see a purple jersey coming my way. Instead of heading away from him, I change course and barrel into him, using the momentum to thrust him into the end zone with me.

We end up in a tangled heap in the end zone, and my yell of pain is covered with the sounds of the cheering crowd. I lie there, unable to move as my team piles into the end zone with me, pulling me to my feet and hoisting me up. For the first time I'm grateful for the action, otherwise I'd just be laying on the cold grass like an idiot. My jaw is clenched so tightly my teeth hurt, but it's the only way to keep back the screams and tears that push behind my helmet.

They carry me all the way into the dressing room, dropping me on my feet. I collapse on the bench, barely managing to stay in an upright position. The offensive coach is beaming, but Coach looks like a storm has been captured behind his eyes. He glares at me, and I wait for the explosion. It never comes. Guess he'll wait till later, when no one is around. Lucky me.

It's only through sheer determination—and a little help from the guys pulling off my helmet and shoulder pads—that I manage to get dressed. By the time I do I feel like I've done a decathlon.

"Wanna go celebrate?" Daniel asks. Everyone is still riding high on the adrenaline from the win.

I shake my head. "Nah, I think I better get home and get some rest. I work tomorrow."

Worry crosses his face again, and I turn away. I don't want to see it. "Need some help getting there?"

"No, Charlie will take me."

He hesitates, but some of the guys start jostling him, trying to get him to go with them. He relents. "Okay, if you're sure."

"I am." I lift my fist for a bump, that simple action taking monumental effort. "I'll talk to you tomorrow." He hesitates again and I nod my head in the direction of the door. "Go."

After a few seconds, he nods and then jogs to where the others wait. I sit, trying to muster the effort to stand. Coach rounds the corner. *Fantastic*. He comes and sits next to me.

"You know, kid, killing yourself to impress a scout doesn't do any good when you can't play another day."

"I'll be able to play, Coach. I just need a few days to recover."

He sighs and shakes his head. "I shouldn't have let you play. I knew better."

"Coach . . . I'm going to be straight with you. If I don't get a scholarship, I don't have a chance for college. I don't have a chance to get out of here. So yeah, I'll do whatever to get that chance." I look at him. "Including take care of myself, so they won't send me home from college after the first practice."

He sighs again and pats my knee. "Okay, son. I don't like it, but I guess I don't have to." He holds a finger up. "But I swear, Nefer, if I think you're endangering yourself for one second . . ."

I grin at him, hoping it looks like a grin and not the grimace it feels like. "I hear you, Coach, and I give you my word I'll take care of myself. I won't do anything that'll cause harm." *Except live with my father*.

He nods and heads back toward his office. After a few minutes, I shove myself up off the bench and make my way from the dressing room. Charlie waits for me, just as I knew she would. She smiles, and suddenly I feel a little better.

"Hey, new girl, glad to see you didn't abandon me."

"Well, I considered it," she teases. "But then I figured I'd have to pay for my own dinner, so I waited."

It's painful, but I manage to get an arm around her shoulder. I pull her close for a kiss, which she enthusiastically returns. She puts an arm around me and together we walk to her car. If I'm leaning on her a little more heavily than usual, she either doesn't notice, or just doesn't say anything.

"Where are we going?" she asks once we're in her car.

"How about if we just go to your place and chill?"

She shoots me a look, but shrugs and pulls out of the parking lot. I really just want to go home and crawl into bed, but that would be too clear an indication of how much I'm suffering. So I'll sit on her couch and watch movies with her, and pretend.

FORTY-EIGHT
CHARLIE

I can't help but envy the careless happiness of my mom, and all of her friends, as we sit circled around the large dinosaur display in the middle of the museum. A few Dayspring residents listen with rapt attention as the curator talks about the different types and characteristics of some of the dinosaurs, but most of the Dayspring group is just staring in awe at the towering resin model of a tyrannosaurus rex, which occasionally moves, sending them into delighted giggles. I'm just grateful they're all sitting in place and we haven't had to chase anyone down for the past thirty minutes.

I've been volunteering as a chaperone for the field trips as often as possible, when it doesn't interfere with school or work. I also spend what time I can at Dayspring to be with my mom, but usually end up helping out. I considered asking Benjamin to volunteer as well, but since the incident with his dad, he's been . . . distant.

He tries to hide the pain he's still in, but I see it clearly. He pushes himself at football practice, and has been picking up extra shifts at work. I don't see much of him other than at lunch or between classes, and then he barely looks at me.

A tugging on my leg catches my attention, and I smile at my mom as she points up at the dinosaur model, which is once again moving. I sigh silently. Dinosaurs are definitely not in my realm of interest. How much more information can we possibly be told? I'd rather be up, moving around, exploring.

My phone vibrates and I pull it from my pocket, glancing down. As I read the message from Alexis, I suck in a breath. Dread flows heavily from the top of my head to the ends of my toes. I quickly cover my mouth with my hand to stifle the loud sound of my deep breathing.

I glance up to see Mariam looking at me questioningly. *I have to go.* I mouth the words but realize she can't see since I still have my hand plastered there. I pull my hand down and almost repeat the sentiment, but catch myself.

I glance at the group sitting on the floor. Sixteen adult children, with only me, Mariam, and one of the nurses for chaperones. There were supposed to be two others, but at the last minute one came down with the flu, and the other was in the ER with her little boy for stitches from a fall. There hadn't been time to call anyone else in, so we decided to just make do.

I can't leave. Panic sweeps through me, nearly pushing me to my feet and out the front door. It's an effort to remain seated. Mariam still watches me so I shake my head. I can't go. The thought swirls in my head, tangling with the even louder sentiment that I *need* to go.

My mom laughs and the sound cuts through me. Selfishly, I wish, yet again, for a mom who could take care of *me* at a moment like this instead of the other way around. Immediately guilt joins the argument in my mind, tears pricking the corners of my eyes.

I lift the phone and read the message once again.

Daniel just told me that Benjamin's dad was killed in a car accident. Come quickly!

Forcing myself to drive the speed limit takes monumental effort as I try to get to Benjamin's house. When I do turn in to the drive, I see it's empty. Still, I run to the door, pounding.

No answer.

The handle twists beneath my hand, but the house is as empty as it feels from the outside. Even though I know it's useless by now, I press the send key on my cell to redial Benjamin's number yet again. After seven rings his voice comes on telling me to leave my number.

Where is he?

No one knows where he is. Daniel had driven him to the hospital to identify the body, and then gave him some time alone. No one has seen him since.

I drop onto the couch and bury my head in my hands. Vaguely I realize this is only my second time at Benjamin's house, and my first time sitting on his couch. I've been everywhere I thought he might be—this is my third try at finding him at his house. Several other people are looking for him as well. I don't know where else to look. So I sit, frozen with indecision.

After some time passes, I lift my head and look around. The house is as cold and empty of homey touches as I remember, just like Benjamin's room. No photographs, no family heirlooms, nothing to indicate a family lives here.

There's an old TV in front of me and a small table between the couch and a battered chair. It's not exactly a pigpen, but not really clean, either. Beer cans litter the table, a few fallen to the floor. A pair of shoes are kicked carelessly next to the TV. Not Benjamin's. A T-shirt lies across the arm of the chair. I stand and look around. The floor needs to be cleaned, the sink is full of dishes, and the counters look like they haven't been wiped in a while.

An hour and a half later, the house is cleaned, mopped, and vacuumed. I even organized the fridge, though there was so little food in there it didn't take much time. I ignored the amount of cans and bottles that filled the trash can as I carried the bag out-side. I stayed out of the bedrooms, feeling those were too intimate for me to clean, but the bathroom was fair game—and in desperate need.

Now there's nothing left to do but wait. Every fifteen minutes or so I've checked in with everyone, and still no sign of Benjamin. My worry is turning from the need to help Benjamin to worry that he's hurt somewhere and in need of a very different kind of help than I was thinking.

Thirty more interminable minutes pass pacing a hole in the already threadbare carpeting before a car turns in to the driveway. I rush to the window and see Benjamin's car. Relief tidal-waves through me. Then my stomach tightens and suddenly I think I shouldn't be here. What was I thinking, coming into his house? He'll think I'm invading his privacy. And he's right—I am. I should have waited for him to call. I should sneak out. Stupid! Of course he knows I'm here—he pulled in right behind my car.

He comes in through the door, the dusky light barely showing him. I didn't even realize I've been sitting here in the near dark until now. I stand stock still, unable to move as he stands silently in the doorway, looking at me. I can't read his expression.

"Charlie." My name is a gasp, a choke, thrust out on a surge of grief and I move, rushing to him.

He pulls me tightly against him, his arms crushing my ribs, his face buried in my neck as sobs rock him. We sink to our knees, Benjamin rocking me. Or am I rocking him? My tears match his own. Grief is something I've known my share of, and I know there aren't words to make his grief any less, so I don't try to comfort him with talking. I just hold him and cry with him.

Finally, his shoulders stop shaking beneath my hands, though he doesn't relinquish his hold on me or lessen it at all. We sit in silence as the darkness deepens around us.

"I really don't know why I'm crying," he finally says, his voice low and hoarse.

"Benjamin," I murmur, "your dad . . ." I can't bring myself to say the words.

He pushes away from me and stands, pulling me up with him. "I didn't even like him, let alone love him." Anger lines his words now. "He was a loser in every way. I can't remember him ever being anything more than a drunken, angry man who liked to bully everyone in his path. It's his fault that she left, his fault that Mia was taken—"

He picks up a chair and throws it across the room, where it crashes violently into the wall, sheetrock raining down on top of it as it hits the floor. I flinch at the action, surprised but not scared. Somehow I know Benjamin won't hurt me. Apparently he doesn't know the same thing if the look he turns on me now is any indication. He looks as surprised as I am, but also filled with guilt and self-recrimination.

"I'm sorry," he says, holding a hand toward me.

I quickly put my hand in his. "Don't be," I say.

My words seem to open a floodgate of fury as his eyes narrow and his mouth tightens. His hand squeezes mine painfully, but I force myself not to grimace or pull away. "Don't say that," he growls through gritted teeth. "Don't ever excuse someone's violence." He leans closer. "Do you hear me? Promise me. Promise me you won't ever do that again."

"Benjamin, you're hurting. Your dad just . . . it wasn't violence, it was just a reaction."

He thrusts my hand away from him and strides across the room until he stands in the living room before swinging back toward me. Pointing, aggressiveness in his wide stance and hunched shoulders, he repeats himself. "*Never*, Charlie, never say it's okay. It's not okay, not *ever!*" He drops his hand and turns away. "You sound just like her," he mumbles.

I'm stunned by his reaction. My mind whirls as I realize what his life must have been like, why his mom and sister left. Why was Benjamin left behind? Sympathy for what he's been through, for all of the things I can only imagine but won't ask him about, tightens my heart. I walk up behind him and slide my arms around his waist, leaning my face against his back. "I promise."

He turns and takes me in his arms again, leaning his cheek against the top of my head. "What are you doing to me, Charlie?" he whispers. Seems like a rhetorical question, so I don't answer. After a few minutes he lifts his head and looks around. "Did you clean my house?" I just shrug and the edges of his mouth lift. It's the first smile I can remember seeing on Benjamin that seems as genuine as it appears. Strange that it would come now, on the heels of his father's death.

FORTY-NINE
BENJAMIN

Charlie sits at the table with me and eats frozen burritos, never once grimacing in disgust at them. She doesn't press me for information, just tells me about her day at the museum when I ask. I know she'll never ask, but she deserves to know, so I tell her the gruesome details.

My dad, drunker than usual, got into his car. I don't know where he was headed, but it wasn't toward home. Wrapped his car around a tree. No seatbelt, ejected through the front windshield, he wrapped around the tree as well. Died on impact. I'm just grateful he didn't take anyone else out with him. That's a miracle in itself.

I didn't try to explain to Charlie my unexplainable crying. I haven't cried since I was a kid. I certainly didn't cry for the jackass who I haven't cared about for years. If anything, his being dead is a relief. After she leaves, I pace in my blissfully empty house as I try to figure out where the tears came from. I really have no idea. I just walked in and saw Charlie there, standing in the middle of my house, waiting in the near darkness for me, twisting her hands in worry for me, and something inside broke.

My chest tightens as I remember—another panic attack just beneath the surface. I sit down and take some slow, deep breaths and the truth hits me like a sucker punch.

Not a panic attack. Panic, yes, but panic caused by what my heart apparently knew before my head just figured it out.

Love.

I love Charlie.

I drop back against the couch. *No.* No, it's not possible. I don't *love.* Not her, not myself, not anyone. I can't. To love someone requires feeling, and I repressed that ability in myself a long time ago.

Or did I?

I groan and look for something to throw. There isn't anything, not a single can or bottle. Charlie cleaned them all up as she waited. Stumped in my intention, I sink back again. I *can't* love anyone. I won't. Love doesn't fit into my plan. Football and college, getting out of here. That's my plan.

Protecting myself from ever being hurt again, from risking the pain that came from loving someone and watching them be hurt, watching them leave, feeling crushed as they walked away from me. Making sure I'm never open to that again—that's my plan.

And once I remember that, I know what I have to do.

&

It appropriately and with great triteness rains on the day of the funeral. *Funeral* is maybe too expansive a word since it's me, Charlie, Daniel, Alexis, Phoebe, and Cozi at the graveside. Might have been a few more friends from school if I'd told anyone, and probably even a few of my teachers. Definitely Coach. But I didn't want them here. Not a single soul who worked with him showed, or any of his bar cronies. Guess that says something as to the kind of person he was. As if I didn't know better than most.

Cozi says a prayer, then kindly reads some passages from the Bible about death and heaven, though I doubt this particular soul will see much of what she's reading about. I suspect he'll be a little toasty where he's going. Ten minutes and the whole thing is done.

The guy who arranged everything—paid for by a small life insurance policy my dad had through his work—offers to give me some time to say good-bye before they lower the coffin. I don't need it. What's there to say? *Thanks for being a jerk who couldn't show an ounce of kindness to your son after driving away your wife. Thanks for molesting your daughter, the only bright spot in our house, so that she left also. Thanks for beating the crap out of me on a daily basis.* I'm pretty sure I won't be having *Father of the Year* carved into his headstone. Or even the word *father* at all.

We head back to my house, and Mrs. Davis comes across the street, no small feat for her, to bring us a casserole. I'm not a fan of casseroles, but it's better than frozen burritos, so I thank her and find enough plates for everyone to have some. It's surprisingly good.

A couple of hours later, Charlie glances at her phone. "I need to go," she says, looking at me apologetically. "I promised my mom I'd come by before she goes to bed."

"I'll go with you," I say.

"Are you sure? It's okay if you don't want to after . . ." She trails off uncomfortably. Even now, Charlie can't imagine that I prefer the company of her undemanding mother over most people, and definitely over sitting here in this house that holds no good memories.

"I'm sure," I say, standing. Everyone else stands also, and after a round of hugs that I tolerate, we leave.

⚬

Sitting across the table from Cora, playing Candyland, I realize I'm going to miss her almost as much as I'm going to miss Charlie. She's my princess, after all.

I drive Charlie home, relieved that her aunt isn't there. We sit on her couch and I take a breath to begin. Oddly, I feel nauseated at the thought of what I have to do, instead of relieved like I expected. Still, it has to be done. Before it's too late.

"Charlie, I want to thank you for today," I begin.

She smiles at me, an open smile, just like always. It's never been a game for Charlie. It's never been anything less than what it seemed, and guilt worms into my brain.

"Of course, Benjamin. I'm just sorry today had to happen at all."

I know she's speaking the truth, because that's how she works.

"Listen, I wanted to . . . there's something we need to talk about. That I need to say, that is."

She puts her hand in mine, threading her fingers through my own. I nearly cave. But I can't. I have to do this. Otherwise everything I've built since the day my mo—since *she*—left will be undone.

"You can tell me anything, Benjamin."

I can't look into her eyes. I don't want to see the hurt I know is going to be there. I stand, pulling my hand from hers.

"This can't . . ." I turn toward her, but don't look at her. I wave a hand between us. "This isn't working."

Silence. Then, quietly, "What do you mean?"

I push my hands into my front pockets. "I mean, it's not in my . . . nature to have a girlfriend. I like to . . . you know, date around." I dare a glance at her, and she's staring at me, her eyes wide, mouth flat.

"Are you breaking up with me?"

I don't want to say the words, I really don't. Which is why it's so imperative I do. "Yes, I am."

Her eyes drop to her lap and she swallows loudly. "Can I ask why?"

"I just told you why. I mean, it's been fun and all, but—"

"Benjamin, if this is because of your dad—"

"This has nothing to do with him!" She jumps at my outburst, but still doesn't look at me. I sigh loudly. Why is this so hard? I've done it hundreds of times. "Sorry. I shouldn't have yelled. It doesn't have anything to do with him, Charlie. It's me. I feel . . . stifled." Her shoulders hunch at my words. "Look, it's just time, okay. I mean, I usually only go out with a girl twice. We went out a lot more than that, so—"

"So I should feel lucky?" Her gaze flies to mine, anger sparking. She shoots to her feet. "Seriously, Benjamin? You're going to try to tell me that what we have is the same as you've had with anyone else?"

"No." I turn away. "No, it's different. Like I said, I've been with you longer than I've ever been with anyone. And it was fun, right? But now it's time to move on." My words sound lame and completely unconvincing, even to me. So I'm surprised when she swings away and angrily stalks to the door.

"You should go," she says, opening the door.

"What?" I close my gaping mouth. Usually at this point I'm faced with tears and begging. Alexis's eyes flash into my mind again. *That's* what I expected, only on a larger scale. I thought Charlie felt something more for me . . . maybe that she even loved me.

"Just go," she says, her voice rough with anger.

I walk slowly to the door and step out. I turn her way, only to see the door closing, shutting her off from me. And then something happens I couldn't have imagined ever happening to me.

My heart breaks.

FIFTY
CHARLIE

Are you coming to lunch with us today?"

I barely glance at Cozi as I shake my head, pulling books from my locker. "No, I told Mrs. Rallison I'd help her grade papers. I brought lunch from home so I can eat while I work."

Cozi sighs loudly, rather overdramatically, if you ask me. "Charlie, you can't avoid him forever."

"I'm not avoid—" My voice catches and I grit my teeth. "I know, Cozi, but just . . . not yet, okay?"

She stands silently for a few seconds longer then says, "Okay. But tomorrow, all right?"

I don't answer, and thankfully she leaves without pressing me for a commitment. I blink a few times to rid my eyes of the tears that hover before closing the locker door and turning around. I lean heavily against it, jaw clenched. I can't pretend yet that I'm not bothered by being around Benjamin.

I head to Mrs. Rallison's room. She signs in to her computer and leaves me to correct yesterday's tests while she heads to the teacher's lounge. Guess it's a good thing I'm honest. Not long after I start going through them, Alexis ducks into the room.

"Hey," she says.

"Hey." I don't quite know what to say to her. She warned me—they all did. I should have listened to her particularly, since she was Benjamin's last victim. She sits down across from me and watches while I go through a few more tests. It's pretty simple since the computer does all the answer checking. I just have to manually enter the grade based on the percentage of correct answers.

"You know, you could just give people whatever grades you want," she says.

"Right," I laugh. "Mrs. Rallison always leaves me in here alone. Guess I have an honest face."

"Nah, she probably knows she can trust you."

I smile and shrug. "How's it going with Daniel?" I ask. She and Daniel are pretty exclusive now.

"Good. He's really . . . he's different than I expected him to be. Guess that shows me I shouldn't judge people before I know them, huh?"

"I guess." I pull up the next test and watch as it autocorrects. "Sometimes, though, people are exactly what they seem to be."

Alexis grabs my hand and I look up. "Charlie, I'm so sorry he did this to you."

I shrug again. "My fault. You all tried to warn me, and I didn't listen. I let him charm me." And then the floodgates open. I pound the desktop. "He's such a jerk! Why did I think I was any different? Do you know how many times I questioned, 'why me?' But I didn't want to look at that too closely, you know? Because the answer was obvious."

"What's the answer?" she asks.

"The answer is that I was just something new, someone who hasn't watched him do this to others over the years, so for him it was just a challenge, see if he could completely fool the new girl." My heart twists at the last words, his nickname for me. "And he did fool me, didn't he? Utterly and completely. I dared to think what we had was different—different from anything I've had before, different from what you guys told me. Like I'm something special. I'm so stupid!"

Alexis comes around the desk and hugs me. "You're not stupid, Charlie. Okay, well, maybe a little."

I laugh and lean away from her as she pulls a tissue from the box and hands it to me, getting one for herself as well. "Thanks a lot."

"Not for the reason you gave, though. Charlie, I've known Benjamin for a really long time. I've watched him go through all the girls. As you know, I *was* one of the girls. But with everyone else it was the girl who looked at Benjamin like he was the best thing since chocolate cake. Not with you. With you it was him looking at you like that."

"That's crazy. He doesn't even like me anymore. I don't think he ever did. What's so different about me that would make him like me more than any of the others?"

Alexis shrugs. "Maybe because you didn't just fall head over heels for him. I mean, maybe in the beginning it was just a challenge for him. But not after a while. I've never seen him look at *anyone* the way he looks at you. He's different with you. Better."

I drop my head into my hands. It'd be so easy to believe her. But if I do, it becomes that much harder to know he doesn't want me anymore.

"Can I ask you something?"

"Can I stop you?" I mutter.

One corner of her mouth lifts at that. "Did you ask him why? When he was breaking up with you, did you ask him why?"

"Yeah, he said he felt stifled, and that it was time."

"And did you ask him if that lame excuse was the truth?"

"I . . . no, I . . . no, of course not. He'd just buried his dad. Besides, it seemed obvious."

"What, that he'd just decided to dump you like everyone else, even though you guys have been together for so long? Charlie, this is why you're stupid, because you can't see him. You can't see *you*. Trust me on this. Ask him."

I shake my head. "No. It's his decision. He doesn't have to give me a reason . . . does he?"

Alexis stands and walks to the door. "Ask him," she says as she walks out of the room.

ⅭⅯ

As I exit the school, digging through my backpack for my keys, I bump into someone. "Sorry," I mutter as they steady me. I look up into Benjamin's face, and my heart skips a beat.

"It's fine," he says, his face tight as if I hurt him.

"No, I'm really sorry," I say, worried that I might have caused him genuine pain. "Did I hurt you?"

He smiles, that same empty smile he used to look at me with. "I'm not that fragile, Charlie."

"Oh, okay." An awkward silence descends and I turn away. I take four steps before I stop and swing back. He stands in the same place, watching me. I return to face him. "Can I ask you something?"

He glances away, but nods. "Sure."

"Why did you break up with me?" His eyes shoot back to mine. A slow, lazy grin turns his mouth up, but before he can give me the usual, sarcastic Benjamin speech he already gave me, I cut him off. "I know what you said. I don't buy it."

His jaw clamps as his mouth tightens into a thin line and he looks away again.

"I mean, I don't think I was imagining that things between us were . . . different. I think you felt something, too. I'm not trying

264

to convince you to change your mind, or anything. I just want the real reason."

His glare pins me in place. I'm surprised by the anger. "You want to know why?" He takes an aggressive step closer. "Because you're not good for me, Charlie. My life was fine. You had no right to come in and mess it up." My jaw drops at his words. How did I mess his life up? He leans toward me, and I take a step back from the passion emanating from him. "I'm leaving this hellhole as soon as I graduate to go to college. I don't have the time, or inclination, for a girlfriend when I'm just going to be leaving soon. Did you imagine this would last forever?"

I can't answer his question. I hadn't really thought about it. I hadn't looked that far ahead. Behind the anger, his words make sense. I nod and turn away again, but before leaving I say, "I miss our friendship."

I hurry to my car, wishing I can retract my words, wishing I can take back even asking him. It was better not knowing, because now there isn't any hope. I didn't realize I've been holding on to hope. Guess I'm wrong.

FIFTY-ONE
BENJAMIN

Charlie's words haunt me as I pace in my kitchen. I feel bad for hurting her, for only giving her part of the truth. But it's all I can give. I can't tell her what she's done to me. But her last words, *I miss our friendship*, nearly tore my heart out.

I miss it, too, but I don't know how to be her friend without loving her. Loving her is the one thing I really, really can't do. My phone vibrates and I glance down at it. Another voice mail. I look at the caller ID. The U of Michigan.

I've talked to several universities about playing football for them. It's what I've always wanted, increased a hundredfold. I'd only ever hoped for *one* school to want me on a scholarship. Now, I have my choice of several. So why do I feel so empty?

The sound of a car in the gravel outside gets my attention. I hope it isn't Charlie—even while my heart begins pounding at the thought that it *might* be her. I step to the kitchen window and I see a strange car pulling in front of the trailer. I watch as a woman wearing a business suit gets out. Her dark hair is pulled back into a tight bun and she's wearing sunglasses. Probably a rep from another school, though usually it's the coach who contacts me.

I glance around the place, see that it looks clean if not exactly nice. I can't do anything about that. With only me living here, it's been easy to keep clean since my dad decided to dance with the tree.

She knocks and I pull the door open, plastering a smile on my face. The woman looks at me and slowly pulls her glasses from her face. My smile fades as I stare into eyes that are identical to my own. She's just as beautiful as I remember, as if time has stood still for her. She's definitely dressed better than I remember, and I can't see a single bruise or cut on her as I'd come to expect as a boy.

It feels like an eternity passes as we stare at each other, my stomach flopping around in my gut, my heart frozen into silence. It's my most prized dream and worst nightmare rolled into one and standing on my porch.

"Ben?"

Her voice startles me and I jerk. "I go by Benjamin," I say roughly. The response is automatic. I haven't allowed anyone to call me Ben since she left so long ago.

She clears her throat and nods. "Can I come in?"

I want to say no, shove the door closed in her face, but I also don't want the nosy neighbors watching, so I step back, shoving my hands into my pockets as she passes me.

She stands in the middle of the kitchen, looking around. "Hasn't changed much," she says.

I shrug and move into the living room. She follows.

"Why are you here?" I ask. "There isn't any money."

Hurt crosses her face, but I steel myself against it. I don't care.

"I didn't come for money, Ben . . . Benjamin."

"Then what?"

"I came . . ." She sighs and sinks down onto the couch. "Please sit."

I'm not going to sit on the couch with her, and that only leaves Dad's chair. I'm not going to sit there, either. I'll stand.

"No thanks, I'm good."

She sighs again. "Okay." Awkward pause, then, "I wanted to come see you."

"Oh really?" I keep my voice calm, controlled. Cold. "You haven't come in all these years, but now . . . now that he's gone you come. Why the sudden urge to see me?" My phone vibrates at that moment and it's suddenly clear. She's heard about the scouts. She thinks she can somehow profit from that.

"Benjamin, there are things you don't know—"

"I know enough. Listen, lady." Her forehead creases with hurt as I call her that. "I didn't need you before. I don't need you now. I'm not giving you anything, and you're not going to be a part of my future. I'm eighteen. I don't need a parent."

She clasps her hands together so tightly that her knuckles turn white. She clamps her lips together and as she does a scar appears above her lip. The memory of how she got that scar, not long before she left, comes rushing back. The feelings from that day—fear, loathing, shame at not being able to protect her—assault me, and I sit in his chair because I'm afraid my legs won't hold me any longer.

"I'm not trying to . . . interfere. I hoped . . ." She gulps as if she's trying not to cry. I did it enough in my young life to recognize the sound. "I'm so sorry, Benjamin. I shouldn't have left you here. I should have found a way . . ." She holds a pleading hand my way. I don't take it. "He threatened to kill us all. And he would have, he would've tracked us down and followed through on it."

I have no doubt she speaks the truth. Still. "And you didn't think to call the police?"

"I called them more times than you can imagine, Benjamin. They would arrest him, and a day later he would be out." Remembering his arrest after his assault on me, and my refusal to press charges knowing it would only anger him, I know she's telling the truth again. I understand her reasoning. Doesn't make it easier to stomach. She was the *mom*. It was her job to protect us. "It didn't take long for me to realize that it only made things worse when he was arrested. I was *trapped*. I didn't have anything, any money. I had no one and nowhere to go."

"But you did," I argue. "You left."

"It was the hardest decision I've ever had to make, Benjamin. I thought if I could just get away, and earn some money, I could come back for you both."

"You came for Mia," I say, her name getting caught on my tongue.

"You know what he did to her, right?"

I nod tightly. Of course I knew—I was the one who called her. I went to the school counselor, and told her I needed to talk to my mom. She pressed for reasons, but I refused to say. Finally, though, she gave me my mom's number, something the school somehow had access to. Hardest phone call I've ever had to make—and the worst because I thought she'd take me as well. Instead, she took Mia and left me with the brute. That's when I stopped feeling anything, the day she and Mia drove away.

"Would you have had me leave her here?" she asks.

I push out of the chair hard enough to send it skittering backward. She flinches, and I feel shame for scaring her, but I'm angry enough to ignore that.

"You couldn't take me, too?"

"No, Benjamin." A sob escapes her and she presses a fist to her mouth. "*If* they could have convicted him, he would've served maybe three years. Then he would've come after us. Only he promised that this time he'd kill me, and make you and Mia suffer worse than ever. The things he threatened to do . . ." She closes her eyes and swallows loudly. "He was very graphic in his threats. So I compromised with him, made a deal with the devil. He'd allow me to take Mia without a fight if I left you here."

"King Solomon, huh? Sacrifice one for the good of the other?"

"Not exactly how that story goes—"

"You want to give me biblical lessons now?" I shoot at her, even though I really don't know the story and she's probably right that I'm way off.

She stands and holds her hands up in surrender. "No, of course not. I just . . . I didn't know what else to do. You were older by then, bigger, I thought maybe you could take care of your-self . . . defend yourself. Besides, he promised not to hurt you."

"And you believed him?" My voice cracks in disbelief like a twelve-year-old.

She drops her hands. "No. I mean, I think I managed to con-vince myself it was true just so I could walk away. I'm not stupid, Benjamin. I know better than anyone what he was like. And I guess all these years I've known that he wouldn't leave you alone." Silence stretches before she says, "I came to one of your football games once." My mind reels at the thought that she'd been in the stands, that close to me at one point, and I didn't know. "I saw how big you were, how strong and fast. I guess I hoped he'd changed—"

"Yeah, well, you were wrong. He put me in the hospital a week before he did a header into that tree."

She drops back to the couch and drops her face into her hands. Long seconds pass while she shakes. "I don't blame you for hating me, Ben—Benjamin. I truly don't. I only wish you could under-stand how trapped I felt, how much I didn't know how to fix it, how much I wanted to protect Mia from being hurt like that again. It took years of therapy for her to be okay—or as okay as she can be. Who knows if she'll ever be truly whole again?"

I swallow the surge of emotion her words bring. Not because of what she says about herself or me, but because of her words about Mia. The one thing in this world I thought I could love—well, the one thing I once thought was the only thing I could love.

"Is she okay now?" I ask quietly.

"She's doing really well," she says with a small smile. "She's a freshman, and she went on her first date a week ago."

I try to imagine my baby sister, the little girl I once knew, grown up enough to *date*. I wouldn't know her if I saw her on the street. The thought lodges in my throat.

"Do you want to see a picture of her?" she asks.

Yeah, I do. I nod and she turns her phone on, scrolling through some pages before handing it over to me.

I look down at the girl who smiles up from the phone. She has olive skin like me, long, dark, curly hair, with piercing green eyes. She's beautiful. She looks happy. I could stare at the picture all day, but not wanting to show emotion to her, I hand it back. She might have been completely selfish to leave me behind at the mercy of my dad, but she did the right thing by taking Mia away. I try to imagine what Mia would be like now if she'd stayed, and I shudder at the thought. No, whatever else happened, Mia needed to be far away from the monster that raised me.

She smiles down at the photo for a second before turning the phone off and pushing it back into her pocket. She returns her gaze to mine.

"Does she know about me?" I ask.

She nods. "She remembers you. She asks about you."

"And what do you tell her?"

She doesn't answer at first, and I realize I'm not going to like the answer. Finally she takes a breath. "I tell her you wanted to stay here."

I huff out a mirthless sound. "Makes you look good, huh? Wouldn't want her to realize you left your son behind."

She grimaces. "It's selfish, I know. But I didn't know how to help her heal, how to effectively become whole again if she had to live with a mother she resented. So yes, I told her what I needed to."

"Whatever helps you sleep at night," I mutter.

"I didn't come to ask your forgiveness, or even your understanding," she says. "I don't deserve one and don't expect the other. But you were wrong when you said there was no money, Benjamin. There is money, from a life insurance policy. And because we never divorced, I'm the sole beneficiary."

FIFTY-TWO
BENJAMIN

I didn't think anything my mother had to say could surprise me, but I was wrong. I'm dumbfounded.

"What insurance policy?" The question is inane, but it's the only one I can think to ask.

"Years ago, when we first married, we took out policies. He forgot about them, but I kept paying them. I changed the beneficiary on mine, but he didn't."

I shake my head in amazement. "You never divorced him?"

"No. I was afraid if I tried he'd know where to find us and he'd come after us. I figured the less he was reminded of us, the better." She waves a vague hand around. "I took all of the pictures with me when I left so that there wasn't anything here to remind him."

"Not all of them," I say.

"No. I left one with you."

"To torture me?"

Her mouth drops. "Of course not! I just wanted you to have one . . . something for you to remember me—*us* by."

"Yeah, well, thanks a lot." I fill my voice with sarcasm just in case she doesn't understand that. "Tell me about the money, and why you're telling me about it. If you have his money now, you can't possibly want this piece of crap I live in. And I'm *not* going to live here with you."

She flinches again and I turn away, not caring about her hurt. Or at least trying really hard not to. Trying to push down the images of having Mia in the house again, having laughter here.

"I don't want the house, Ben—Benjamin. I also don't want the money."

Okay, she has my attention now.

"It belongs to you, and to Mia. That's why I kept it all of these years. I figured it was only a matter of time before something like this happened, with the way he drank. I'm surprised it took him this long. My biggest worry was that he would end up in prison instead."

I laugh sarcastically. "*That* was your biggest worry?"

"No, I mean . . . no. Only in regards to the policy. My biggest worry was that he'd take you with him. I wanted the money to be for you for college, or if it was later, maybe for a house or whatever you needed. But as it turns out you don't really need it."

So she does know about the college scouts? I look at her suspiciously. "What does that mean?"

She shrugs. "I was worried that you wouldn't get the money by the time you needed it. So I started a savings account for both you and Mia. I left under bad circumstances, but I was determined to make good in some way. So I got some grants and went to college myself. I make decent money now, enough that I can afford to put you and Mia both through school—whatever you want."

I take a few deep breaths to control the rage that threatens to burst. When I feel I have control, I say, "Do you really think I want anything from you? That I'd willingly take a single penny from you?"

Her tears start again. "So much anger. I'm sorry," she whispers.

"If you're making so much money now, why couldn't you come back for me?" I didn't mean to voice the thought since she'd already explained why she didn't come back. Even if I thought she was a selfish witch for not coming to get me, I couldn't fault her reasons. I'd do anything to protect Mia as well. I probably would have left her behind and taken Mia away if I could've. I *really* didn't mean for the sentence to come out sounding all whiney and pleading.

"Benjamin." Just that. Just my name, but so much regret and emotion in the single word that my heart twists.

I turn away and stride to the door. "I don't want it. I don't want anything from you. You can't buy my forgiveness with a few dollars. And you can keep *his* money as well. I don't want anything from either of you." I pull the door open with a violent tug, and stand aside. "Leave, please."

She doesn't move for long minutes, and I begin to think I'm going to have to pick her up and toss her out the door. Finally she stands and comes toward me. She stops right in front of me, raising a hand and touching my cheek lightly. I freeze beneath her touch, refusing to give her the satisfaction of any reaction from me.

"I've always loved you. You can't imagine how much, Ben."

She steps out and I slam the door behind her before sliding to the floor, burying my head in my arms, and wondering how my life got to this point.

FIFTY-THREE
CHARLIE

Wallowing in self-pity seems to be my thing these days. If I'm not at school or at Dayspring, I'm lying on my bed, crying. It's ridiculous. I used to mock girls who fell into despair whenever a boy broke up with them, and here I am doing the same thing. I just couldn't fathom their pain. I mean, there are a lot worse things happening in the world than a breakup, right?

Now I understand. The pain is deep, searing, feeling as though my heart has been viciously, unceremoniously ripped from my chest. A torn, gaping hole is all that remains.

I quit my job at Tony's to avoid seeing Benjamin and having that extra reminder. It's hard enough pretending I'm fine at school without having to do it at work as well. I gave the excuse that now I'm spending my free time at Dayspring—which is true enough. But it isn't the whole truth. Luckily, Debbie was nice about it and offered to give me a reference in the future. I think she understood why I was really leaving.

As I sit in my window seat, my laptop open on my bed waiting for me to finish my homework, a knock sounds at my door. Probably Naomi, bugging me about my blood-sugar levels, which have been off. Stress will do that. I wipe my face and school my features before calling, "Come in."

"Charlie!" my mom cries, bounding into the room. I stand just in time to catch her in my arms. I glance beyond her to Naomi, who waits in the doorway. I lift a brow in question.

"Sometimes a girl just needs her mom," she says, shrugging and closing the door behind her.

I close my eyes as we hug, wishing once again that I could talk to her about Benjamin, that she could give me some kind of advice that would make my heart stop hurting so much. I squeeze my mom, then release her.

"Mom, I'm glad you came to visit."

"Mimi says I can sleep over." The excitement is clear in her bright eyes, and she's bouncing on her toes.

"Here, sit by me." I lead her to the window seat.

As we sit she studies me, her forehead scrunched.

"What's the matter, Mom?"

"Mimi says you're sad."

I smile and shake my head, cursing Naomi. "I'm fine, Mom."

Now she's shaking her head. "No. Mimi says." She lifts a finger and swipes it beneath my eye, surprisingly gentle for her. "You're sad right here. I can see it."

My breath hitches, and my stupid, disloyal eyes well up. I can only nod, not trusting myself to speak without bursting into tears.

"Mimi said Prince Benjamin won't come over again. Mimi said he isn't going to be our prince anymore."

Tears slip out, and I take a breath. Still, my voice is shaky. "He isn't going to come over anymore, Mom, but he'll always be your prince."

"But not yours?"

"No, Mom, not mine." I can't help the sob that escapes even though I try to catch it in my throat.

She cups my cheeks with her hands, slowly stroking up and down. "Does he still love us?" she asks, worry in her puckered expression. Her face smooths. "Yep, he does. Don't worry, Charlie, he still loves you, too. It's okay."

She pulls me into her arms, holding me tightly and rocking back and forth, stroking my back, making cooing sounds . . . almost like any other mom. And I take it, take her comfort and blind acceptance that everything will be okay. For the first time in my life, it's her taking care of me, even tucking me into bed and sliding between the sheets next to me so she can hold me through the night.

FIFTY-FOUR
BENJAMIN

A week is as long as I can stand staying away. I've driven past their house nearly every day, hoping for a glimpse of Mia, and dreading seeing my mother. Still not sure what to do with my feelings about her. After years of hating her beneath my oppressed feelings, it's hard to deal with this wanting. I never want to see her again, even as I long for her. Every time I think of my mother, betrayal and hurt consume my heart. Then memories flood me, of her loving me when she was there, protecting me and Mia as much as she was able.

It was so much easier when I didn't feel anything. And *that* thought brings to mind the reason I *do* feel now—the person who caused it—and the hurt comes back full force.

Now, I can't believe I'm standing here, on the doorstep of this house that really belongs to strangers. It's a nice house, not overly large, but two stories, with a nice yard. Almost as big as Charlie's house. I quickly pull my mind away from that train of thought and knock before I can change my mind.

Enough time passes that I consider leaving—running—when the door opens. The girl standing in front of me isn't a little girl. She's nearly a woman. The photo of her on my mother's phone didn't do her justice. Or maybe I'm biased.

"Can I help you?" Her voice is different, deeper, older . . . not frightened.

She's dressed casually in jeans and a pink T-shirt, wearing socks, and I suddenly remember that about her—she always wore socks around the house, insisted on it. I cringe when I remember her being beat a few times because it bothered my dad for some reason, but she refused to go barefoot. I'm glad she hasn't changed that one little quirk.

I realize I'm staring and smile. Her expression jumps from annoyed curiosity to recognition and she draws a breath, her hand flying to her mouth. Tears spring up in her eyes and she shakes her head.

"Ben?"

I nod and she flies against me, squeezing my neck so tightly I can barely breathe. Or maybe that's from emotion, it's hard to tell anymore. I give as good as I get, careful not to hurt her. I realize she's nearly as tall as me. I didn't have to lean down as I usually do—did—with Charlie. *Or any other girl*, I quickly amend.

"Ben, I can't believe it's you!" she squeals, pushing away to look at me. I can feel the dumb, wide smile on my face, unable to bring it down and act any kind of cool. She throws herself back into my arms, and then practically drags me inside, without relinquishing much of her hold.

"Come in," she says uselessly, since I'm inside whether I wanted to be or not. "Mom!" she yells. "Look who's here. It's *Ben*."

My mother comes into the entry from somewhere else, wiping her hands on a towel. She freezes when she sees me standing there. She presses her lips tightly together, not in anger but with suppressed emotion. Her eyes are shiny with tears, and finally she smiles.

"He goes by Benjamin now," she says to Mia, never pulling her gaze from mine.

"Oh, sorry," Mia says, finally releasing me, though she keeps one hand on my arm, as if that will anchor me here.

"It's okay," I say, putting an arm around her shoulder and pulling her close. "Ben is fine."

"Come in," Mia says again, putting an arm around my waist and pulling me further into the house until we're in the family room. She swoops up the remote and shuts the TV off, then pulls me down onto the couch next to her. She's strong, although honestly she couldn't have gotten me past the front door if I didn't want her to.

"I'll give you two some time," my mother says.

"Don't you want to see him, too?" Mia asks.

"I've already . . . I went to see Ben a week ago."

"What? You didn't tell me?"

"I'm guessing she didn't want to give you false hope," I say. "I wasn't exactly welcoming. I'm sure she thought she'd never see me again."

Mia turns a confused gaze on me.

"I wasn't sure, either," I admit.

"But here you are," my mother says.

"Here I am."

After an awkward silence, my mother leaves us alone to get to know each other. I'm grateful—though I don't want to be grateful to her for anything—so that I can talk freely with Mia, the one I came to see.

I ask Mia about school, and tell her about football, about Daniel and some of my friends, about the scouts calling with scholarships, which Mia squeals over. Finally, a seriousness settles over her.

"Ben, why didn't you come with us? Why did you stay with . . . *him?*"

She thinks I betrayed her by staying—that's clear in her tone. She thinks I preferred that fiend over her and my mother. I decide it's time for us all to be honest about what we've been through. He can't hurt us anymore unless we let him.

"I didn't have a choice, Mia. My moth—Mom didn't have a choice but to leave me there."

"Why not? She took me, why not you?"

I won't tell her it was to protect her. That isn't a burden she needs to carry. "He wouldn't let her. Do you remember what he was like?"

Mia shudders, her shoulders hunch in protective shame, head drooping. "Yes, I remember." Her voice is small.

"Look at me, Mia." I wait for her to lift her head. "Never hang your head for that man. Ever. He isn't worth it, okay?"

She nods, though her body remains in the hunched position.

"He was a monster, but he's gone now. We survived him—all of us. He made all of us do things that we shouldn't have had to. And he did things to us that were beyond our control. It doesn't matter now. He's *gone*."

Mia licks her lips nervously. "My therapist told me that if we hold on to anger and guilt then that gives the power to the person who hurt us."

I nod. "Sounds like good advice." Not that I think I'll be able to follow it, but I want Mia to live a happy, carefree life, even if I can't.

"He's gone," she repeats.

"Gone. Gone, Mia, as in never coming back. I watched them close his coffin, and lower it into the ground."

"Were you sad?" she asks.

"Nope. Not at all."

Her body uncurls a little. "Me neither."

"I'm happy you got away, Mia. I couldn't protect you anymore. It made it easier to be there knowing you were safe." As I say the words, I realize how true they are. I survived because I knew she would. I didn't have the burden of trying to protect her, or my mother, once they were gone.

"I'm sorry, Ben. I'm sorry I left and you had to stay." Her face crumples with her words.

"Mia, it was okay. I mean, he was a complete jerk, but I want you to look at me." I hold my arms out to the side, flexing my muscles a little, and her eyes take me in. "I held my own."

A small smile tilts the corners of her mouth up. "I hope you kicked his butt. At least once."

"Over and over, for you." I don't tell her that I didn't have much choice in fighting him, or that he almost always kicked *my* butt.

Her smile widens and her body completely uncurls. "Good. I mean, is that okay if I feel that way?"

"Of course."

She glances toward the door where my mother disappeared. "Do you hate Mom for leaving you there?"

I follow her gaze. Do I hate her? "I did. For a long time. But I don't think I really hated her as much as I just wanted her back. I couldn't understand why she never came."

"She did come, once," Mia says. I lift a brow as she continues. "She doesn't know I know. But I overheard her on the phone. She said she'd seen you at a football game, that you were the star and that everyone cheered your name. She said that you looked happy. Were you happy, Ben?"

Of course I *looked* happy. It was all part of the act. "Don't I look happy?" I say instead.

She tilts her head as she studies me. "You kinda look sad," she finally says.

A vision of Charlie pops into my head at her words, and I can't speak.

"A girl?" she asks.

"What? Are you Dr. Phil now?" I try for a teasing tone, but it doesn't come out that way.

"Dinner's done," my mother says, sticking her head back into the room. "Do you want to stay?"

Relieved at not having to further this particular conversation, I stand. "No." Both of them look at me with puppy-dog eyes. But I can't do this. Not yet. "Not today. Maybe another time."

∽

Two weeks later, after seven or eight other visits, I finally concede and stay for dinner. Sometimes I spend time with just Mia, but other times my mother is with us as we talk or watch TV. She seems to be trying to give me space, but can't always make herself stay away. And as much as I don't want to, I admit she's wearing me down. It's exhausting being angry all the time.

I *crave* a family. That's what she offers. Forgiveness might be hard to achieve, but I'm starting to think I might do it, forgive her and let her give me what I've always wanted.

We begin eating when Mia pops up with, "Ben's having girl troubles."

My mother's eyes fly to mine and I groan. "It's nothing."

"What's her name?" my mother asks. Apparently they're going to gang up on me.

"Charlie," I say, proud of myself for getting it out without sounding all pathetic.

"A guy?" Mia's eyes widen in surprise, and I smile as I remember thinking that Charlie was into girls when I first met her. How incredibly arrogant I was to think that was the only reason she wouldn't like me.

"No, it's short for Charlotte."

"Oh, cool. So what's the story?"

I shake my head. She isn't going to let this go. So I'll give her the short, unemotional version.

"No story. Just a girl I dated."

They both continue to watch me, and suddenly I find myself pouring out the story, telling them about meeting her, and how hard I worked to get her to date me. I tell them about her diabetes, about her mom, my "princess," about her aunt and Dayspring, and how I had to break up with her because it was too hard being with her. Loving her.

By the time I'm done, my mom is holding my hand in hers, which weirdly I don't mind. Mia has her hand on my other forearm. Like a real family.

"Ben," Mia says sympathetically. "You're an idiot."

My mouth gapes. I was expecting some kind of supportive, sisterly love and instead I get a dig.

My mom nods. "It's true. You're an idiot."

I pull my arms away from them and lean back in my chair, crossing my arms over my chest. "Well, thanks for the compliment."

They both laugh. Mia's smile is the same as my mother's, a smile I rarely saw as a child. My mom reaches for me again. "Ben, it's clear you love this girl. Why do you want to make yourself miserable without her?"

"Yeah," Mia pipes up. "So you're going away to college. What if she goes to the same place?"

I admit the thought crossed my mind. But knowing she's planning to stay close to Cora, I know the chances of that are slim to none. "What if she doesn't?" I counter.

"So what if she doesn't?" my mom asks. "I mean, seriously, with cell phones and Internet, and Skype, and airplanes, how far apart can you really be?"

"Besides, you don't know if it'll work or not if you don't give it a chance," Mia adds.

I stare at them both, eyes flicking between them as their words cause a little bloom of hope in my chest. "I don't want to hurt her."

"Too late," Mia says. "You already did. Now you need to fix it."

Mia can't possibly understand how many ways I can hurt Charlie by staying with her. Or how many ways she can hurt me. I stare at her. Actually, maybe if anyone can understand, she can. I realize she's right—they're both right. I hurt Charlie not to protect her, but to protect me. Selfishly.

"What if she won't take me back?" I ask. After all, she was angry when I broke up with her, not crying. And when I see her at school, she seems fine. Maybe she doesn't care all that much.

"She will," Mia says firmly.

I look at my mom. She shrugs and says, "Or maybe she won't. You won't know unless you ask."

FIFTY-FIVE
BENJAMIN

Standing on the sidelines, I look into the bleachers again. She's still there, with Cozi and Phoebe. I watch intently until she looks my way. I hold her gaze, but then she pulls away, and from here I can see her sigh. Charlie clearly doesn't want to be here. My watching her is making her uncomfortable, but I can't seem to help it.

Something changed after my visits with Mia and my mom. Something inside of me shifted, and a lot of my anger at my mom has drained away. The hurt hasn't been erased—that remains and probably always will to some degree. But I understand her running. Given the chance, I would have run myself a long time ago. Her running got Mia away from him so that she has a shot at a normal life—with normal emotions, instead of thinking that she has to shut off all feeling just to survive.

The night my mother first came, I dreamed. Not really dreams, memories. Even though I was young when she left, the things my dad did to her remain clear in my mind. I remember her lying on the floor, crying, begging for her life. I remember him finding any infraction, no matter how small or insignificant, as an excuse to hurt her. I also remember her stepping in when he came after me or Mia and taking the beating intended for us. She was always bruised, bloody, broken. No one knows his temper like I do, and I don't question for one second that had she stayed, he would have killed her. And maybe Mia, too. I think that somehow being his son protected me from that same fate. He had zero respect for females.

There was a time when he'd used excuses for beating me up as well, after she left. I can't remember when he stopped even pretending to need a reason. I do know that none of his reasons were good, and nothing she did, or I did, ever warranted what he did to us.

Now, I'm going to see them again this weekend, my family, and I want Charlie to come. And yet, I don't want her to come, because it would mean that I'm allowing myself to love her. I can't do that—can I?

It's our turn at offense again, so I jog out onto the field. We're winning by a large margin. We shouldn't be since we're fairly evenly matched with this team, but for whatever reason I'm completing every throw today, making handoffs without a problem, and even ran in two touchdowns myself. I don't even feel the pressure that there is a scout here from Alabama State.

The ball is snapped and I make the long pass. The crowd cheers, teammates pound me on the back, and I look up in the stands again. Charlie is leaving, making her way up the steps alone. In that second, before I really have a plan, I make a decision.

Running over to the sidelines, I grab Coach's shoulder. "Coach, I've gotta go."

His jaw drops. "Go? What does that mean? Do you know what's at stake here, son?"

I look up at the scoreboard. "There's three minutes left in the game, we're ahead by twenty-eight. I think Ashford can handle it from here," I say, nodding toward the backup quarterback. Coach is shaking his head. "C'mon, Coach. You know I wouldn't do this if it wasn't important."

Emotions war on his face. He wants to make me stay, that's clear enough, but he's also aware of what I've given over the last few weeks. Reluctantly, he nods. "Hit the showers, Nefer. Monday you can tell me what's so important that you're risking Alabama State for."

I grin and jog away from him, away from the locker room, toward the parking lot. He can make of that what he will. Right now, all that matters is that I get to Charlie.

She's nearly to her car when I exit the gate. "Charlie!" I call. She doesn't hear me, or she's ignoring me, because she keeps walking. I run faster. "Charlie!"

Now she hears me, stopping in her tracks before glancing back over her shoulder. When she sees me running, a look of concern crosses her face.

"What's wrong? Did something happen?" she asks worriedly as I get to her.

"Yeah, something happened. You happened."

"Um . . . huh?" Her forehead scrunches in confusion.

I place my hands on her shoulders and give them a gentle squeeze. "I don't know what you did to me," I say. "Before you came I was content with being an unfeeling jerk. I didn't care about anyone or anything. I built up walls to keep everyone and everything out. You seemed like the perfect girlfriend because you didn't want to get that involved, either."

"Benjamin, look, I get it, okay? You don't have to expl—"

I cut her words off with a hard kiss, my mouth pressed against hers. In true Charlie fashion, she immediately responds. I have to pull away to laugh.

"I *do* have to explain, because you *don't* get it. My dad—what you saw on me at the hospital—that was not really that much worse than what he did to me on a daily basis."

Charlie gasps and brings a hand up to touch my jaw softly. I nearly lose my train of thought. I take her hand in mine, press a kiss into her palm then keep hold of her hand.

"He did it to my mom for years until she was forced to leave. She left me and my sister behind. She came back for my sister when he . . . he hurt her in a way that nearly destroyed her." Tears well in Charlie's eyes. "And me . . . I was helpless. I couldn't protect her. I couldn't protect my mom when she was there. Then she came back and took Mia and left me there. Which sounds horrible, I know. And it is, but it's also sorta understandable. She did the right thing, at least for Mia. Only I couldn't see that."

"Benjamin." My name is a breath as her tears fall. "You don't have to—"

"Please, I want to. I want you to know everything. I boxed to hide the bruises because I was humiliated that I allowed him to beat me. It worked. I fooled everyone. But in order to live in that house, I had to turn off my emotions. And I did it, Charlie, I didn't care about anything."

Charlie nods. She swallows some tears and says, "I saw that in your eyes sometimes. You'd smile, but your eyes were . . . empty. I suspected about the bruises. I should have asked. I'm so sorry."

I hug her, releasing her before saying, "Why would you be sorry? If you had asked, I would've lied, and I would've convinced you, too. I had lots of practice."

"Benjamin, I'm so sorry you had to live like that."

I smile. "Yeah, I know you are, because you're good like that. Don't be sorry. Be happy. If it wasn't for you, I'd still be that same, unfeeling jerk, going through life hurting people and using them and not caring. I probably would have ended up just like him."

"But what did I do?"

"You just accepted me. You didn't expect more of me than I could give. Even when I broke up with you, you didn't have a dramatic breakdown . . . which kind of hurt, just so you know." I grin, and finally a small smile lights her face.

"Whatever. You aren't big on displays of emotion."

"You're right. You know that because you know me better than anyone else does."

"Well, just so you know, I did cry. A lot. At home, in bed. Alone."

I kiss her then, a real kiss, deep and intense. My heart thumps a little harder.

"I'm sorry," I say.

She shrugs. "You hurt me, Benjamin. It's hard to know what to believe. Everyone told me you were . . ." Her cheeks grow pink. I know exactly what everyone told her, and they were right. Thank heavens she didn't listen. "But then you seemed different. *We* seemed different. And then we weren't." She blows out a breath. "I know I'm not making sense . . ."

"You are, Charlie. I get it. I know what I did to you was completely selfish. No, that's not right. What I did to Alexis, and every other girl before her, was selfish. But you . . . I knew how much worse it would hurt you and I did it to protect me. Selfish isn't a big enough word for what I did. And I know it's going to be really hard to make it up to you, but I'm asking you to let me try."

Cheers from the stadium interrupt the silence between us. "Shouldn't you be playing football?" she asks. Avoiding my request?

"I had something more important requiring my attention."

"Me?" she asks.

"You. And telling you this: I love you, Charlotte Austin. I don't know what the future is going to bring, or how much you hate me now, but I love you. *Thank* you for making me learn to love again."

She shrugs, a small smile lighting her face. "I don't hate you *that* much."

"So you're saying you love me?" I feel like a fool grinning like I am, but I can't seem to stop. Luckily, she grins right back.

"Sadly, yes, I love you, Benjamin. You're not the easiest person in the world to love, you know?"

"I know."

She rises up to kiss me, but just before her lips touch mine, she says, "That's a lie. You're *very* easy to love. So get used to it."

"I think I can do that," I whisper before slanting my mouth across hers once again, feeling a happiness I never thought I'd be capable of surge through me as she gives back as good as she gets. "Now, new girl, let's go see my princess. I miss her."

"She misses you like you can't believe."

"Oh, I can believe it," I say, with as much smugness as I can muster.

Charlie laughs, taking my hand in hers as we walk across the parking lot. Together. The way I can only hope we'll always be.

ACKNOWLEDGMENTS

Writing and publishing a book takes the effort and input of many people. My name might be on the cover, but really there are so many people who deserve to have their names *somewhere* on the book because it couldn't have happened without them. This seems like a really great place to give them the recognition they deserve.

To my beautiful daughters, Lindsay and Lexcie, who make it possible for me to do this by encouraging me, and by cooking dinner sometimes when I just can't seem to escape my characters, and who give me great input on plot points, current teen lingo, and my covers. Lexcie wrote me two mini-pages of notes clarifying diabetic issues I'd gotten wrong, questions she felt should be in the book, and gave me the names for Charlie, Benjamin, and Daniel. Lindsay kept me supplied with cupcakes and cookies to keep me going. I'm so grateful to have you both!

To the Wigz: Sherry Gammon, Camelia Miron Skiba, Jeffery Moore, and Juli Caldwell, my critique partners and first editors. You guys rock my world. You give me the feedback I desperately need (and whether I like it or not, I always definitely *need* it) and supply laughs via email when I need it most. How did I get so lucky to end up with such an amazing group of great authors?

To my beta readers, who were willing to take the time to read the book and give me feedback on strong points, weak points, and plot holes. All of this couched in praise that makes me blush and brings tears to my eyes and a smile to my face. To sweet Emma Frost, Rachel O'Hara, Amy Wood, and Alexis Coffman (yes, Alexis in the book is named after her). Thank you so, so much!

To those wonderful authors whose names are in the first few pages, who read the book when it was full of typos and other blips, and then went so far as to write me an endorsement, I can't begin to thank you enough: All of the Wigz, Shannen Crane Camp, Heather Frost, and Jamie Canosa. I love you all more than words can say. Seriously.

Last, but hardly least, thanks to Courtney and Vivian at Skyscape for taking a chance on my book—Courtney for finding it in the first place and approaching me, and Vivian for believing in it enough to take the leap. I appreciate you both! You've been amazing to work with.

ABOUT THE AUTHOR

Photo © 2014 Lindsay Bennett

Cindy C Bennett is the author of several YA books. She lives in Utah with her two daughters. Both of her sons have married, giving her two more daughters (in-law) that she adores as much as her own kiddos. She loves gooey cookies, dark chocolate, and cheesy popcorn. She hates housework and cooking, and has no plans to become a domestic goddess. She occasionally co-hosts a geek podcast with her son called *Geek Revolution Radio*. Her favorite pastime—other than writing—is riding her Harley.

Find Cindy at:
www.cindycbennett.com
www.facebook.com/authorcindycbennett
www.twitter.com/cinbennett